Stems Of Completion

Stem Series Trilogy

Book 1: *Stems of Affliction*
Book 2: *Stems of Inception*
Book 3: *Stems of Completion*

The Stem Series Trilogy is a continual story. The author recommends reading the series in order, as they are not meant to be stand-alone novels.

Stems Of Completion

BOOK 3 IN THE STEM SERIES TRILOGY

M. J. Brookes

ISBN: 978-1-7276-8181-9

Dedicated to all the fans who stuck with me on this trilogy journey

Table of Contents

Chapter 1	1
Chapter 2	12
Chapter 3	19
Chapter 4	26
Chapter 5	34
Chapter 6	43
Chapter 7	51
Chapter 8	58
Chapter 9	65
Chapter 10	73
Chapter 11	81
Chapter 12	90
Chapter 13	101
Chapter 14	108
Chapter 15	117
Chapter 16	126
Chapter 17	133
Chapter 18	139
Chapter 19	151
Chapter 20	160
Chapter 21	166
Chapter 22	176
Chapter 23	182
Chapter 24	195
Chapter 25	202

Chapter 26   207
Chapter 27   215
Chapter 28   222
Chapter 29   226
Chapter 30   230

Acknowledgments   233
About the Author   235

Chapter 1

Setting his coffee on a nearby desk, Jake Morgan inched toward the door to the meeting room in the security office of the casino and hotel that would soon belong to his company. Having discussed the original purchase of this property with Mike Valente, he was familiar with the layout. Knowing the room was soundproof and the privacy glass kept others from seeing inside the room, he wasn't surprised that his best friend and colleague, Cal Mitchell, would use it to hold the person who had stalked him and his fiancée, Samantha Andrews.

Three weeks ago, when he and Samantha were in Las Vegas, she had sensed someone following her. She had first noticed the man by the spa, wearing a hooded gray sweatshirt during the hottest time of the year. Then she had felt the presence of someone again the night they went to dinner. Video from the security footage showed the same man taking a photograph of them with his phone. No pictures of them had surfaced in any form of media, leaving Jake wondering why someone would take a photo.

After he learned about Samantha's past and the threats that had lurked around every corner over the death of her father, the thought of any photos of her being released to the media had weighed on his mind every second of the day. The dangers of her past were now over, but she had been through hell and back again, barely escaping a madman. The physical scars would heal, but the emotional scars would be with her forever. Though she appeared to be coping with the aftermath, he wondered how many afflictions she was hiding from him. He wished he'd been as successful shielding his own ugly traits from her, but she'd witnessed them, more times than he cared to count.

It was an innate characteristic. The first time he felt the anger flaming in his gut, he was four years old. He didn't understand it then. As he grew older, playing football gave him an outlet. When he joined the army, he took out his anger against the enemy that threatened the country he loved. When he left the army, he relied on alcohol and women to ease his anger. If not for his grandfather, he would have spiraled into a deep abyss, driven by the demons of his past. He'd been able to control it since then, until the day he learned of Samantha's past. It was then he felt the unwelcome rage return. Though she had a way of calming him, as did his counselor, neither were here now as he was about to face the man whom he'd buried long ago. Boring holes through the door with his eyes, Jake clenched the wallet still in his hand, fighting for control, focusing on his breathing, but it was no use. The man behind this door may as well be a goddamn gas can, pouring fuel on his blaze of fury.

Jake exhaled, looking down at the wallet. He couldn't comprehend how he hadn't recognized him. Yes, he had been distracted when Samantha told him about her past, but still…he should have known this man was his own brother. Shoving the wallet in his back pocket, he latched on to the doorknob, hesitating, unsure of what he was going to say or do to the ghost of a man that haunted him in more ways than one.

For the sake of his mother, he had tried to find his brother, Kyle, after his grandfather passed away. He and Cal had braved the gang-ridden streets, scoured rat-infested alleys, searched through abandoned homes, and called in favors from friends who were more familiar with the underground drug network than either of them were. When his efforts turned up empty, he checked with the local hospitals and morgues, thinking Kyle had finally succumbed to the nasty crack he craved, which had almost destroyed their family. When he had scoured all logical places and burned through his resources, he buried him in his mind, secretly reveling in never having to see his face again. His silent celebration was about to come to an end. Once he opened this door he would be faced with his past. The feelings of hatred and guilt troubling his psyche would be roused up in the form of anger, and he wasn't sure he could control it.

Taking a steadying breath, Jake turned the knob, opened the door, and stepped inside, getting his first glimpse of the man who had terrorized his thoughts for the last six years. He wasn't sure what to expect, but he didn't expect the clean-shaven man in front of him. A sheepish smile cracked the somber look, the same sort of sheepish grin he remembered from when they were kids. Kyle was six years older, and they had a brotherly bond he never thought would be broken, but Kyle had managed to do just that, severing their relationship forever.

To Kyle, drugs were more important than his family, and because he was an unwelcome irritant, Jake had almost done the unthinkable the last time he saw him—the night his anger and hatred climaxed in one decisive moment. It was a moment he couldn't erase from the depths of his mind, and when it passed, he was left broken while Kyle was committed to rehab again. Kyle promised he would stay, again, like he had every other time. Jake held out little hope that treatment would be successful, and even if it was, after what happened that night, their relationship would never be the same. *He* wasn't the same, but he had to walk away. Leaving Kyle's treatment plan in the hands of his mother and sister, he had returned to his duties in Afghanistan, where what he'd almost done tormented him, forever impacting his life more than anyone would ever know. Jake grimaced at the thought, then swallowed hard, pushing it from his mind, focusing instead on the apparition in front of him.

Six years ago, Kyle's appearance was entirely different. Back then, he needed a shave, his hair was disheveled, his eyes were hazy and droopy from the drugs, his lips were thin, his skin was pale, his face was hollow, his body was a frail, barely one hundred and thirty pounds, and his mind was all but gone. The drugs controlled him then, his body shook, and he was wasting away, dying a slow death because he didn't have the strength to walk away, to admit his addiction, and get himself the help he desperately needed.

Today, the man in front of him had replaced the sweatshirt he had worn in the videos with a black T-shirt that accented his yellowish-pale skin, such a contrast from the skin that was once tan when they were kids. The muscles in his neck bulged as did those in his arms. His eyes crinkled when he smiled at Jake. They were clear, but not the bright blue Jake remembered. His dark-brown hair was pulled back in a short ponytail, hanging just past his shoulders, the same dark-brown color of hair their father had. As Kyle strode toward him,

Jake could see what he saw in the videos, a well-built man, probably a minimum of two hundred and twenty pounds. Jake closed the door behind him.

"Little man," Kyle said, embracing him. Jake kept his arms at his side, his hands balling into fists as Kyle patted his back twice. "Come on now, is that any way to greet your older brother?"

Shrugging from Kyle's grasp, Jake stepped away from him. "What the hell are you doing here, Kyle?"

Kyle laughed out loud. The attempt at humor and the laughter were both tactics Jake remembered him using as a kid to make light of any situation. He waved his arms to the side. "I came to see you, little man."

"Like hell you did! If you came here to see me, then why not call the office, or ask the front desk? Why sneak around in the middle of the night?"

"I needed to make sure it was really you."

"Did the drugs fry your brain to the point where you don't recognize your own brother? I haven't changed since I saw you six years ago!" Jake paced around the conference table, glancing at the faces in the other room, aware the black glass offered the privacy he needed. "What do you want this time? More money?"

"It's not like that, Jake." Kyle's voice softened.

"Then tell me what it is like, Kyle!" Jake pounded his fists on the table, his eyes darkened as the anger at his brother that had rumbled beneath the surface began to bubble, like a volcano ready to erupt.

Kyle leaned against the opposite solid white wall, his hands behind his back, watching Jake as he spoke in a calm manner. "Like I said, I came to see you. I tried a few weeks ago, but you were with that pretty lady, and it didn't seem like the right time to approach you."

"And when exactly would be the right time, Kyle?"

"Look, Jake, I know you're angry with me and you have every right—"

"*Angry?*" Jake cut him off, mocking the word, throwing his hands up when he pushed off the table. "You think I'm fucking *angry*? Hell, I was *angry* twenty-two years ago when you first came home in a drug-induced stupor, stealing from your own mother! I was *angry* every day of my teenage life watching the brother I once looked up to waste away! I was *angry* when you promised to stay in treatment and take care of our family when I enlisted in the army, only to find out you disappeared within days after I left! I was *angry* when every time I came home on leave, I had to spend my time tracking your ass down to sober you up! I was *angry* six years ago when I found you so strung out you didn't know who the hell you were! I was *angry* when I'm out of the country in the midst of a goddamn war zone and find out you walked away from rehab! Again! That was *angry* Kyle!" Jake moved toward him, backing him further against the wall, but keeping his fists at his side. "Now you show up here, unwelcome, stalking my fiancée, taking pictures, disrupting my life again! Now, Kyle…now, I'm fucking *furious!*"

Seconds ticked by, and Kyle swallowed, his Adam's apple protruding from his neck from the effort. "If you want to hit me, go ahead. I deserve it."

Jake's nostrils flared. His lips pressed tight against his teeth as he opened and closed his fists. Every cell in his body wanted to bloody and bruise him, pay him back for all of the suffering he had brought on his family over the years. He turned away, kicking the chairs and shoving them up against the table, needing to distance himself before he regretted his next move. Though the space between them was less than he needed, Kyle was safe from his wrath, at least for a few moments.

"You're a lot like him, you know."

With Jake's energy beginning to drain, Kyle's voice infiltrated his teetering mind, forcing him into the present. "Like who?"

"Our father."

"I'm nothing like him!" Jake shot back.

"You have a temper like he did."

"Only because I have a sorry-ass excuse for a damn brother—an irresponsible, squandering, self-gratifying, drug-addicted asshole!"

Kyle pushed away from the wall and took a deep breath, filling his cheeks with air before exhaling. "I deserve that. But that's not me anymore. I've changed. I'm clean now."

Jake spotted Kyle's hand twitching by his side. He quirked an eyebrow and snorted. He could remember the twitching limbs when he and the medics strapped Kyle to a stretcher after Jake had found his all-but-lifeless body inside an abandoned home occupied by drug addicts. Kyle lifted his hand, staring at it, before letting it fall to his side again. "Side effect of the long-term drug use. It's likely I'll always have involuntary muscle movements."

Running both hands through his hair, Jake clutched the back of his neck, staring up at the ceiling. The minutes passed as he tried to calm himself. At least Kyle was smart enough not to antagonize him further. "How did you know I was here?"

"You're buying the casino."

"And how do you know that?"

"It's not like it's a big secret. Anyone who follows the regulatory authorities knows all about it, and there are a lot of employees here. They talk."

"OK, so, you know I'm buying the hotel and casino, but that doesn't explain why you were following Samantha?"

"Is that her name? The pretty blonde—well, now brown-haired lady, the one you left at the spa?"

"Yes, that's her name! Why were you following her?"

"I wasn't following her. I thought you would be coming back to pick her up, so I waited around."

"You waited an entire day because you figured I was coming back? Right."

"I wanted to talk to you."

"So you thought it was acceptable to hang out by the spa all day, in a hooded sweatshirt in the middle of the goddamn summer? You realize you scared her, don't you?"

"How did she know I was there?"

"Because she fucking saw you, not once, but twice! Why were you hiding? Why not just find me? Why not call? Why the secrecy?"

"I didn't want to be seen."

"By who? I would have never recognized you."

"No, the others."

"What others? Are you running from someone? Your dealer?"

"No, that's not what I meant." Kyle took a deep breath. "My coworkers, them." Kyle nodded toward the employees in the security room.

Jake followed his gaze. "You work here?" Jake's voice cracked, and Kyle nodded. "Jesus Christ! This day just can't get any better." Shaking his head, he let out a cynical laugh.

"They know you're my brother, but they don't know about my past. That's my office right there." Kyle pointed through the privacy glass toward an office on the other side of the room.

"You're one of the security supervisors?"

"Yeah, I've worked here for about four years now."

"Unbelievable! This is how you had the security code to the penthouse floor?"

"Yes."

"Why in the hell wouldn't Mike tell me, and why were you not around when I asked to meet all of the security team?"

"I asked Mike not to tell you. I wanted to talk to you first, so he made sure I was off whenever you were here, at least until I had a chance to talk to you. Everyone sort of covered for me."

"Is that right?" Jake shook his head, surmising he needed to make immediate changes with the security personnel. "So everyone out there knows you're my brother and that I'm buying the hotel?" Jake waved his hand toward the outer room.

"Pretty much."

"*Christ!*" Jake sagged over the table, hanging his head before looking back to Kyle. "Did you take a picture of me and Samantha when we got off the elevator three weeks ago?"

"Yes."

"Why?"

"I don't exactly have any family photos."

"Why would you? You chose drugs over your family, remember?"

Kyle pursed his lips together and nodded. "The old Kyle did, yes." Kyle took a step toward Jake, then stopped. "I wanted a picture, and you looked so happy. I couldn't remember the last time I saw you that happy."

"What did you do with it?"

"Nothing. Your men took my phone. The picture is still on there, or at least it was."

"So why today? Why in the middle of the night?"

"You were always an early riser. I figured if I called the room from the hallway, you might meet me outside. I wanted to talk to you before your meeting with Mike and Vanessa today. You found out she comped the room I stayed in last time, and I didn't want you to be angry with her before the sale."

"The room, Christ!" Jake spit out. The pieces were falling into place. It all made sense now.

"Yeah, I thought you might figure it out, like when we were kids. I was always Superman. You always wanted to be the cop, and you always used a combination of our ages for your badge number. I didn't realize you had security with you twenty-four seven, otherwise I wouldn't have attempted to go to your room."

"They're not security; they are my friends, and they all work for Morgan Industries, but more importantly, we served together; we have each other's back because that's what *brothers* do, something you know nothing about!" Jake ignored the grimace on Kyle's face at his angry words. "So, what do you want? What is so urgent that you needed to sneak up to the penthouse suite? Is it money?"

Kyle shook his head, chuckling a little. "I didn't sneak up to the room. And I told you I don't want your money or anyone else's money. I wanted to see you before your meeting today. I wanted to say I'm sorry…for everything, for leaving you with all the responsibilities before you were a teenager. I'm sorry for all the things you said before. I'm clean now, Jake. I know what I did was wrong, and I wanted to say I'm sorry."

"Feel better now?"

"It doesn't feel as good as I thought it would. I didn't realize you were harboring so much resentment toward me. Mike said since you were in a relationship, you were different, calmer. He thought you would be more receptive toward me."

"Did he? I'll be having a few words with Mike about why he kept this from me, but now that you said what you wanted to say, you can check it off your list—until next time!"

"There won't be a next time, little man."

"Don't fucking call me that!" Jake pointed at Kyle. "You lost your right to call me that! You lost your right to call me your brother when you chose drugs over your own goddamn family!"

"OK." Kyle held his hands up in front of him. "But please hear me out. I'm done with drugs and that life. I know I have amends to make." Kyle blew out a breath. "But I also wanted to thank you."

"Thank me?"

"Yeah, for always being there for the family, for looking out for me, and… well…you know, for not killing me when you had the chance six years ago."

Jake squeezed his eyes closed, a desperate attempt to rid the images from his head of that night. Everything that led up to that final showdown, all the anger Jake had concealed over the years, boiled to the surface. The images filtered through his mind: his sister Shannon, his grandfather looking helpless, the open safe, money scattered everywhere, and Kyle.

"Look, Jake, I asked Mike not to tell you, so don't blame him or Vanessa. They were only trying to help."

"Why? How did you end up here?"

Kyle peered at the floor, shuffling his feet back and forth. "After I left Phoenix House, I started using again. I wanted a fix to ease the withdrawal, you know." Kyle ran a hand through his hair, pulling a few strands loose from his ponytail. He looked up, his eyes latching on to Jake's. Jake watched him, not wanting to see the difference in Kyle, not wanting to see the honesty in his eyes, or the emotion creating a wet sheen over them. "One time led to a second time, then a third, and by then I couldn't face everyone, not again, not after all the mistakes I made over the years. I hated myself and what I had become, but I couldn't stop." Jake watched Kyle struggle with his words. He looked away, not wanting to give him any sympathy only to be disappointed again. "I ended up in Utah for a while, hitched a ride, and eventually came here. I guess, for the first time in my life, I had a new perspective on things, and I reached out to Grandfather and told him I was ready to get the help I needed."

"Grandfather knew?"

"Yes. He kept it a secret, except for Mike and Vanessa. He told me I had to prove myself this time. He and Mike put me into treatment, and this time it was different. I was the one who wanted to get clean, and I was ready. Once my treatment was successful, Mike gave me a job, and since then I've worked in every department, proving to myself that I didn't need the drugs to live."

Jake shook his head, still unable to believe his own brother was standing in front of him. If he worked at the hotel, it was no wonder he was able to hide from the cameras. Jake pulled out the wallet Cal had handed to him and threw it on the table. It landed with a thud, falling open so Kyle's identification was visible. "So how long have you lived here?"

"A little over four years."

"And you know Grandfather died, right?"

"I know." Kyle hung his head. "I usually checked in with him once a week, so he knew I was following through this time. I spoke to him that morning, and later that day, Mike found me in one of the hotel suites and told me the news. Mike and Vanessa were so good to me, staying with me every night for a month, recognizing his death might be the stressor that would set me back."

"And yet you didn't show for his funeral."

"I wasn't ready."

Jake snorted. "That was four years ago. Why did it take you so long to contact me? Did you start using again?"

"I told you I'm clean, Jake, and I did try. I've called your office every day for the last six months. Sometimes I hang up before anyone answers. Other times I make it as far as asking for you, but I—"

"Chickened out?" Jake said, interrupting Kyle again. "So how long are you clean for this time?"

"I've been clean over four years."

"Until the next time. Isn't that how it goes with you?" Jake stood against the wall with his arms crossed and his legs spread, allowing the heat from his anger to flush through his body. He wasn't prepared for any of this, not today, not this weekend, not ever. "Until you show up at your job stoned out of your mind waiting for your little brother to save your sorry ass? Not this time, Kyle!"

Kyle didn't react but slowly nodded his head. His slight reaction made Jake seethe. He wanted an argument, a fight. "I made mistakes. I know that, and I'm ready to face them now. I know I have other amends to make, to Mom and Shannon."

"Like hell! You hurt our family enough, and I'll be damned if I let you back into our lives to do that again!" Jake moved toward the door.

"Do you speak for them now?"

Jake halted. Turning back to Kyle, he bristled at the challenging words. "I suggest you start looking for a new job. I need a security team in place I trust, and that definitely isn't you." He scanned the outer room. "Or your friends."

Jake walked out the door, slamming it hard. He could feel the faces turn toward him. They were all watching him, but they were smart enough to look away when he glared back at them. He stalked toward the exit, shoving aside chairs and anything else in his way, making his way to the hallway with Cal right behind him.

"I guess that didn't go so well," Cal said, catching up to him.

"It was fucking great!" Jake hissed out.

Jake felt like the walls were closing in on him. Samantha was safe from her past, but there was still the vandalism, which had started in Atlanta three months ago. The cryptic messages left behind at the scenes had him stymied: letters, numbers, shapes, and symbols—none of it made any sense, and now he had to deal with Kyle. Ever since he could remember, Kyle had been a distraction, and the last thing he needed right now was a damn distraction. Jake rubbed at his chest, heaving a deep breath. He couldn't go back to the hotel suite, not in this state. He needed a release, something to numb the pain.

Chapter 2

Samantha poked her head through the bedroom door, observing Jake leaning against the opposite wall. His head was resting against his arm, and his face was turned away from her, so she had no idea what he was thinking, but the deep breaths he was taking made his shoulders rise and fall, informing her without words that whatever had happened that morning couldn't be good.

As they were a newly engaged couple, she had envisioned an entirely different scenario when she woke. Instead of being greeted with a morning kiss from Jake, she was greeted by Ammo, his friend, a vice president in the company, and a former comrade who served with him in the army. He refused to tell her what was going on, only that Jake had urgent business to attend to. Samantha tightened the towel around her chest, twirling a strand of her wet hair as she worried her bottom lip. Jake was the strongest man she had ever met, but right now his body emanated defeat.

Opening the bedroom door, Samantha took cautious steps toward him until she was standing behind him. She wondered if the urgent business had been more vandalism, or if something had gone wrong with the sale. Whatever it was, she wanted to help, to be there for him, like he had been there for her. "Are you OK?" When he didn't respond, she wrapped her arms around his torso, resting her head against his back. She inhaled, breathing in his fresh woodsy scent, a smell unique to him, one she would never tire of. "What happened?"

"Not now, Samantha."

She ignored his response. "Is it more vandalism?"

Covering her hand with his, he took another deep breath. "I need a minute."

Continuing to hold him, she closed her eyes, tightening her grip around him. They had been through so much because of her past. When they visited the cemetery and she told him about her father, he held her, providing her with his strength, and now it was her turn. She would be strong for him. "Tell me, Jake."

"I said I need a minute, Samantha!"

His angry words made her flinch. Though she had tried to push him away when her past began to close in on her, things were different now. They were partners, engaged to be married. She wouldn't let him shut her out. "You don't need a minute. You need me." She rubbed her hands up and down his chest, his muscles contracting under her touch. He remained silent. "Don't shut me out, Jake. Talk to me."

He grasped one of her hands, removing it from his chest. Without warning, he spun her around, trapping her against the wall with both arms pinned above her head. She gasped, her heart beating rapidly, fighting the instinct to escape from him. His face was a mere inch from hers, his eyes boring into hers, the prominent odor of whiskey on his breath. She inhaled, trying to calm herself while her body quivered under his powerful gaze. She licked her lips, praying he could see her through the darkness blanketing his eyes, but it was more than anger causing the black sheen. There was something else…something deeper… something more troubling than the anger.

She wanted to ask him who had hurt him, but he didn't give her a chance to speak when his lips crashed over hers, hard and demanding, his tongue forcing its way through her closed lips, invading her mouth, tangling with hers. Inhaling through her nose, she struggled for a breath, needing the air to clear her mind to figure out what was happening between them.

She felt a slight hesitation when he placed his palm on her neck. His hand moved slowly toward her towel, his finger following the top of it toward the knot. Tugging at it, the towel dropped to the floor. With the same urgency with which he'd captured her lips, his palm covered her breast in a frenzied grasp, his fingers pinching her nipple hard, the biting sting eliciting a whimper. Squirming under his provocative ministrations, she tried to free her hands, but his response was a low growl emitting from deep in his chest. Tightening his grip around her wrists, he held them against the wall, his knee separating her legs.

Her body and her mind began to battle. This wasn't the Jake she knew and loved, but the way he was demanding a response, the way he was needing her, sent a thrill of excitement flowing through her veins, causing chill bumps to form on her skin. His hand moved to her other breast, drawing out her nipple between his thumb and forefinger, his manipulation a direct link to her heated core, provoking a desire so powerful her insides trembled. As wetness pooled between her thighs, her mind told her this was wrong. She tried to fight through the fogginess of the sensual state he'd put her in, but her body had always responded to him, like it was now. She was helpless over his sexual prowess.

She didn't care that this ardent sexual display was a manifestation of something else. He needed her, and she was not about to make the same mistake she'd made before and let him slip away from her. Despite the vulnerable position of her body, she swallowed hard. If she had any chance of calming the storm raging inside of him, she would have to put aside her need for control. Closing her eyes, she let her body relax and go limp under his imperious touch. It was what he needed, his resolve to take her this way mimicked a feral animal with its mouth and hands holding its prey captive.

Her anticipation escalated when she heard the zipper of his jeans. She tried to free her hands, wanting to do whatever she could to ease the ache he'd built up inside of her, but she was met with another growl and more resistance as he again tightened his grip around her wrists. As he skimmed his hand down her torso, she arched forward, craving the brush of his fingers against her clit. His fingers, slick with her arousal, entered her, and his growl turned to a guttural moan. He penetrated her with hard, fast strokes, then slowed to a rhythmic, sensual teasing in and out, again and again. Pressing his thumb against her hard nub, he rubbed in small circles, tormenting her, sending her toward the height of her release. She moaned into his mouth, her release building, the familiar tingling spreading through her veins, warming her from the inside out.

She was close, but the abrupt withdrawal of his fingers was unexpected. Freeing her hands, he broke the kiss and moved away from her. The T-shirt that had been rubbing against her breasts was no longer creating a delicious friction against her nipples. The magical fingers driving her toward her orgasm were gone. The lips owning her mouth had disappeared. Making a desperate attempt to pull herself out of the erotic haze he cast her into, she opened her eyes.

He stood less than a foot from her, his hands fisted by his side, his breathing ragged. "Fuck!"

Samantha dropped her arms to her side, her fingertips scraping at the wall as she tried to steady herself. Their eyes met, the blackness in his fading to blue, the passion in hers burning with heated desire, the intense ache in her core still pulsating.

"I'm so fucking sorry." His voice was raw, gravelly.

"Don't be. Use me."

"What?"

"You need me."

"No!"

"I know you need me."

His determination began to fade as he scanned her naked body. He took a step toward her. She silently pleaded, wanting him to know she would be there for him, however he needed her.

"I do, but not like this."

"Take me," she whispered, resisting the urge to touch him.

He bent down, snagging the towel from the floor. "I'm so sorry, baby. I never meant to hurt you." He held it to her chest, waiting for her to take it.

"You didn't hurt me. I want this."

"No, you don't."

Samantha tossed the towel to the side, placing her hands on him. She caressed his chest, sliding her hands lower to the waist of his pants. With his zipper open, she tucked her fingers inside, intending on pushing them down, but he seized her wrists, gripping them tight.

He shook his head. "You don't want me this way."

"I want you in every way."

"I—"

"Shh." She shook her head at him, leading him over to the sofa. He released her wrists, allowing her to push his pants over his hips and to the floor. He sat and she straddled his legs, holding herself above his growing erection, waiting for him to make the next move.

"Samantha, I can't."

"Touch me." She tilted her body over his, her breasts less than an inch from his lips.

With his eyes fixated on hers, he placed his hands on her thighs, slowly moving them up to her torso, grasping a breast in each hand, his thumbs rubbing gently over her sensitive nipples. "Aah," she panted as the pleasure he'd built up earlier returned. She let her head fall back, breaking away from the confusing stare he gave her. Pushing her breasts together, he continued massaging one while his lips covered the other, his teeth scraping over her nipple.

Bringing her hands to his head, she ran her fingers through his hair, guiding his head closer to her, encouraging him to continue the sensual suckling. Releasing her breast, his hands slid up, grasping her neck until she was facing him again. Opening her eyes, she was met with the bright blue of his. "Jake."

His response was an intimate kiss, reigniting the embers. Grasping her hips, he guided her, his steel shaft sliding into her slick entrance. With their gazes locked, he lifted his hips, penetrating her wet core with a hard thrust, followed by a slow drag as he pulled himself out. Samantha held on to the back of the sofa, granting him control. He lifted her slowly from him, then back down, the erotic friction of each deep stroke creating a renewed sense of pleasure. She was nearing the peak, the place she'd been before he abruptly withdrew from her. Sensing her needs, Jake's movements became faster until he was lifting himself, hammering into her, rubbing against every nerve ending. Unable to hold on, she closed her eyes, his name leaving her lips in a raspy groan as her orgasm washed over her. Her walls clutched his shaft, and he inhaled, holding his breath as he stilled inside of her, spurting himself into her tight channel. With both of them panting, he drew her into him, burying his face into her chest. Resting her cheek on his head, she fought back tears at the intensity of what had just happened, but also because he was hurting. Something had affected him so deeply, and she vowed to be the one to take away his pain.

Opening her eyes, Samantha squinted at the bright light entering through the window. She sat up on the sofa, drawing a blanket up around her and rubbing her eyes, the view of the hotel suite kitchen coming into view. "Jake." The eerie quiet sent a sudden panic through her. Pushing off the sofa, she bustled the blanket around herself and ran to the bedroom. She dropped the blanket and snagged a pair of shorts and a T-shirt from her suitcase. Slipping on a pair of flip-flops, she hurried through the suite, running her fingers through her hair in a lame attempt to look presentable.

Grabbing the key card from her purse, she pulled the door open, racing toward the elevator. Cal ducked inside as the door was about to close. "You scared the crap out of me!" Samantha held her hand to her chest. "Where were you?"

"Right outside your door. I guess you didn't see me, and talk about scaring the crap out of someone! You came out that door so fast you nearly gave me a heart attack. What's your hurry?"

"Sorry. I need to find Jake."

Cal pressed a button on the elevator. "He's on the executive floor. He locked himself in one of the offices and hasn't responded to any of us for the last three hours."

"Three hours? What the hell time is it?"

"Almost ten."

Samantha closed her eyes and rested her head against the wall. She remembered holding him to her chest and how her body felt so tired and her eyes heavy after their lovemaking. If it was almost ten, that meant Jake left her there almost right after. She'd tried to calm him, bring him back to her, but maybe she hadn't. Maybe the powerful storm raging intensely inside of him was too much for her to get through to him. "What happened last night?"

Cal slung his backpack over his shoulder. "I'm sure he'll tell you."

The doors to the elevator opened, and Samantha stepped on to the executive office floor, lit up by the bright morning sun shining through a wall of windows in every direction. It was going to be another day of blistering, dry heat. "Where is he?"

"Down that hall." Cal pointed toward the narrow passage where the tile ended and gave way to an orange pile carpet. "Corner office."

Samantha bolted toward it, eager to get to him, to try to reach him. She had no idea where things stood with him, how he was doing, what he was feeling, or what the hell had happened, but he was not going to shut her out, not after everything they had been through. She tried not to run, but as soon as she reached the carpet, she jogged toward the closed door at the end of the hallway, making a note to herself to ask Jake if she could redecorate this place. The dark paneling and orange carpet were depressing, not to mention old. The smell alone was beginning to nauseate her.

She knocked on the door. "Jake!" She breathed a sigh of relief when she heard scuffling noises coming from the other side.

"Samantha?" Jake pulled the door open. "What's wrong?"

"Wrong? Um…" Looking around the room, her eyes landed on the older gentleman she recognized as one of the attorneys from Clay's office. "Sorry, I'm interrupting, aren't I?"

"Is everything OK?"

Samantha rubbed her temples. She'd been worried when she'd woken and found him gone. She didn't know what happened the night before, but she didn't recall him having any meetings this morning. "I'm sorry. I didn't think you had any meetings."

"I didn't, but something came up. I'll be done before noon."

"I was just…"

Jake's upper lip twitched. "Worried?"

Samantha nodded. "Yeah."

Jake kissed her forehead. "I need to finish prepping for this meeting. Cal, can you escort Samantha back to our room?"

Samantha gripped on to his hand. "Whatever happened, I'm here for you."

Jake leaned over, kissing her lips. "I know, baby. Go spend some time with your brother or go shopping. I'll see you later."

Chapter 3

*J*ake threw the highlighter down on the desk, then shoved the pieces of paper into his briefcase as he walked toward the conference room. This entire situation with Kyle was something he didn't need to deal with—not now, not ever. The only good thing that came of it was knowing he was the mystery stalker, but there were too many other memories conjured up by his presence. Once again, Kyle was distracting him from what he had planned for Samantha this morning. He winced when he thought about what he'd almost done to her. As soon as she'd fallen asleep, he'd covered her with a blanket, needing to get away from her, afraid that if he kept reflecting on his conversation and his history with Kyle, his anger would reappear. He needed to keep his distance from her, at least until he was sure any residue of his anger was completely gone.

He checked his watch, cognizant of how long he'd made Mike and Vanessa Valente wait for him. He gripped his briefcase, reassuring himself they deserved what was to come after what they'd tried to pull over on him. The fact that Kyle worked at the hotel pissed him off. Not once while they were discussing the sale did they mention it or give him any indication they had been in contact with him. He should have known something was up when they were adamant about keeping all personnel on staff. It had been a sticking point early on during negotiations, and after Jake agreed not to make any changes for the first thirty days, they had still negotiated six-month severance agreements for any supervisory positions he wanted to replace. Jake wanted his own team running the show after observing the multiple inadequacies, and now that he knew Kyle was employed here—as a supervisor no less—it infuriated him.

The worst part of this entire mess was the fact that Mike and Vanessa were friends of his grandfather, and he didn't want their departure to be on less-than-amicable terms, but at the same time, he wanted answers. He always thought he could hold his own as a CEO of a large corporation. In his few short years of leading his grandfather's company, he had circumvented unscrupulous people and met stringent deadlines for the regulatory authorities, contractors, and the like. He had sat through exhausting meetings, patiently waiting for the other party to put a final offer on the table, and he unpleasantly had to manage ambitious employees who would stop at nothing to get ahead.

He had been successful thus far by following the values his grandfather instilled in him and because he understood people. He had mastered the skill of reading people, gauging whether or not they were being truthful. He had known Samantha was hiding something from the first time they met, but he'd led with his heart, and he couldn't help but think maybe he'd done the same thing with Mike and Vanessa, two people who had been part of his life since he was a young child. Every year they visited New York, always staying with his family and bringing gifts for everyone. They were like the aunt and uncle he never had, but they had so blatantly lied to him.

Mike and Vanessa had betrayed his trust, and he refused to be duped again. Taking a deep breath, Jake walked in, and both Mike and Vanessa looked at him from their seated positions at the large conference table. *Guilty.* The first word that popped into his head was reflective of the way they were looking at him, and Jake was keenly aware that Kyle had told them about their early-morning meeting.

Mike stood, holding out his hand. "Morning, Jake. It's going to be another hot one out there today. Must be why you want to get your meetings out of the way. Another trip to the lake planned?"

"Not today." Jake took Mike's outstretched hand, holding on to it longer than necessary as he searched Mike's eyes. Mike lowered his gaze, yanking his hand away from Jake's tight hold. Jake turned to Vanessa, holding out his hand to her. "Thanks for coming in early."

Vanessa took his hand in both of hers. "Is everything OK? I mean, with the purchase? It's still going through, right?"

"I hope so," Jake said. He sat at the head of the table with Mike and Vanessa to his left. Shifting in his seat, he crossed one leg over the other, folding his hands in his lap. "It's hard to believe this day is finally here. It seems like we've been in discussions about it for years."

Mike laughed. "Hell, your grandfather and I were discussing the sale of this place before you were old enough to drink."

"Yes, he mentioned it several times. But you and I have been having this conversation for what...six months now?"

"It was right after Christmas," Mike confirmed.

"I remember. I signed the purchase agreement on the second of January."

"Yep, and the rest is history," Mike said with a hearty chuckle.

Jake opened his briefcase, removing the original purchase agreement, perusing it slowly as though looking for something specific. His procrastination was getting the desired effect as he watched Mike squirm. He wanted to speak, but Jake held up his hand, making a silent request for him to be patient. "Aah, here it is." Jake placed the document in front of Mike and Vanessa, tapping his finger above one of the contract clauses he'd highlighted.

Mike read the short paragraph and stared at Jake, concern etched across his brow. "I don't understand, Jake."

Jake continued to look at both of them, seeing the lies written on their faces, realizing in that moment how wrong he'd handled the entire acquisition of the hotel and casino. Had he been involved in the transactional exchanges rather than the attorneys, he would have realized Mike and Vanessa's demeanor was more than a bit odd. Jake reached over and turned the page of the document, pointing to another clause. "And this one."

"I'm not sure what you are getting at, Jake. We gave you everything you need for this sale...financial statements, vendor contracts, assets. Your auditors were here for weeks going through our books."

"Who else knows about this sale?"

"We've told no one," Mike said.

Jake frowned. He'd hoped Mike would come clean and they could get this all out in the open. He sighed and pulled another document from his briefcase.

"You provided *almost* everything and you told *almost* no one." Jake tried to keep the emotion from his voice.

"With you and your team being here, requesting access to so many different things, there were rumors," Mike said. "Some of the employees took it upon themselves to check in with the regulators. We couldn't stop the gossiping, and we neither confirmed nor denied it."

"But you did tell one of your employees."

Mike shook his head, his lips moved, but the words were mute.

"The schedule in this document indicates when the purchase agreement is signed we will be provided with an employee list, and again a current list will be provided at the close of the sale. This is the list you provided as of the purchase date," he said, laying the two-page document in front of Mike. He pulled his final piece of ammunition from the file in his briefcase and placed it on the table next to the other one. "And this is the list you sent through email as of the end of the day on Friday." Jake sat back in his chair, his victory foiled by their pale faces. Mike and Vanessa were older, and they had worked hard for everything they had. They deserved better than this, but they lied to him.

Mike sat back in his chair, crossing his arms in front of him. "I don't understand what you are getting at."

Jake reached his limit and stood from his chair, pinching the bridge of his nose to try to hold back his frustration. He needed to tread thoughtfully, lest his anger be unleashed and this whole agreement would be off. He rested his palms on the table, glaring at Mike. "One question, Mike, and I want a straight answer this time. No more lies, no more hiding the truth. Did I or did I not meet all of your security personnel?"

"I believe so," Mike said.

Jake held Mike's gaze. The man had been in the gaming industry for years. No doubt he could use the current poker face to win a few hands, but Jake had laid out the evidence, and yet Mike was still attempting to lie about it. There was no reason to keep it from him any longer. "Since the two of you are leaving the country, I agreed to a midmonth purchase date to accommodate your schedule. Funds are scheduled to be transferred to your account tomorrow at 12:01 a.m." Jake checked his watch. "Which means that in a little more than twelve hours, should you decide to fully disclose everything per our original agreement, you are free and clear to walk away from here. If not, I can legally back out of the agreement, cancel the fund transaction, and walk away. Now, let me ask you one more time, did I meet all of your security personnel?"

"Kyle working here isn't relevant!" Vanessa shouted, clearly upset.

Jake winced when a tear fell to her cheek. He didn't want her to cry; this was simply business. *Wasn't it?* "Finally, the truth comes out!" Jake pushed off the table. "You had an obligation to disclose his employment to me and rather than doing that, you purposely manipulated the employment lists, removing his name, and adjusted the schedule so I didn't find out."

"Jake—"

Jake held up his hand. "After being awakened by an early-morning phone call, I met with Kyle. Imagine my surprise when he told me he worked here. Afterward, I reviewed every employee list you ever sent to me, and nowhere is he listed as an employee. Why in the hell would you keep this from me?"

Vanessa placed her hand on Mike's. "When Kyle first came here, it was your grandfather who told him he needed to be the one to come to you. We wanted him to tell you earlier, but he was worried about your reaction. He tried several times, but he could never seem to find the right words. Regardless of any of that, his employment here changes nothing with the agreement we entered into."

"That's where you're wrong, Vanessa. Your name is on that agreement. When you were negotiating for severance packages for your supervisory staff, I asked to meet them, *all* of them! I checked them off the employee list I was provided. I made calculated decisions based on who I might or might not keep and what additional costs that might entail. But let's be honest, the only reason you negotiated for those severance agreements at all was because of Kyle."

"No," Vanessa said. "He may be part of the reason, but he's not the only reason. These employees are like family to us."

"Enough, Vanessa," Mike said. "Jake, your grandfather asked me to help him. I figured by the time we got to the closing date of the agreement, he would have come to you." Mike shook his head, staring at the documents in front of him. "Kyle has changed. He's been clean over four years. He's been through a lot during that time. I didn't want to push him."

"You would do well to respect the life he has fought for," Vanessa added. "We witnessed him struggle and juggle—" Vanessa stopped when Mike placed his hand over hers.

Jake glanced between them, furrowing his brow. "You witnessed him struggle and juggle what?"

"The difficulties of a recovering addict," Mike finished for her. "He's clean now, our best employee. Kyle knows more about this hotel and casino than any one of us sitting at this table. Imagine how easy it would have been for him to go to your mother, to ask for money to get on his feet again, but he didn't do that. He worked hard, every day, picking up shifts, helping the other workers. Not once, in four years, has he been late for work or missed a shift. He has never screwed up and has never lost his focus on changing his life for the better."

Jake bit back the words on the tip of his tongue. He had no idea who the hell they were talking about. Kyle didn't have a responsible bone in his body. In fact, he was one of the most irresponsible people Jake had ever known. He shirked his responsibility to his family years ago, dependent on them for money, for a place to live, and to finance his drug habit. "Are we still talking about Kyle?"

"You know we are. I can vouch for him. He's clean," Mike stated.

"For now, but one thing about Kyle is there is always a next time. Don't let him fool you."

"You are the only one who is a fool."

Jake quirked an eyebrow. He pointed back to the documents. "Are you sure about that?"

Mike glared at him, his aging features looking stern. "We never lied to you. We didn't tell you because Kyle wanted to be the one to tell you."

"You risked a hell of a lot by covering for him, yet you call me the fool."

"You are a fool for not allowing your brother another chance and for saying you would walk away from this arrangement because of him," Mike stated.

Jake turned from them and walked to the window. His decision had been made. "The way I see it, there are two options." Jake placed his hands in his pockets. "I could cancel the funding transaction and walk away, but my grandfather's wish was to own this place, and since you sold your house and don't intend on staying in the area, that leaves both of us with the second option."

"Which is what?" Mike asked.

"My attorney is waiting on the other side of that door. He's prepared to amend the agreement, to remove the severance agreement addendum we added and to incorporate language offering no protection to any of the employees. You in turn, will provide a full list of employees and agree to the changes, no questions asked."

"You would terminate your own brother?" Vanessa gaped at him.

"Vanessa, you may find this hard to understand: Kyle is dead to me. As far as I'm concerned, he died six years ago."

Mike stood. "Your grandfather wanted this place, but I don't think he ever thought you would treat your brother this way."

"I knew what my grandfather wanted in business, but as to Kyle, I guess we'll never know."

"Jake, don't do this. Kyle needs the insurance. You can't just leave him on the streets without a job," Vanessa said, scolding him.

Jake eyed her with disdain. "Once you agree to the changes, what I do or don't do isn't your concern, Vanessa."

Mike walked over to Jake. "Your grandfather was right about you. He always called you the boy who was a man by the age of ten, the one who had to give up everything to tend to your family and later your grandfather's business." Mike put his hands in his pockets. "I'm sorry we didn't tell you, Jake. You leave us little choice, so we'll do it your way, but I doubt this is how your grandfather envisioned this purchase. He would never put such an ultimatum on the table without talking about it first." Mike pulled his hands out of his pocket and pointed at Jake. "And George would never turn his back on family, regardless of what happened. He was a forgiving man, so unlike you."

Jake forced a swallow past the dryness in his mouth. He may have turned the tables on both Mike and Vanessa, but Mike was acting more like the winner here, knowing his words had a much bigger impact on Jake personally than anything Jake could have done to impact Mike's financial situation. It was a good thing they were leaving the country; he wouldn't want to face Mike in the coming days after he took care of the Kyle situation.

Chapter 4

*S*amantha gazed out at the pool, the water as blue as the cloudless sky above with the midday sun reflecting off the mosaic tiles surrounding it. Music blared in the distance, and a cacophony of voices and splashes sounded around her. The blistering July heat was intensified with the dry air, and she'd give anything to join her brother, Charlie, in the pool.

Charlie was walking up the stairs at the shallow end of the pool, oblivious to the hoard of females with drinks in their hands ogling at him as he passed them by. He walked to the deep end of the pool, fluently launching himself off the edge. For a moment, Samantha was taken back to her first swim meet after her mother had died. She had nailed her entrance with minimal splash, the cheers of the crowd disappearing once she submerged herself into the water. It was then that everything left her mind, her focus solely on winning. She didn't want the win for herself; she wanted it for her mother, who for years had sat along the side of the pool, cheering her on. Even as she swam, she could hear her mother's voice. She had rarely taken first place, usually coming in second or sometimes third, and she only wanted one win, just one for her mother. Her arms stroked through the water, her legs kicking to give her momentum. Every third stroke, she turned her head and inhaled, slowly exhaling as she continued her swim. Tears stung her eyes through the goggles she wore, making the crystal-clear pool appear murky. She put everything she had into the last few feet and came out victorious. From that moment on, she wouldn't lose again during her final senior year, and she owed it all to her mother.

Samantha drew her knees to her chest, fingering the stitches still sewed in her leg, the memories of what happened at the cabin barely two weeks before spewing forth in her mind. Carlos Casano was her father's cousin, an evil man who drove a knife into her leg, all because he wanted something she didn't have. Her friend, Tess, who was with her at the cabin, had been shot in her shoulder, probably ruining her career as a police detective. So much had happened over the past few months, but it was over now. She no longer had to hide from anyone; she had both of her brothers, Chase and Charlie, back in her life, and she had Jake. Her life felt complete, for the first time in over ten years. But thoughts of who or what hurt Jake continued to confuse and concern her.

Charlie came to the edge of the pool, placed his palms on the cement surround, and hoisted himself onto the edge. He looked tired, with dark circles under his eyes, appearing as though sleep had eluded him for most of the night. With his legs dangling in the water, he crossed his arms over his chest, clenching his fists as he stared at the row of hedges bordering the pool. Leaving the comfort of her chair, Samantha joined him at the edge of the pool.

Charlie instinctively held his arm out holding her back. "You can't go in with those stitches."

Samantha nudged him. "I know," she said, putting her feet in the water. "You seem different these past few days."

"Do I?"

"Yeah, you do." She'd noticed a change in his behavior when they left Jake's mother's house. He seemed to drift off during conversations, sometimes his hands shook, and whenever they walked past the gaming area, he was on edge, sometimes jumping at the loud pinging from the slot machines. "You seem distracted."

Charlie smiled and shook his head. "Me? Distracted? I don't miss a thing."

"I know. I'm sure you could tell me precisely how many people are in this pool area, their gender, hair color, and perhaps what they are drinking."

Charlie didn't smile or laugh. "Forty-six, twenty-eight females. The two men on the other side of that hedge are arguing about the female in the two-piece red swimsuit who's pretending to enjoy that strawberry margarita. The dude to your left wearing the khaki shorts, oversized flowered shirt, and sunglasses is an undercover cop. He has a piece under his left arm and a hitch in his step, probably an old injury judging by the missing hair on the front of his left calf. The guy he's watching is at the bar, blue striped trunks, muscular build, gold spearheaded pendant necklace that matches the tattoo on his right shoulder—no doubt some sort of gang affiliation."

Samantha gaped at him. She crossed her arms, splashing her feet in the water, waiting for a few minutes to pass while she processed her thoughts. "Do you ever get tired of it? I mean, it must get exhausting, to watch people like that."

"I like to be aware of my surroundings. I call that being observant, but you seem to think that's being distracted."

"After I moved here, I was keenly aware of my surroundings, though not to the extent you are, but that night at the cabin was the second time I experienced something traumatic in my life. I can't think about what might happen anymore. I want to chase my dreams and live in the moment."

"You make it sound easy. I was trained to be observant, and I survived because of it. I can't snap my fingers and shut it off. This is normal for me."

"But by doing all of that, aren't you distracted from life...reality maybe?" She regretted her choice of words when he flinched. "Forget it. Just forget I said anything."

"Already forgotten."

Samantha gawked at the individuals Charlie had pointed out, wondering if he was right. The man in the striped trunks flashed her a smile, and Charlie was quick to put his arm around her, pulling her into his chest, kissing her temple. His tactic worked when the man turned away from her.

"So what's the deal with you and Tess?"

Charlie dropped his arm from her and chuckled. "I didn't know we had a deal."

Samantha rolled her eyes. "Stop being so literal. You like her."

"I like a lot of people, others not so much."

"You know, when we were kids and Dad asked you something you didn't want to answer, you used to rub the back of your neck, and your lip would twitch. It looks a lot like what you just did."

"Then you should know I don't want to talk about this."

"Why don't you ask her out?"

Charlie looked away, but she saw a glint of a smile as he stood and held out his hand. Samantha took it, and he helped her up. "If you didn't have those stitches, I would have thrown you in the pool already."

"Because you can be an asshole. What's wrong with asking her out?"

"Because I can be an asshole, like you said." He snatched up their towels and her small bag. Taking her by the elbow, he led her from the pool area.

"Why are we leaving?"

"Because something's about to go down in there, and I don't want you anywhere near it." Charlie nodded to Cam and Manny, who followed in step behind them. "What if she says no?"

"Are we talking about Tess?" Samantha rolled her eyes when he nodded. "Are you twelve or thirty-two? Just ask her out! I have money on this!"

"You bet on me?" He feigned hurt.

Samantha bit her top lip to keep from laughing with him. "It was Chase's idea. He said you would be too chicken to ask her out."

"Now you're only trying to goad me. Chase would never call me a chicken when it comes to women, but how much?"

"Never mind; I'm hungry. How about if I shower and change and meet you downstairs in an hour?"

"I'll come to your room in an hour."

Samantha entered the hotel suite, holding her hand to her chest upon seeing Jake leaning over the kitchen counter. "Hi."

Jake pushed off the counter, his eyes roaming over her. "We need to talk."

"OK." Setting her things down, she walked over to the counter.

"I'm sorry, Samantha. About what happened this morning."

"You don't need to apologize."

"Yes, I do. My plan for this morning looked much different." He took her hands in his, his thumb mindlessly rubbed over her engagement ring. "I promised you no more secrets."

"We promised each other no more secrets."

"The first night we met, I told you I had two siblings, but it was only me and Shannon now. I never told you about my older brother, Kyle."

There was something weighing heavy on his heart and in his mind. Samantha pulled her hands from his and stood on her tiptoes, running her fingers through his hair. "Do you want to tell me about him now?"

Clenching his jaw, he reached for her hands, leading her over to the sofa. "I was only four when my father walked out. Kyle was ten. I knew then that our lives would never be the same, but with Kyle there, I thought things would be fine. I used to look up to him, but almost right away, things started to change. Something was different with him. He was quiet and rarely smiled. After a few years, he started acting strange, lying to our mother, staying out all night. He was no longer the brother he had been before that night."

Even though Shannon had told her about their father and about Kyle, she realized in that moment how much she didn't know about his past. She'd always been more concerned with the present, afraid if she asked him too much, he would pry into her past.

"After a few years, we moved in with my grandparents. Grandfather worked in the city and because Grandmother was ill, we all took care of her. Most of the time, it was just me and Shannon. When Kyle did come home, he wasn't the brother I remembered. He didn't care about anything, including himself. He started stealing pills from my grandmother and money from our mother. We started locking everything—cabinets, doors, cars. Then one night, someone broke into the house. Shannon stayed upstairs and called the police. I was scared, but I had to protect my family, so I went downstairs with Mom. It was so dark, but then I heard Kyle laughing. I turned on the light, yelling for Shannon."

Leaning forward, Jake folded his hands. "Because Mom worked most days, she left a jar of money in one of the locked cupboards so Shannon and I could use it for emergencies. Kyle had broken in through the patio door, gone into the cupboard, and taken the money jar. He must have dropped it on the floor, and it shattered. I have this image in my head that won't go away. He was on his hands and knees, crawling through broken glass, and his clothes and his face were dirty. He was sweating so bad his shirt was wet and his hair was slicked back. I just stood there, watching his hands shake as he tried to pick up the dollar bills on the floor, talking to himself and laughing, not realizing we were standing there watching him. There was blood everywhere from the glass…on his hands, his legs. I'll never forget that image."

Jake paused, inhaling and exhaling. Samantha remained silent, affording him the time he needed to tell his story his way. "Shannon called his name, and he looked up at us, and I remember his eyes looking so blank, like he didn't know who I was. He stared at us for a long time, and he had this look on his face, and for the first time in my life, I was scared of him. It took him only a second to jump up and grab ahold of Shannon. He had a piece of glass in his hand, and I'm not sure what he was going to do with it." Jake shuddered. "It was like this rush of adrenaline came over me, and even though he was bigger, I went after him. I don't even remember him hitting me, but afterward, I had bruises on my face and stomach and cuts on my arms from the glass. I heard the sirens in the distance, and I only had to hold him off for a bit longer, but he heard them too. He got away from me and ran out the back door."

"Was it drugs?" Samantha asked, though she knew the answer.

"He was high on crack, and from that night on, we wouldn't see him unless he needed something or got himself into trouble again. Sometimes we wouldn't even see him, we'd just find something missing."

"I'm so sorry. I can't imagine how hard that was for all of you."

Jake nodded. "It was the hardest on our mother. We tried committing him several times over the years, but it never helped. He was wasting away. The last time I saw him, he was skinny and frail, and his mind was gone."

Samantha reflected back on their conversation the night in his brother-in-law's office. She had asked him why he would help Brittany, his former friend and lover, if she didn't mean anything to him. He had told her then it was because he hated to see someone throw her life away on drugs. She now understood the depths of his misery and what he experienced seeing his brother waste away from drug use. Her heart ached for the little boy he was then and for the man he is today, both so strong, but hurting because of losing a brother.

"What happened to him?" She was afraid of what his answer might be, wondering if it was the reason for his distress and what had awakened him so early that morning.

"Six years ago, we committed him to rehab again. And again, he walked away. When I was discharged from the army and Grandfather was ill, I searched for him in the usual and not-so-usual places. After Grandfather died, I searched again, but I never did find him, but I guess I don't need to look any longer."

"Oh no." Samantha gasped. "Is he…"

"No, he's not dead. I don't need to look, because this time he found me."

She gave him a quizzical look. It was not what she had expected to hear. "What do you mean, he found you?"

"He's here, in Vegas. Working at this hotel and casino."

"Oh! Wow!" Samantha said, unsure how to read his expression. "I'm sure you must be relieved to know he's alive and well."

"Relieved?" Jake pursed his lips together. "No, not really. I buried Kyle a long time ago."

"But he's your brother."

"No." He shook his head. "Brothers don't choose drugs over family."

"Is he still using?"

"He says he's clean and has been for four years."

"But you don't believe him."

"He's like the boy who cried wolf, Samantha. After he says it so many times, you stop believing him."

Samantha heard the anger mixed with pain in his voice. "Drug addiction is an illness, Jake. If he says he's clean and he's here now, why not give him the benefit of the doubt?"

"Yeah, he's here," he repeated her words softly. "He was the man in the hooded sweatshirt who has been following you, or us."

"That was Kyle? Why would he do that?"

"The first time, by the spa, he was waiting for me to come back to get you, and he didn't want his coworkers to recognize him. God knows *I* never would have recognized him. He's put on at least a hundred pounds and wears his hair in a ponytail. He's not the Kyle I remember. What I remember is the torment he caused our family, and I won't put them through that again!"

She didn't anticipate this type of reaction. He took so many risks bringing her family together. Something didn't make sense. "Won't you at least try? If not for you, then for your mother and sister?"

"No!" Jake jumped from the sofa and paced the room for a few moments before coming back and standing in front of her. "We will never talk about Kyle again! Do you understand?"

"But——"

"Never again, Samantha! The subject is closed, and not one word of this to my mother or sister!" Jake lifted his briefcase from the floor and walked past her toward the door.

She crossed her arms over her chest. "Are you mad at me or at Kyle?"

Jake stopped but didn't turn to look at her. His shoulders rose and fell several times. "Can we just drop the subject of Kyle? What's done is done."

Samantha shut her eyes when he slammed the door behind him, mulling over everything he'd told her about his brother. She couldn't help but think there were many pieces still missing from his childhood and many stories about Kyle he had left out. Jake was a wonderful man, a devoted brother. He wouldn't give up on Kyle that easily. *So, what happened? What happened to make him give up on the brother he once looked up to?*

Chapter 5

Samantha walked between Ammo and Charlie toward an apartment building on the north side of Las Vegas. The yellowish stucco-like structure appeared in need of a coat of paint. The rocks and red sandy areas were planted with bushes and shrubs, appearing to be more than a little overgrown. Sounds from children screaming and laughing could be heard from the playground and pool area a short distance away as the sun began to set.

"Remember what we talked about," Ammo said. "It's late and we maybe have thirty minutes. After that we need to hightail it back to the hotel."

"What did you tell Cam and Manny?" Samantha asked.

"That you wanted to check out the competitors so you could decide on a marketing strategy for the hotel, and if that doesn't work, Max is prepared to step in and help us out."

Samantha stopped at the foot of the stairs, grasping Ammo's arm. "Thank you, all of you, for helping me. I don't want Jake mad at any of you, though."

"JT is like a brother to me...to all of us. He might say Kyle is dead and buried to him, but you ask me, Cal, Max, or Shorty, and we know better. We have all served in the army with JT, and we have all worked for him. He's our friend, and he's always been about family. It's why he worked so hard to bring your family together again. JT needs to face his brother; he needs closure."

"Closure?" Samantha quirked an eyebrow, surprised by his use of the word. "What do you mean by that?"

"Nothing. Just go; you're wasting time." Ammo nudged her toward the outdoor concrete steps.

Once they were on the second-floor landing, Samantha took a deep breath, following Charlie down the cement walkway to a brown door, though the paint was peeling, revealing a red color underneath. The doorknob was faded from years of use, and the screws appeared looser than they should be.

Charlie raised his hand to knock, glancing at Samantha. "You sure about this?" She had confided in Charlie, telling him everything, and they'd both agreed they would find a way to bring Jake's family together, like he had done for their family. First, they needed to meet Kyle, to hopefully find out what happened between him and Jake, and then determine their next move.

She nodded to Charlie, feeling a bit uneasy but knowing she couldn't turn back now. Samantha stepped from behind Charlie when the door opened. The man standing before her had yellowish skin; it was the first thing that connected in her mind: the same color skin as in the videos she'd seen. His brownish hair was pulled back in a ponytail, accentuating his strong jaw, the shape so similar to Jake's. He wore a pair of jeans and a black T-shirt with some sort of writing on the front too small to read.

"Hi," he said. "This is a surprise."

"Kyle, right?"

"Yes, and you're Samantha." He eyed Ammo and Charlie, then leaned his head out the door, looking in both directions. "Is Jake with you?"

"No, he's not." Samantha held out her hand. "It's nice to meet you."

Kyle took her outstretched hand, his grip firm like Jake's, but the disappointment on his face made her worry he didn't want her there.

"This is my brother Charlie, and I think you know—"

"Ammo." Kyle shook his hand, then turned to Charlie. "Charlie, it's nice to meet you," he said. Placing his hands on his hips, he raised an inquisitive brow, assessing the three of them. "Why are you here?"

"Who is it, Daddy?" a tiny voice asked from behind Kyle.

Surprised, Samantha looked down as a little dark-haired girl with huge blue eyes came out from behind Kyle, clutching his leg. The little girl looked up at Samantha, her eyes widening and her lips curving into a smile, showcasing her tiny teeth and a familiar trademark dimple in her cheek. She squealed with excitement, looking up at Kyle when he placed his hand on her head. "Is it really her?" she tried to whisper, but Samantha heard.

"Yep, that's her, sweetheart." Kyle looked at Samantha. "This is my daughter, Sofia."

Samantha smiled and tossed a quick glance over to Ammo, hoping the shock on her face didn't show. Neither Jake nor Ammo had mentioned Kyle having a daughter. She knelt down so she was face to face with Sofia. "Hi, Sofia. You have a very pretty name."

"I know. It was my great-grandma's name."

"How old are you?"

"I'm four," she said. Kyle cleared his throat. "I mean three, but I'm almost four."

Samantha held back her laughter and smiled at Sofia. "You seem very smart for someone who is only three."

"She's been talking like an adult since she was two. She likes to say she's four so she can go to school, but she has another year to wait."

"I'm sorry I lied," Sofia said. "Daddy, can they come in?"

Kyle smiled and nodded. "Sorry. Please come in." He stepped aside, allowing them to enter.

Samantha expected to walk into a bachelor pad with empty soda cans and pizza cartons, but the inside was clean and cool, a welcome relief from the evening heat. There was a hint of lemon ammonia, as though he had cleaned not long ago. A small dining-room table with four mismatched chairs sat directly across from the small L-shaped kitchen. A coffee pot and toaster were on the counter, both shiny and clean. One lone pink plastic cup with what appeared to be a princess on it sat next to the sink.

"You have a pretty name too," Sofia said once they were inside. She tapped Samantha's leg. "What happened to your leg?"

Samantha bent down again. "It's nothing the doctor couldn't fix, but I'm curious, how do you know my name?"

"Daddy told me. You're Samantha, and you're going to marry my uncle Jake, so that makes you my aunt."

"How did you know I'm going to marry your uncle Jake?"

"Because Daddy is Uncle Jake's brother, silly, and brothers and sisters share everything."

Charlie and Ammo both chuckled behind Samantha. "Well…you're probably right about that, but Sofia, since you never met me before, how do you know who I am?"

"You look like you do in the picture Daddy gave me."

"The picture?"

"Come on, I'll show you." Sofia took Samantha's hand, leading her down the hall and into one of the bedrooms. Kyle, Charlie, and Ammo followed. It didn't take long for Samantha to figure out this was Sofia's bedroom, with everything in pink except the white walls: a pink dresser, a pink lamp, a pink bedspread, and pink handles on the closet door. Sofia grabbed a pink picture frame from her bedside table and handed it to Samantha. "See? That's you and Uncle Jake. You look pretty."

"Thank you," Samantha told her. The picture was taken of them when they were on their way to dinner over three weeks ago. "Your daddy gave you this?"

"Uh-huh, and he bought me the frame too so I could keep it close to me because I don't ever want to forget my family."

"That was very thoughtful of him."

"I know, right?"

Sofia's exaggerated nod forced Samantha to bite back her laughter. She said she was almost four, but her tiny frame made her look so much younger than Jake's nephews, who were also three. She spoke in full, coherent sentences, unlike the playful gibberish she often had to decipher from his nephews.

Kyle chuckled. "I work nights sometimes, and I can only get teenagers to babysit, so she picks up on more than she should."

Sofia tugged on Samantha's shorts, drawing her attention from Kyle. "Did you know Daddy can color a picture without going outside the lines? He's really good. Can you color too?"

"I sure can." Samantha wanted to pick Sofia up and squeeze her. She was like a precious doll with long, dark, curly hair pulled into a pony tail and perfect skin that looked so soft and smelled of baby lotion.

"Would you color with me?"

Charlie stepped in front of Samantha and knelt down. "I'm Charlie, Samantha's brother, so you can call me Uncle Charlie if you want. I was away in the army for a long time, and I can't remember the last time I held a crayon. Would you mind if I colored with you?"

Sofia looked up at Kyle, who didn't respond, allowing her make her own decision. She looked back at Charlie and shrugged. "I guess, but you have to stay in the lines."

"I'll do my best," he said, snickering.

Sofia took his hand and led him out of the bedroom and back into the dining area as Samantha, Ammo, and Kyle followed. Taking out one coloring book and a small box of crayons, she put them on the table and pointed to one of the chairs, a silent order for Charlie to sit down. She flipped through the coloring book until she found an empty page, then placed it in front of Charlie.

"She's adorable, Kyle," Samantha said when they approached the dining room to watch Sofia and Charlie.

"Yeah, she is. She's a handful, though." Kyle ran a hand through his hair. "Does Jake know you are here?"

"Does it matter?"

Kyle blew out a breath. "I'll take that as a no." Kyle gestured behind her to the living room, which was smaller than the one in her apartment. It was furnished with a mismatched sofa and a leather recliner worn through on the armrests. The end tables and coffee table were all made of different types of wood, the colors and styles also not matching. The television hung on the wall next to a small curio cabinet displaying pictures of Kyle and Sofia. Samantha sat on the sofa and Ammo sat next to her. Kyle perched on the edge of the recliner seat and leaned forward. "Can I ask why you are here?"

"Oh…well…I wanted to meet you."

"So, Jake told you I was here, but yet he doesn't know you are here. Are you checking up on me to see if I'm clean?"

"No, no, Kyle; that's not why I'm here."

"So, this is what? A nice gesture? Or now that you are engaged, is this your way of ordering me to stay out of the family?"

Samantha was taken aback by the statement, but the torture in his eyes was evident, resembling the same torture present in Jake's eyes that morning. She inhaled, trying to steady her breathing as she thought about what to say. "I don't think that's fair. I would never tell you that. You are Jake's brother; that makes you family, and family is important to me."

"I don't think you and Jake would agree on that." Kyle sat back, studying Samantha for a few minutes. "When did you get engaged?"

"Last night."

"Well, congratulations then. You seem to make him happy, and that's all I want for him."

"You and Jake spoke this morning, but he didn't mention anything to me about you having a daughter."

"I never told him. We never actually got around to having a civil conversation. He was rather upset I was there, and when he found out I worked for the hotel, things went downhill fast." Kyle shifted in his chair. "But it's not like I expected him to welcome me with open arms either."

"What did you expect?"

"I don't know." Kyle sighed. He slumped forward, rubbing his hands down his face.

Samantha worried her bottom lip, concerned about the aura of devastation emanating from every pore of his body, so similar to what she'd witnessed that morning with Jake, but solidifying her original thought that there was more to the story than what either one of them was telling her. She scanned the room, her eyes landing on the pictures. "Is it only you and Sofia?"

"Are you asking if I'm married?"

"Are you?"

"Sofia's mother isn't around, not anymore."

"Oh. I'm sorry." Samantha clasped her hands together. "Um…the picture you took, the one Sofia has in her room—why did you take it?"

"It doesn't matter now." Kyle leaned back in his chair, turning away from her.

Charlie stood from his chair. "Mind if I use your bathroom?"

"End of the hall," Kyle said.

Sofia continued to color after Charlie left. Her little fingers could barely hold the small nubs of the crayons. Samantha leaned forward, speaking in a whisper like Kyle had done earlier. "I don't understand what that means. What doesn't matter now? Jake said you were the one following us the last time we were here. Obviously, you wanted something. Was it the photo?"

Kyle leaned forward again, their faces mere inches apart. He clasped his hands in front of him. "I did follow you, and I'm sorry if I scared you. Mike and Vanessa thought I should talk to Jake before the sale went through, so when I was at the spa, I was waiting for Jake to come back. When Ammo came instead of Jake, I asked Mike what your plans were, and he said you were going to dinner, so I waited by the elevators, but he looked so happy…it just didn't seem like the right time."

"So why take the photo? What were you going to do with it?"

"Exactly what I did with it, which is give it to Sofia." Kyle ran a hand through his hair, causing a few strands to come loose from his ponytail and fall on to his cheek. "Look, Samantha. I don't know what Jake has told you, but he made it pretty clear to me where things stand between us. You shouldn't be here."

Samantha ignored his concern. "I understand you have been working at the hotel for a while, so can I ask why you never reached out to Jake or his mother or sister before now?"

"It doesn't matter, Samantha. I really think you should go." Kyle stood from the chair. "I have done enough harm over the years; I don't need to cause any more."

Samantha and Ammo both stood. She shook her head at him. "I don't understand. How are you causing harm now?"

"By you being here. Please, Samantha, you should go."

"But, Daddy, they just got here," Sofia whined.

"Her auditory skills are impeccable," Kyle said with a roll of his eyes.

Samantha looked over at Sofia just as she threw her crayon across the room and bolted toward Samantha, grabbing both of her legs. Samantha winced when her arm rubbed against the stitches. "Will you come and visit me again?"

Samantha bent down, hugging Sofia, holding her head to her chest. "Yes. I will come back and see you. How about tomorrow?"

"Don't, Samantha. She's only a child. Don't make promises you can't keep," Kyle said.

"How about if I plan something special for the two of us? Maybe a movie or shopping."

"Really?"

"Samantha, don't do this. She won't understand," Kyle pleaded.

Samantha kissed Sofia on the cheek and breathed in the baby-fresh scent. She stood, studying Kyle. Though Sofia added an entirely different dimension to her mission of reuniting Jake with his family, Kyle didn't know her. She wasn't about to lie to a child, much less her soon-to-be niece. "Think what you want, Kyle, but I'm coming back. I'll be here at ten."

Samantha turned on her heel and left with Charlie and Ammo right behind her. Once she'd made it down the stairs, she stopped and took a breath, swiping at the tears. She didn't understand how that little girl had gotten to her in such a short time, but she had, and now there was no turning back and pretending she had never been here. But she had to find out more, and it was obvious Kyle didn't want to tell her anything. If he wanted something from Jake, he would have taken every opportunity to get close to Samantha, but he didn't even want her there. She knew so little about drug use and whether his jaundiced skin was a sign of using or something else, but he sure didn't act like someone who was on drugs.

She peered across the apartment grounds as darkness set in. One lone out-door light buzzed, then flickered on. While it wasn't the worst place to live, it didn't appear to be the best place to raise a child either, but it's where Kyle called home when he could have made one phone call and be living in a much better place right now. Something didn't make sense.

Charlie nudged her from her thoughts. "He's not using."

"I don't think so either."

"Then that makes all three of us," Ammo said.

"But while I didn't find any drugs hidden in the bathroom, there were some rather peculiar medications in his cabinet." Charlie held up his phone to show her a photo.

"That's a lot of medications," Samantha said.

"They are all issued to Kyle. Ammo, do you think you or Max can figure out what these medications are for?"

"We'll try."

Samantha rubbed her temples, wishing away the headache forming behind her eyes. "Do you think it has something to do with his jaundiced skin? Is it something to help with side effects from long-term drug use?"

"Let's not jump to conclusions," Charlie said. "Now, you made a promise to a little girl, so we'd better figure out how we are going to make sure you keep that promise."

Chapter 6

*J*ake stared out at the city of Las Vegas on Sunday night, the neon lights filling the dark skies for what seemed like miles in each direction. He swirled the glass of scotch in his hand, taking a long sip, the flavor filling his senses. According to Cam and Manny, Samantha had left the hotel with Ammo and Charlie, something about checking on the competition. When she didn't answer her phone, he'd called Ammo, and they were due to arrive at any time. He checked his watch, noting less than a minute had passed since he last checked it.

Knowing Samantha, she was presumably checking out how the other hotels marketed themselves, but he couldn't fathom why Cam and Manny couldn't go along. They had strict orders to stay with her. Cal, Max, and Shorty didn't think it was a big deal, merely shrugging when they found out she was with her brother and Ammo. Jake seemed to be the only one who had an issue with it.

He peered into his glass, the ice cubes sparkling, capturing the colors from the streets below. It had been a long day, starting with Kyle, and he wasn't sure how or if he was going to tell Shannon or his mother. He wanted to call Clay, Shannon's husband, and ask him to write up a severance agreement for Kyle, but Clay was more than an attorney; he was his brother-in-law. Informing him about Kyle would place him in a difficult position with Shannon, and he didn't want to do that, but he needed to talk to an attorney, preferably not someone who knew Clay. He wasn't worried about leaving Kyle without a job. A trust fund in his name from their grandfather would provide him with a nice lifestyle, unless, of course, he chose to throw it away on drugs like he had done with every dollar handed to him in the past.

Jake jerked his head around when he heard a key card slide into the door lock. Samantha walked through, her cheeks rosy from spending time in the sun earlier, her smile as bright and cheery as always, and her eyes twinkling when she saw him. He let his eyes roam over her, drinking in every beautiful inch of her from her white tank top contrasting her bronzed skin to the cutoff jean shorts showcasing her sexy legs.

"You know, Ms. Andrews, if you make a habit of dismissing your security, I may very well need to put a monitor on that sexy ankle of yours."

She rolled her eyes at him. "Well, Mr. Morgan, or should I call you Mr. Cranky?" She placed her hands on her hips, scrutinizing him.

"Jake will be fine."

"Well...*Jake*...I didn't think it was an issue since you track my phone anyway."

Jake smiled at her. It was precisely what he expected. She never hesitated to call him out on his own shit. "There is no need to check your phone now, unless of course you continue with this type of behavior." He took another sip from his drink to hide his smile.

She giggled. "And what type of behavior is that?"

Jake was enjoying the playful banter and made a promise to himself that he would do everything he could to make her giggle the way she just did. "Besides dismissing your security, I see you are still wearing that thing you call a bathing suit."

Samantha lifted the brown strap that had fallen from her shoulder. "It's a bikini, not a bathing suit."

"Either way, it doesn't cover much."

"Um...isn't that the point?"

Jake raised his brows. He wanted to tell her no, that she should only be wearing a barely there bikini when he was with her so he could make sure every other man staring at her knew who she belonged to. He took another sip from his glass.

"If you don't like it, I could take it off." She smiled at him like a Cheshire Cat.

"If you take it off, we're going to be late for the dinner I had planned with your brother and the guys."

Grabbing the hem of her tank top, she pulled it over her head. "And you're never late for anything, are you?"

Jake's breath caught in his throat when she pulled on the string of her bikini top. She let it fall from her hand, exposing her breasts. Leaning back, she placed her elbows on the counter, her breasts fully exposed. She was a goddamn goddess. She licked her lips, the sultry look one he couldn't resist. "Never." He stalked toward her, setting his drink on the counter, caging her in. "But there's a first time for everything."

He covered her mouth, devouring her taste, inhaling her scent, no longer caring about the little dinner party he had planned, or what had happened earlier that day with Kyle. All he wanted and everything he cared about was right in front of him.

His hunger for her intensified with every stroke of his tongue. Grabbing her around the waist, he pulled her closer, pressing his hard shaft against her. His hand roamed over her bare skin, palming her breast, his thumb rubbing over her nipple. Breaking the kiss, he scorched a path of hot open-mouthed kisses up her neck to her ear where he lingered and nibbled on her lobe. "Tell me I'm not rushing you."

"What?"

With his other hand he clutched the back of her neck and kissed her again, swallowing her question, his need to make her his permanently stimulating his every desire for her. Pinching her nipple between his thumb and forefinger, he waited for her moan. He knew her body, how it responded to every delicate caress or demanding touch.

She tore her lips away from his, her heavy breathing matching his. "Jake."

He couldn't get enough of her. He continued to kiss her face, her neck, her ear. He needed her more now than he had ever needed anything. He'd been an ass when he walked out earlier, but he couldn't let her leave him. "Things happened so fast between us," he said, nipping at her ear. "I don't want to rush you into anything." He continued kissing her, moving slowly down her cheek, across her jawline until his lips were touching hers. "Did I rush you by proposing too soon?"

She pushed off his chest, meeting his gaze, the crease between her eyes deepening. "What is this about?"

He tried to pull her back to him, but she resisted. "I can't lose you."

"I'm not going anywhere. I love you, Jake. I would have married you last night."

Her words made his heart pump faster. "You would have?" He reached for her again and this time she came willingly into his arms. He was in awe of her. She could make his legs weak with a simple smile. Bringing his lips to hers, he nipped gently. "Maybe we should set a date? Like next month."

Samantha's eyes sparkled with amusement. "Clearly you have no idea how long it takes to plan a wedding."

The wedding didn't concern him. He wanted her, and the sooner she became his wife, the better. "Clearly. But since you said you would marry me last night, perhaps I can convince you next month is perfect timing."

"I doubt that."

He pinched her nipple, making her gasp. His palm glided down her torso to the top of her shorts. He unhooked the top button, sliding the zipper down. Dipping his hand inside, he rubbed it against the brown bikini bottoms, soaked with her arousal. "Oh, Samantha. I know I can convince you. One month and you are all mine."

After they had both showered, Jake exited the bedroom, noticing Samantha painting her toenails. "What are you doing?"

Samantha glanced up, licking her lips, her eyes wandering over him, conveying the same sultry gaze she'd given him less than an hour ago. "Um…painting my toenails."

"In pink?" He held up the bottle. "You don't even like pink."

She pulled her gaze from him to her toes. "Just because I don't wear a lot of pink doesn't mean I don't like it."

"Why don't you go to the spa?"

Samantha plucked the bottle from his hand, placing it on the counter. "You know what? That's a great idea. I think I will."

Jake caught her arm and pulled her into him. "Excellent." He held her, careful not to let his hands roam too far or they would be late for dinner. "I have something for you."

46

"Jake," she started to protest.

"Let's not argue. Just get used to the fact that I like to buy you things." He removed the small jewelry box he'd tucked into his pocket, turning it toward her, he opened it.

"Jake, it's beautiful."

Jake had planned to give her the gift that morning, complete with a bowl of strawberries and chocolate, but his plans had changed. The black orchid charm represented the hotel and everything his grandparents had done to shape him into the man he was today; the diamond sparkling in the center of the orchid was who she was to him, the center of his world, the reason he lived and breathed. "I hope to fill your bracelet with a charm for every occasion."

"And what occasion does an orchid signify?"

"My grandfather wanted to buy this hotel and casino for a long time. He had a corporation established with the name of my grandmother's favorite flower."

"An orchid. What a beautiful story." Samantha placed the charm back in the box and wrapped her arms around him. "Thank you."

"There's something else we need to talk about, and before you say anything, just hear me out. We've talked about it before, but what do you think about moving to a bigger apartment?" Jake heard her sigh. He lifted her head from his chest, holding her face in his hands. "I want a new start for us, but if you're not ready to move, we can wait."

She pulled out of his grasp, ambling over to the counter. "Other than Richard's house, my apartment is the only place I've lived in New York."

Jake nodded. He knew her uncle, Richard Bauer, had brought her here when she was still a teenager. Bauer had found her an apartment, a place she felt safe and comfortable. He didn't want to push her, not after everything she had been through the past few weeks. "Is it more than just the fact you haven't lived anywhere else? You've had a lot of changes these past few months. After what you went through at the cabin, maybe you should think about talking to a professional, a counselor."

"You and Richard think alike, but I'm fine. I just need to go back to work and get into a routine." She let out a heavy sigh. "I think a new place is exactly what we need. Besides, if Charlie decides to stay in New York, he's going to need a place to live too."

"If you're sure; otherwise I'll call Tobin and put a stop to it."

"Put a stop to what?" She turned to face him, inching a brow upward. "Jake Morgan, did you already find us a place?"

Jake walked over to her, placing his finger over her lips when she was about to say something else. "I wanted to surprise you, but yes. I found us a new place. You told me once the only stipulation was that it be in Brooklyn, and that's where it is, right along the East River on Furman street. I know you're going to love it."

Jake removed his finger from her lips, and she pursed them together, continuing to scold him with her eyes. He envisioned the argument that was sure to follow. He shouldn't have acted so quickly, but he wanted to do this for her, to give her a home, a place she could call her own. And with the renovated building filling quickly, he didn't have much time.

Samantha turned away, walking back into the bedroom. "I did say that was the only stipulation, didn't I?"

Jake followed her, unsure what her reaction meant. "So…you're good with the apartment then?"

"Sure."

"You're sure?"

"What were you expecting me to say?"

"Well…to be honest, I was expecting——"

"What? An argument?"

"Something like that," he said, realizing too late that the small chuckle that followed his words would have been better kept silent.

"Do you want one?"

"Um…no. I'm good."

"Good." She tried to walk past him, but he snagged her around the waist. "Thank you."

She settled against his chest. "You're welcome. Do you have more meetings tomorrow?"

"Yep. And I was thinking, maybe after you go to the spa, you should go shopping for a dress."

Samantha dropped her head back. "As in a wedding dress?" Her eyes narrowed toward him.

Jake chuckled, leaning toward her. "I told you I could convince you."

"Wipe that smile off your face. Withholding an orgasm is hardly playing fair."

"Aah, but you laid out the challenge without any rules."

"I call a do-over."

Jake laughed. "Didn't you do that once before?"

"You can be such a shit." She playfully slapped him. "Do you have any idea what goes into planning a wedding?"

He shrugged. "It can't be that hard; people do it all the time."

"Pfft." Samantha snorted and pulled away from him.

"Well, you do like to plan things. Besides, Charlie is here. I think he'd like to do that with you."

"Yeah, I'm sure that's exactly what he wants to do, but I guess it will give us time together since you are going to be in meetings."

"I think it might just be what Charlie needs."

Samantha nodded and crossed her arms over her torso. "You've seen it too then? How distracted and jittery he seems?"

Jake had noticed the little things the minute he and Cal had returned from Colorado. It was worse after the incident at the cabin. Jake doubted Charlie slept, and the only time he seemed to relax was when there were only a few people around, like this past weekend at the lake. "I noticed."

"The funny thing is, I didn't see it when he first came here. But I didn't know what was normal. I mean, it's been a while since I was around him. Should I call Chase?"

"You should talk to Charlie first. He might just need some time to adjust, sort of like you. He's had a lot of changes, and I can tell you first hand, adjusting to civilian life isn't easy, and discovering the sister he thought had died was alive, and..."

"And what?"

"Nothing."

"Well I already tried to talk to him earlier today. I told him he seemed distracted from life. I mean, he knew how many people were in the pool. He even pointed out an undercover cop."

"Ah, yeah. I heard about that. It seems we had a dealer staying here at the hotel trying to pass himself off as some business owner from Florida. Probably one of Kyle's crones."

"Jake! Why would you say that? Didn't he tell you he was clean?"

"I've heard it too many times, Samantha."

"Well, why not give him another chance?"

"I thought we decided not to talk about Kyle." Jake felt his gut beginning to coil.

"You decided, but either way, you brought it up."

"Well, now I'm dropping it, and so are you!"

Samantha narrowed her eyes at him when he raised his voice. He took a deep breath, counting to ten, but the seed had been planted. His stomach was twisting into knotty vines at the very mention of Kyle, remembering the many times he's wanted to kill him. "Can we just go?"

"Are you going to change that pissy attitude of yours?"

Jake had promised her he was working on his anger, and he was, but Kyle added an entirely new scenario, one he neither planned for nor wanted. An appointment with Dr. Kinzie was in order. Maybe two, or three. "Yeah, consider it changed."

Chapter 7

*I*t was barely past five in the morning when Jake exited the hotel with two cups of coffee in his hand. Ammo had sent him a message telling him about Charlie. He yawned, his body and his mind both tired from the past two early-morning wake-up calls, not to mention the dinner party carrying on past midnight. But it also meant Samantha wouldn't be waking anytime soon, which would give him time to talk to Charlie. The guilt of allowing Charlie to go with Cal to Colorado was weighing heavily on him, and he couldn't help but think that was the incident that triggered something in Charlie, and seeing Tess and his sister held at knifepoint at the cabin was likely what sent him over the edge. The man saved his life. He didn't know if he could help him now, but he was sure going to try, not only for Charlie, but for Samantha.

He told Samantha he had seen the signs Charlie was struggling, but he didn't have the heart to tell her what he witnessed the night they stayed at his mother's house over the Fourth of July when he and his friends, Chase, and Charlie, went to town for more beer. What he saw that night solidified his assessment of Charlie. Rattled by fireworks being shot off in the street, Charlie had tackled a group of kids. He was enraged, his mind in another place, another country, another time zone. It took four of them to control him. That had been the reason they were gone so long, deciding not to return to the house until they were all confident Charlie was in the here and now.

If Jake couldn't get through to him, then he'd make a call to Bauer, and that phone call would likely lead to further conversation, and Jake would end up telling him about Kyle. Much to his chagrin, Bauer was probably already aware of what was happening, even from the middle of the ocean on a cruise ship. He knew he should tell his mother and sister about Kyle, but he was afraid. There was no doubt in his mind they would haul his ass back to New York, and Kyle would end up hurting them again, and that would hurt Jake, and he'd be right back where he was with hating him.

He yawned again. He was restless the night before, tossing and turning, thoughts about Kyle infiltrating his thoughts. When sleep finally took over, the same nightmare he'd had time and time again returned, and this time it was Kyle he lifted from the ground and threw over his shoulder, racing to the safety of the chopper in Afghanistan. It made sense when it was Samantha in his dreams, when he thought he couldn't save her from her past. *But why Kyle? And why was it always the chopper?*

The pool area didn't open until eight, and at this hour, only a few people mingled in the outdoor courtyard. Jake placed the two cups inside the fence, then climbed over it, just as Ammo said Charlie had done. He gathered the coffee cups, peeking over the hedge enclosing the walkway, finding Charlie sitting alone in a lounge chair, five empty beer cans lying next to him. Jake walked toward him, slowing his steps as he approached him from the side.

"What are you doing here, Morgan?"

"How did you know it was me? You didn't even turn your head in my direction." Jake plopped down in a lounge chair next to him.

"I recognize your footsteps. Your gait is fast, but I hear a slight drag with your right heel. If that didn't give you away, it was the keys jingling in your left pocket. You always put them in your left pocket, which is odd since you are right handed."

"You are observant."

"Is that from the war? Your heel drag?"

"A little nerve damage. Nothing serious."

"When we were out on the boat the other day, I saw the scars on your back. Is that from that night I pulled you up into the chopper?"

"Yes."

Charlie opened another can of beer, downing it as if it were water. When he was finished, he crushed it in his hand, dropping it in a pile next to the others. Jake noticed him trembling, but Charlie quickly folded his hands together in his lap, as if he knew Jake was watching him.

"So why are you here?" Charlie asked.

"I thought you might need some coffee." Jake offered a cup to him, but Charlie had yet to look his way.

"I prefer beer," he said. "Don't you have some meetings to attend or a company to run?"

"Yes, but my meetings don't start for a couple of hours." Jake set the coffee on the cement between them. "What are you doing here?"

"Just having a beer."

"Looks like more than one."

"I should have brought more."

Jake chuckled. "Try the coffee. I want you to be sober if you are spending the day with Samantha."

"I am sober."

"Look, Charlie, your sister is worried about you, and so am I."

"Nothing to be worried about."

"Yeah, I know. I told myself the same thing. I thought once I was out, my life would go back to normal. For the most part it did, but there are things that remind me of my time over there. Car horns, people talking in Arabic, someone brushing up against me, the pings from the slot machines, or fireworks."

Charlie didn't respond, keeping his eyes focused on the pool in front of him. The bags under his eyes were dark, almost purple. He was sweating, as evidenced by the wetness on his shirt. He kept his hands folded in front of him.

"Do you want to talk about it?"

"Are you my fucking counselor now?" Charlie finally showed some emotion.

"No. I'm not your counselor, just a friend, a brother, hopefully someone you feel you can confide in."

"That works both ways, right?"

"Sure."

"Then maybe you can explain to me why my sister needs all this security and I'm not good enough."

"With this vandalism at the clubs, I worry about her."

"And you don't think I'm sane enough to watch out for her?"

"I didn't say that."

"She's a big girl, and she doesn't like Cam and Manny following her everywhere."

"I know." Jake sighed. "It's only until I figure out who is behind this."

Charlie nodded. "She said you are going to counseling for your anger. Is it helping?"

Jake shrugged. "It takes time, but yes, I think it helps to talk to someone."

Charlie unfolded his hands, holding them about six inches above his legs. They shook uncontrollably. He made a fist with each of them, but the shaking didn't stop. "Did this ever happen to you?"

Jake watched Charlie put his hands back on his lap. While he did shake sometimes, it was never to this extent. "I didn't sleep much. I used alcohol to numb the pain. It was my depressant, something to help me forget. There were times I would go on a two-day drinking binge and have a lot of sex to try to forget about what I'd done. At some point I passed out, but when I woke up, I started again."

Charlie clasped his hands together again. "So now you know why I drink beer."

"I know why you do it, but it isn't the answer." Jake followed Charlie's gaze out toward the water. "I was lucky. I had a grandfather who cared about me. He used to take me out on a boat like Bauer's where we would talk for hours, about the company, life, that sort of thing. Like me, you have people who want to help you too."

"What did you do when he died?"

"I had responsibilities. I didn't have the luxury of time to process things. I managed for the most part, but the signs were still there, and I had to figure out a way to make it through the day sober."

"How?"

"Boxing, running. Alcohol only made it worse, so I limit myself to two or three drinks a couple of times a week. What have you tried?"

"They teach all that crap in the army: the breathing, the counting—shit like that to calm yourself down. It's all bullshit. It doesn't work."

Jake could only nod. He was familiar with the techniques the army trained. He'd tried them, and he too, had failed.

"Do you know how many people I killed, Morgan?"

"No."

"Me either. I stopped counting after the first five because I didn't want to be that guy, but I can't forget them. I see their faces when I close my eyes. I've tried to count them. Certain ones stick out in my mind more than others. I often wonder if they had families, a mom and dad, kids, siblings..." Charlie's voice trailed off, and he closed his eyes. "I remember what they were wearing, how the bullet from the gun I was holding hit them square between the eyes, or how the blood streamed from their mouth when I shoved a knife in their gut, or how their body fell limp when I sliced a knife across their throat." He opened his eyes, shaking his head. "I hate that I see them. I hate that I was the one who ended their lives. I hate that I was the one chosen to do it."

"You were chosen because you were the best, Charlie. What do you think would have happened to Tess if you hadn't taken out Casano? You were trained to do what you did. We both know what Casano was capable of. It's the same with the enemy, Charlie. They would have taken you out too."

"I wanted them to." Charlie rolled his head to the side, his eyes dull and bleak. "After losing Mom, and after what happened to Dad and Christie, I didn't want to live any longer."

Jake grimaced, not because Charlie referred to Samantha by her given name, but because he didn't like what Charlie said about not wanting to live. He set his coffee down and relaxed back in the chair. "What about Chase?"

"What about him? He's smart, good looking. He's a survivor. I'm not."

"But you are here now."

"Yeah, here I am...a crazy motherfucker with a messed-up head."

"It's war, Charlie. Sometimes the soldier pays a high price for it."

"I don't much appreciate the price I'm paying right now." Charlie took a deep breath, exhaling slowly. "Are you over it, Morgan?"

"I'm getting there, but there are things I saw that will always be with me."

"How do you get it out of your head?"

"You don't, but time makes the images appear less frequent, and being with your sister helps. There are times when we are together when I don't think about anything, except her and that moment. My world is a better place when we're together, and she makes me want to be better."

"What are you saying? If I find a good woman, the nightmares and visions will go away?"

"I wish it were that easy, but no, that's not what I'm saying. We all handle things differently. What works for me may not work for you. Sometimes you just have to let things happen and let life play out the way it should without thinking so much about the past and the regrets. Samantha makes me want more for my future, and she has a way of calming me. If it wasn't for her, I'd lose my shit on a daily basis."

"What if I already lost my shit? What if I can't get my head on straight?"

"It doesn't go away overnight, and you're going to need some help."

"Yeah, Richard said I should talk to someone."

"Bauer has an innate sense about certain things. It wouldn't hurt to take his advice."

"How long have you known Bauer?" Charlie released his hands and picked up the coffee cup.

"Only since Samantha and I started dating. Why?"

Charlie held the coffee cup with both hands, trying to steady the drink as he brought it to his lips. He took a tentative sip, then a larger gulp before setting it down and clasping his hands together again. "I don't know. I like him. He reminds me of Dad in a lot of ways. He's generous, concerned. He watched over Christie all those years, but Chase doesn't see any of that. It makes me think I'm missing something or he knows something about Bauer I don't."

Jake took a drink from his cup, recalling the intimate letters he'd read in Bauer's stash of documents, but what he learned, he wasn't about to share. "Bauer is different than most men I know, but he's seen and done more things than one would think possible. But I do know he loves Samantha and you and Chase. If he didn't, he wouldn't have kept you apart for so long, but he was concerned for your lives."

"Does that mean I should trust him?" Charlie looked over at Jake.

Jake shrugged. "I do. He may not always do things the conventional way, but his intentions are always in the right place. He seems to know things before I do, and whether that's because of the connections he has or his intuition, I don't know, but I trust him."

"So I should take his advice?"

"I did, and if you decide you want some company, you only need to say the word."

"Nah. I think I can handle seeing a therapist on my own, but I might need some help getting out of this chair. I've been sitting here a long time."

Jake stood, holding out his hand to Charlie and hauling him to his feet. Charlie wobbled, and Jake grabbed him around the shoulder, holding him steady.

"Now that I think about it, I could use a little sleep because my sister tells me we are dress shopping today."

Jake laughed. "I'm glad to hear it."

"You sure you want to marry her? She can't even cook, and a man can only survive on peanut butter and jelly sandwiches for so long."

Jake laughed again. "I know, but she's learning, and I would marry her anyway."

"Then don't ever hurt her, Morgan, or you'll have me and my insane brother to answer to."

"I give you my word."

Chapter 8

Charlie and Samantha returned to the hotel after lunch on Tuesday. Samantha felt exhausted but elated at the same time. She wanted to tell Jake about Kyle and Sofia, but after the conversation she had with Jake on Sunday, hearing the desolation in his voice, she didn't want to cause him more angst. She had to trust her gut. There would be a right time when they were both back in New York with Kyle miles away.

After having spent several hours with Sofia over the last two days, she had to admit the little girl was growing on her fast—too fast. She shouldn't be so attached to a little girl with a giggle that sprung out of nowhere, or one who tells stories the only way a three-year-old could, or one with big blue eyes and that damn Morgan trademark dimple.

Do you think Daddy will like my new clothes? She could still hear the excitement in Sofia's voice. Today, she and Charlie took her shopping and on a tour of the M&M Factory. *Daddy likes the chocolate ones, not the peanuts.* Sofia loved her daddy, that much was obvious. But Kyle's reaction to her was less than amicable; in fact, he seemed upset by her presence. She replayed Kyle's words over in her head when he found out she had taken Sofia shopping. *She's three! It's not in her best interest to see her once and spoil her! We don't need the Morgan money! I never should have agreed to any of this!*

"You OK?" Charlie asked as they approached the entrance to the hotel.

"Yeah, just thinking about Kyle and Sofia."

"Me too. She's a little sweetheart, isn't she?"

"Don't tell me you are attached to her already."

"She had me at hello."

"Oh my God, you did not just say that."

"I did, but I'm serious. We bonded over the coloring book. That's three days in row we colored together, and she even told me I'm getting better."

Samantha giggled. She never would have thought Charlie would be so attached to a little girl. He was big and burly, but she knew he was as protective as Jake was, and somehow Sofia had managed to wrap him around her little finger. "What do you make of what Kyle said?"

"He's a great dad. He's raising her the best he can, and here we come, showering her with gifts and spending time with her. From what she said, it doesn't sound like they do much, other than go to a movie every other month."

"That's just it, Charlie. He could have so much more. He didn't go back for his grandfather's funeral, and he hasn't reached out to his family since then. With one phone call, you know Jake's mother, Monica, wouldn't have batted an eye, and he could be living in a much nicer place rather than struggling to make ends meet to provide for her."

"He's providing for her just fine, and furthermore, it's not our business."

"But she'll be my niece. Doesn't that make it my business?"

"Hey, you two, glad I caught you." Ammo greeted them outside the hotel, ushering them away from the front door. "First and foremost, Jake is on a rampage. He found out you left without Cam and Manny again and is demanding to know why." He pointed at Samantha. "And you didn't answer your phone."

"Shit!" Samantha opened her purse, fishing for her phone. "I missed four calls and, ugh, he's not happy by the looks of these text messages."

"He asked me if I knew where you were. I told him you and Charlie had gone shopping. He's still in meetings, but damn, I wouldn't put it past him to walk out of those meetings and start looking for you, especially when your flight is leaving in less than three hours."

"I need to call him right now."

"Wait, I have something to tell you before you leave today, and after you hear it, you may want to tell Jake about Kyle sooner rather than later."

"What's going on, Ammo?"

"I have some news, about Kyle."

"Oh God, don't tell me you found out he's using. I was so sure he was clean. How could I have been so—"

"He's not using." Ammo took a deep breath. "Kyle is a model employee. I reviewed his file. He's never late, never calls off his shift. He's worked in every department of this hotel and casino, and the staff love him. The hotel doesn't have a policy on drug testing except when hired or when there might be a reasonable suspicion of drug use, but he gets tested anyway, every two weeks, and turns his slips in to the Human Resources Department so he has proof he is clean."

Samantha let out the breath she'd been holding. "OK. Well, that's good, right? We have proof to show Jake then."

"Yeah, my guess is he was making a record for just that purpose. But that's not all."

"What else is there?" Charlie asked.

Ammo glanced between the two of them, his eyes stopping on Samantha. "It's about the pills Charlie found in his medicine cabinet. Samantha, there is no easy way to say this. Kyle is sick."

"Like what? Sick as in the flu sick?"

"No. Sick as in dying sick."

Samantha held her hand to her chest. The stinging of tears behind her lids was instantaneous as she thought about what Ammo's words meant. She had only known Kyle a short time, but he was a nice man, trying to put his life back on track, and Charlie was right, he was a great dad and was providing for Sofia by working hard and doing the best he could. *Oh God, Sofia!*

"Dying from what?" Charlie asked.

Samantha was still stuck on the fact Kyle was dying and what would happen to Sofia. She tried to listen to the rest of the conversation through the murky waters of her brain, but each word seemed to sting more than the next: *liver, high number for a transplant, not the right candidate, no long-term cure, his disease has progressed.* She had a million questions about doctors and medical care, but she was suffocating under the heartache she felt for Kyle and Sofia. She'd seen the pictures of them together, and if what Ammo said was true, those pictures would be all Sofia would have left. The tears she'd tried to keep at bay seeped through, spilling on to her cheeks. *Had Kyle's illness been the reason he reached out to Jake when he did?*

Charlie put his arm around her. "What about Sofia?" Samantha was thankful he gave voice to her unspoken words.

"I talked to him today while the two of you had Sofia. I told him I knew about his illness and asked him that exact question. After Jake's reaction to him, he can only do what's best for Sofia. He met with a social worker yesterday. As his illness progresses, more than likely she'll be placed in foster care."

"That's not what's best for Sofia!" Samantha pulled away from Charlie and paced in a circle. "She belongs with her family. *We* are her family! Me, Jake. His mother and sister! They would want to know about Kyle and take care of him. Maybe there are some doctors in New York that can do something." Samantha stopped pacing and placed her hands on her hips, gaping at Charlie and Ammo. "Why is he giving up?"

Ammo looked toward the street, then toward the hotel. "There was another reason I went to talk to Kyle. Jake told me that since I'm running the hotel, it's my job to fire him."

"So you fired him? Jesus, Ammo! Why the hell would you do that?"

"I didn't, but he knows it's coming. I can't hold JT off forever."

Samantha was still staring at Ammo with her mouth agape, not wanting to believe that the man she loves would fire his own brother, without even trying to forgive him for whatever happened in the past. "He never mentioned a word about it when we dropped Sofia off."

"But it explains why he was so riled up about spending the Morgan money," Charlie said.

"If—and I mean if—this happens, will he lose his insurance?" she asked.

Ammo nodded. "He can extend it, but without a job, he won't be able to afford it. He lives paycheck to paycheck."

"Then I'll pay his insurance. Hell, after fourteen years in the army and hardly coming home, I have a nice little nest egg saved up."

Ammo shook his head. "The insurance company denied his request for a transplant. They don't think it would help him because his disease is terminal."

Samantha dropped her head into her hands. She had to do something. "I need to tell Jake. It's the only way. He won't turn his back on Kyle when he's sick, and I know he wouldn't turn his back on Sofia."

"Kyle doesn't want Jake to know. He was pretty adamant about that."

Samantha crossed her arms in front of her. "Then what the hell am I supposed to do?"

"You need to tell him," Ammo said. "Regardless of what Kyle says, if he finds out any other way, it won't be good."

"Samantha!" Samantha jumped at the sound of Jake's gruff voice. She quickly wiped her tears away, hoping he wouldn't notice. She lowered her sunglasses, turning in his direction. "Why the hell do you carry a goddamn phone if you aren't going to answer it? Do you have any idea how worried I was about you? Why did you leave without Cam and Manny? We need to talk." Jake snatched her upper arm, carting her away from Charlie and Ammo.

Charlie put his hand on Jake's chest. "Don't ever grab my sister like that again!"

Samantha watched the silent communication between Jake and Charlie as they stared at each other. Jake let go of her, scrubbing a hand down his face. "I'm sorry. I was just—"

"Yeah, we get it," Charlie said. "You were upset because your goonies weren't attached to her hip, but I was. I told you I can take care of her, and I did that today, and yesterday. If you want to be mad at someone, be mad at me. I told those fuckers to find something else to do because I was spending time with my sister, and if you have a problem with that, maybe you shouldn't marry her!"

"Charlie, calm down. I should have told Jake what we were doing," Samantha said, turning to Jake. "I'm sorry. We wanted some alone time. I should have told you, and I'm sorry, but it's not worth getting so upset over."

Jake looked at both of them, nodding his head. "You're right. I was just worried about you. When Ammo said you were with Charlie and I tried calling and texting but you didn't respond, I thought something had happened."

"I'm sure if something had happened, you would be the first to know." Charlie clenched and unclenched his fists, staring at Jake. "Now, I'm going to pack my things, but don't make me question your word again."

"I think I'll be going too," Ammo said. "JT, I'll send you my report tomorrow morning."

Samantha took Jake's hand. "I wanted some time with Charlie today."

"I know. I'm sorry for overreacting. Let's go pack."

Back in the hotel suite, Samantha set her luggage next to the sofa while Jake finished packing after taking a long shower. Opening her purse, she pulled out the coloring book page Sofia had given her. For a child her age, she colored so well, hardly going outside the lines. The princess picture was colored in shades of pinks, reds, and purples. The letters at the bottom of the page were difficult to read, but Samantha read them again and again: "To Aunt Samantha." For the last ten years, she only had Richard. Then she met Jake, and her brothers were back in her life again, and now she has Kyle and Sofia.

"How am I going to tell him?" she whispered aloud, folding up the picture and shoving it back in her purse.

"You OK?" Jake asked from behind her.

Holding her hand to her chest, she swallowed hard. "Yeah, you startled me."

"Where were you just now? You didn't answer when I called your name."

"Sorry. My mind was somewhere else."

Jake came to her, capturing her in his arms. "I'm sorry, about everything. This is not the life I want for you with security following you wherever you go. If I could figure out who is behind the vandalism, we wouldn't need them. Please try to understand that I worry about you, every second of the day."

"I know, and I should have told you. But tell me, what did Charlie mean by not questioning your word?"

"He and I talked yesterday morning about what he's going through. At the end of the conversation, I gave him my word I would never hurt you."

"You talked to him?"

"Yes. I figured I could relate to some of what he's going through."

"I sometimes wonder if you are real or not. You are the best. Thank you for doing that, Jake."

"If we had more time, I might show you how real I am."

Samantha smiled into his chest. "How did your employee meetings go?"

"As good as can be expected. Are you packed and ready to go?"

"Yeah, but we don't need to go today. I'm sure I could find a doctor here to take my stitches out if you need to stay."

"No, we need to go home. You have your doctor appointment, and I have a meeting with the McClellan Group." Jake let her go and walked over to the counter, looking to his left and right. "Speaking of which, I left a spiral-bound report lying here so I could read through it on the way home. Have you seen it?"

"I put it in my backpack," Samantha said.

Jake went to her backpack and started to unzip it, just as Samantha remembered what was in there. She panicked when he removed the coloring book and crayons.

"Um...did you buy these for the way home?" he asked with a small chuckle

She stared at the gift she bought for Sofia, unable to formulate a reasonable response. She rubbed her temples, cursing internally.

Jake dropped her backpack on the floor and walked over to her, lifting her chin. "Are you trying to hide the fact that you are suffering from another one of your headaches?"

"No. I took one of those over-the-counter nausea pills you bought for me, but I think I'm just tired."

"You're sure?"

"I'm sure." She pulled away from him, thankful for the distraction from the subject of the coloring book. "Can we just go?"

Jake slung her backpack over his shoulder and picked up his briefcase, leading her out of the hotel suite. "So, did you find a dress?"

Samantha looked at him, shaking her head, wondering how many more lies she would end up spewing before the truth came out.

Jake held the elevator door. "You don't have much time."

"Don't remind me."

Chapter 9

*J*ake ran a hand through his wet hair as he entered Dr. Martin Kinzie's office. Taking a seat on the sofa across from the oversized chair where Dr. Kinzie sat, Jake looked around the room. The walls were beige and brown, the furniture a brown leather, and the wooden desk a dark oak that had seen better days. The room was as drab as the weather outside, both of which matched his current mood.

"Is it still raining?" Dr. Kinzie asked.

"Yep."

Dr. Kinzie was dressed in a pair of khaki shorts and a flowered dress shirt with sandals two shades darker than his shorts. It was the same type of attire he had worn the last few times Jake had been here. Through the stories Dr. Kinzie told, Jake learned he was an avid outdoorsman. He talked about golfing, fishing, and hunting, and he had the leathery tanned skin to prove it.

Dr. Kinzie crossed his arms over his chest, and Jake turned away, focusing his attention on the two bookcases. The heavy periodicals in the first seemed to remain untouched since the last time he was here. The other bookcase held the same seven paperback books, still lying haphazardly in the same place as before. Jake read the title of each before scanning the remaining shelves with a variety of games and the same wooden box with sand and small figurines that had caught his attention the last time.

Jake moved his gaze to the next wall, where two framed certificates hung next to one framed scenic photograph that Dr. Kinzie had told him was a gift from Richard Bauer. Dr. Kinzie had confirmed it was one of Samantha's photographs, and Jake wondered if Dr. Kinzie was just a friend of Bauer's or if he had been Bauer's counselor too.

Dr. Kinzie let out a heavy sigh and crossed one sandaled foot over the other, lacing his hands behind his head. Jake was never quite sure what the proper protocol was with Dr. Kinzie. His last counselor had started out talking about the sessions, but Dr. Kinzie had started out talking about his golf game.

"I went golfing last weekend," Dr. Kinzie said. "Damn wind sure has a way to mess with your game. I was on par until the eighth hole, and wouldn't you know it, that damn wind came up, and it was over. Whew! It was a rough day."

Jake waited out Dr. Kinzie, knowing he would ask a question, and Jake would answer with a word or two, then another question, and a few more words. And so it would go, until his time was up and he could hightail it out of there.

"I understand your week was rough too."

Why else would I be here? Though his weekend started out to be one of the best, it didn't stay that way. Jake focused on the floor, following the carpet patterns, as Dr. Kinzie waited for an answer. He started counting the lines in each square of carpet: four red, four blue, four yellow, and four brown stripes within each twelve-inch square. When he deduced each square had sixteen lines, he started counting the number of squares, but Dr. Kinzie started whistling, making him lose count. He restarted, not particularly wanting to be here but keenly aware he needed to get his anger under control.

"Your regular appointment is scheduled for next week, but when you called, you said it was urgent you come in."

Jake nodded, then shifted his eyes back to the corner of the room to restart his count.

"I can tell you how many squares there are in the room, then you can multiply that by each color so we can move on, or I could just sit here and let you count and take your money, but I doubt you would get much out of our session. Why don't you tell me what happened?"

Jake inhaled and dropped his head back, staring at the ceiling. *I have to do this.* He gritted his teeth, but it did little to ease the tight knot in his stomach. Blowing out his breath, he looked at Dr. Kinzie. He was trying to help Jake get to the root of his anger, and if he wanted to be in control, he needed to do this. "I asked Samantha to marry me, and she said yes."

Dr. Kinzie smiled. "Congratulations. I'm guessing that's the reason you are here?"

"Yes. I...she's always had a way of calming me, but this past weekend, something happened, and I almost ruined everything."

"Oh? It sounds to me like you have a fiancée. How is that ruining everything?"

"It's not about that. It's what happened afterward."

"The first time you were here, you told me your anger frightened Samantha. Is that what this is about?"

Jake hunched forward, resting his elbows on his knees, waiting for the words he couldn't seem to speak.

Dr. Kinzie released his hands from his head and sat forward so he was face to face with Jake. "I know you first came here because of Samantha, but you have to want to be here too. You have to want to get help for yourself. I can only help you if you let me."

Jake nodded. "I don't like how I feel when I'm angry, or who I become. I was always able to control it, but last weekend, I...then when I found out...I just couldn't." Jake couldn't breathe. He felt like he was suffocating under a pile of dirt, and rather than help him, everyone was shoveling more dirt on top of him. He had to dig his way out. He needed to find a way to save himself.

"Why don't you start with what happened after you asked Samantha to marry you," Dr. Kinzie said.

Jake looked up at Dr. Kinzie, and before he could stop himself, he blurted out everything, including his meeting with Kyle, and how his anger had almost destroyed everything he cared about, how he'd tried to use sex as an outlet and thought he'd hurt Samantha. He told him how he went crazy when his calls to Samantha went unanswered and how upset he had been and how he riled up Charlie when he grabbed her arm. When he was done, he jumped up from the sofa and began pacing. He had a sudden rush of adrenaline to tell Dr. Kinzie all about Kyle and how worthless he was. Details from his childhood spewed forth, and he was helpless to stop himself. It was if the dam that had been holding in all of his feelings broke loose.

"You never mentioned a brother in our other sessions when I asked you about your family."

"Because at the time, I didn't consider him my brother!" Jake became irritated, wondering why that was the only thing Dr. Kinzie had to say. He expected him to validate Jake's anger toward his brother, then say something so he'd be over it and could move on.

"And you do now?" Dr. Kinzie tilted his head to study Jake's reaction.

Jake pursed his lips together. "No. I don't." He focused on the carpet again, then the walls, seeking out anything to help him avoid the scrutinizing gaze from Dr. Kinzie. He wanted to leave, to walk away and forget about having this conversation with Dr. Kinzie, but he didn't. He removed his jacket and loosened his tie, then started to pace over the same squares he'd started to count earlier. "I run a business, a business someone is trying to ruin with this vandalism crap, and now my brother is here, and I don't have time to deal with him. He's a distraction."

"You called him your brother."

"I what?"

"Called him your brother."

"Jesus! Is this what I'm paying you for?"

"I'm just saying you called him your brother, so you must still feel something for him." Dr. Kinzie sighed. "What didn't you tell me about that night six years ago when you had Kyle committed?"

Jake stopped pacing, wondering how the good doctor had honed in on that particular subject when he'd tried to skim over it. "I wanted to kill him!" He bent over the sofa to steady himself, taking a deep breath as the memory came crashing into his mind. After taking out one of Kyle's druggie friends, his grandfather had signaled to him to stay where he was, but Jake didn't listen, attacking Kyle from behind and wrestling the gun from his hand. Kyle started to say something, but Jake shoved the gun in his mouth, cocking it, his finger on the trigger…he was going to kill him. *Jake, no!* It was Shannon who pulled his attention away, long enough for his grandfather to stop Jake.

"War does things to us that most people don't understand. What we see in war doesn't just go away. It's a part of us, and sometimes when we try to go back to our lives, we see things that aren't there. Sometimes our thoughts are hijacked when a situation arises that is threatening. It's kind of like our dreams. The people in our dreams are in effect just a depiction of someone else."

"It wasn't a dream and I was perfectly sane. I wanted him dead!" Jake squeezed his eyes shut as he imagined the gun going off, pink mist from Kyle's blood spraying in every direction, pieces of his head lying on the floor of his grandfather's restaurant. The thought sickened him, yet he kept going back to it. He hated knowing what he was capable of. Just envisioning it made him nauseated.

"And now?"

"And now I just want him out of my life."

"You don't believe he's changed?"

"Kyle will never change!"

"Everyone is capable of change, if they have the right reasons and want to change."

"Not Kyle." Jake shook his head. "He only pretends to change until he gets what he wants."

"Did he look like he was using when you saw him?"

"I don't know."

"You know what he looks like when he's high. Was he using or not?"

"Why does it matter?" Jake was irritated, ready to leave.

"I'm just wondering if he was using or if you *wanted* him to be using?"

Jake paced over the squares, counting them in his head, no longer wanting to discuss his feelings.

"Let me save you the trouble of counting the squares in the carpet. There are two hundred and twenty-eight squares on the carpet in this office. Nine hundred and twelve lines of each color in the carpet. You're welcome to continue counting, but it's been done before, several times, actually."

Jake let out a sigh of frustration. He looked around, hoping to find a different distraction, but there was nothing. He turned to Dr. Kinzie, who waited patiently.

"I wanted him to still be using because then I could go on hating him," Jake admitted.

"And why do you want to keep hating him?"

"Because he's always been a distraction! Even when I was in the army."

"Hmm. You told me everything about Kyle except what happened after you last saw him. Does this have something to do with the death of your friend more so than it does Kyle?"

"Aren't we out of time?"

"When a client says it's urgent, I clear my schedule. You obviously have some things to talk about. I want to know what's going on in that head of yours, Jake. I want to know about your friend."

"I'd rather not talk about it."

Dr. Kinzie stood up and walked to the book shelf, grabbing the box of sand off the third shelf. "Show me then." Dr. Kinzie placed the box on the table, motioning for Jake to take a seat.

Jake stopped pacing and stared at the ominous sand-filled box, now understanding what it represented. "Show you?"

"Show me how it went down, in Afghanistan, the day your friend Cuddy was killed."

"I can't." Jake sat down, picking up one of the small green army men and twirling it through his fingers while Dr. Kinzie waited.

The smell of spent ammunition burned through Jake's nostrils as that night a few years ago began to inch into his psyche. Image after image flashed through his mind. "We had bad intel. We were told only twelve were in the compound, but there had to be at least fifty there. We were dead in the water."

With his jaw clenching, a cold bead of sweat formed on his forehead. He swiped it away. With a shaky finger, he drew a square in the sand. He clenched the figurine he had been twirling through his fingers. Taking a deep breath, he placed it in the sand. "Cuddy was here." Picking up a second figurine, he placed it in the sand. "And this is Ammo." One by one, he placed the plastic figures in the sand, naming off each member of his team, including himself. Sitting back, he stared at the figures, as the memories poured forth.

"What happened next?"

"We waited. It was eerie, like the calm before the storm. I heard the footsteps, then a gun, and another. Cuddy was always our front man, and by the time I got to him, it was too late. He was just…gone." Rubbing at the tightness in his chest, Jake closed his eyes, wishing away the images flashing through his mind. Sweat dripped down his back, a painful lump lodged in his throat, and he gasped for a breath.

Dr. Kinzie reached over, resting a calming hand on Jake's arm. "Then what?"

"The voices got louder; there was more gunfire. I tried to cover Cuddy from a bomb that went off. There was shrapnel everywhere." Jake shuddered. "I never should have followed the order."

"Did you give the order?"

"Of course, I gave the order."

"I didn't hear you say you gave the order."

"As the commanding officer on the ground, I had the authority to abort the mission, but I wasn't in the right frame of mind. I was distracted!"

"What distracted you, Jake?"

Jake hesitated, remembering that day like it was yesterday. "Before we boarded the chopper to ship out, my mother called. Kyle had walked out of rehab again."

"I see, but Jake, Kyle is not the reason Cuddy died up on that mountain. War is the reason, not one person in particular. Just because you were think- ing about Kyle doesn't make it his fault. Don't you think some of those men in combat are thinking about their wives or their children? They were trained to do a job, just like you were. You wanted to be mad at someone, and Kyle was an easy target. He wasn't around; he couldn't defend himself. It was perfect, wasn't it?"

Jake dropped his hands to his side, grasping at the material of the sofa as his body began to shake.

"Did you go to Cuddy's funeral?"

Jake nodded. "His parents waited until we came home to hold a formal cer- emony. We were all there."

"Did you speak to his parents?"

"Yes, and several times afterward."

"Did they blame you?"

Jake shook his head.

"And yet you wanted to blame someone. Maybe it was Kyle or maybe it was you, just like you blamed yourself for Samantha's injuries."

"Because I should have figured things out sooner. If I had, she wouldn't have been hurt."

"You took on a lot of responsibility at a young age, but it doesn't mean you are responsible for everything that happens around you. You had no control over that any more than you had control over the enemy behind that wall. The only thing you can control is you—your thoughts, your words, your actions."

Chapter 10

Manny pulled up to the curb along Furman street. When Jake had called, he'd sounded distraught, but for the life of her, Samantha couldn't figure out why they were meeting here. She stepped out of the vehicle, staring up at the building with sleek modern edges and walls of windows reflecting the late-afternoon sun as it danced on the water. Tobin pulled up in front of Manny, pulling her gaze from the amazing view. Jake jumped out, striding toward her as both Tobin and Manny took off down the street.

"Hey, baby." He handed her a bouquet of tulips. "These are for you."

She took them, bringing the bouquet to her nose and inhaling the fresh scent while taking in his desolate state. His suit coat and tie were missing. His hair was ruffled, probably from running his hand through it, and his blue eyes appeared a shade darker than normal. "Thank you. They're beautiful."

"Like you." Bringing his hand to her face, he rubbed his thumb over her lip. "Your leg looks good."

Samantha glanced down at the scar on her leg, wondering when he'd noticed it. "Yeah, it feels better too. No more itching."

"And the headaches?"

"Dr. Carlisle ordered some tests. She'll let me know if I need to be concerned about anything."

"And you'll tell me, right?"

"Right. So why are we here?"

Jake turned toward the building, putting his hands in his pockets. "This is the apartment I told you about. I wanted to show you."

"This is the new apartment? It's so beautiful."

"Again, like you," he said, taking her hand.

Samantha followed him into the lobby, his solemn state at the forefront of her thoughts. His voice was too quiet, and his words sparse. Though he was trying to be affectionate, he wasn't here; he wasn't in the moment with her. She tried to smile at the doorman before looking up to the ceilings where the chandeliers shone brightly. Several white pillars were situated proudly throughout the lobby. She slowed her steps, reaching out to graze her palm along one of the pillars, her mind flashing back to the pillars that once stood in front of her home in California. She used to lean against them in the evening, listening to her brothers talk about school and girls, or her parents discuss the next charity event her mother was helping to plan, or just to sit and look at the stars at night. Jake squeezed her hand, effectively bringing her back to the present, her childhood memories dissolving in the confines of her mind.

Following him toward the elevator, she gawked at her surroundings. The lobby was so beautiful and welcoming, she didn't want to leave, but Jake was impatient, pulling her into the elevator. He entered a code, confining them in the small space. Samantha propped herself against the wall, watching Jake clench his jaw through the mirrored walls, his mind seemingly elsewhere. "Do you want to talk about whatever is bothering you?"

Jake stared at her through the reflection of the elevator doors. "Not particularly." He continued staring at her until the doors opened. Taking her hand, he led her down the hall, stopping in front of a lone door. Fishing the key from his pocket, he placed it in the lock, dropping his head against the door. "I had a session with my counselor today. It was…difficult."

Samantha placed her hand on his arm, thankful he was at least talking. "What can I do?"

"Nothing."

She ducked under his arm, nudging herself between him and the door. "Let me help you."

He dropped his hand from the key, positioning his hands next to her head. "You are. Just being with you helps me."

She stood on her tiptoes and kissed him lightly on the lips. "I'm always here whenever you need me."

"We should go in," he said. Samantha moved to the side, and he unlocked the door, gesturing for her to enter. "I took the liberty of ordering new furniture, but I'll leave the decorating to you."

Peeling her eyes off from Jake, she took in her surroundings. The high ceilings created a spacious, airy ambiance, and the oversized windows offered a breathtaking view of the East River and lower Manhattan. To her right was a French door leading to a stone-walled balcony. Jake was leaning against the immaculate white kitchen counter. Behind him were European wood cabinets and a kitchen any chef would die for. She twirled around, throwing her hands up, unable to hold in her excitement. "This room is bigger than my entire apartment."

Jake's lips twitched, and he gave her a half smile. "Would you like to tour the rest?" Taking her hand, he showed her the three extra bedrooms and the two bathrooms and the master bedroom. She stood for a moment, envisioning what she could do to spruce the place up. Jake turned on the light to the master bathroom, and Samantha entered, noticing the same clean lines as the rest of the apartment. It was more than she needed, but she loved the white-tiled walls and the spa tub and especially the walk-in shower. She giggled and turned the water on, watching the glass panel steam up. She glanced at Jake, biting her bottom lip, stifling her giggle, but still smiling.

She stepped out of her sandals. Gripping the hem of her shirt, she pulled it over her head, letting it fall to the floor. Keeping her gaze on him, she unbuttoned her jean shorts, sliding them down her legs with her panties. Jake quirked a brow. After removing her bra, she stood before him, his eyes wandering over her naked body, a heated flush running through her when their eyes locked. "I can see your pain. It's in your eyes, and your body language. Let me help you. Use me Jake, however you need to."

"You should get dressed."

Samantha shook her head, backing up toward the shower. Keeping her eyes on him, she brought her hands to her breasts. Jake unbuttoned the cuffs of his dress shirt. Moving to his chest, he unbuttoned his shirt, never taking his eyes off from her. She continued to entice him, pulling her now-taut nipples between her fingers.

Unhooking the belt from his pants, he lowered his zipper, sliding his pants and boxers down his legs. Kicking out of his shoes, he removed his socks and stalked toward her, his erection at full attention. Samantha licked her lips and took a step inside the shower. The water cascaded down her face, forcing her to close her eyes and swipe it away. When she opened them, Jake was standing in front of her, his body now wet. He placed his arms behind her against the wall. "I can't do this now, Samantha."

She placed her hands on his chest, and his muscles twitched. "You don't need to do anything." She lowered herself to her knees, taking his engorged length into her hands. The water created a natural lube, allowing her to fist him from base to tip. Their eyes locked as she took his length into her mouth, hollowing out her cheeks, sucking on him hard as she took him to the back of her throat. He let out a satisfied moan, but she wanted more. She wanted him to forget everything…she wanted to take away his suffering and make him feel like there was nothing else in the world except them.

She was soon lost in his taste and the heady sensation of pleasuring him. She moaned, pumping him with her mouth and hand. His hands came to her head, but she shook off his tight hold, scraping her teeth along his shaft before sucking him harder than she had before, her mouth savoring every inch of him. His hoarse voice said something unintelligible, and though she couldn't understand the words, the guttural sound stoked the fire in her belly, making her slick between her thighs.

The pressure from Jake's fingers on her head increased, forcing her to stop. He reached down and pulled her up. The pain she had seen in his eyes had been replaced with a predatory gaze. Placing his hands on the tile behind her, he captured her lips, devouring her mouth like a crazed man. His hand came to her neck, slowly moving downward, pinching her nipple between his thumb and forefinger, until she whimpered. His hand slid lower, past her abdomen, his fingers locating her heated core. He penetrated slowly at first, then harder, his thumb pressing against her clit.

She tore her lips away from his, throwing her head back and closing her eyes. "Jake…I—"

He didn't let her finish, instead lifting her up and placing her against the wall. She wrapped her legs around him as he drove his rock-hard length into her. His moves were deliberate, unhurried, stimulating her senses with a steamy stroke and lazy drag, allowing her to savor every satisfying inch. Samantha opened her eyes, locking on Jake's heavy lids, his lusty gaze focused only on her. They were one, two parts of a whole. The closeness, the pure mutual passion burning between them surpassed words. She couldn't look away, afraid of losing the powerful connection that was making her climb to new heights with every stroke. As her walls began to close in on him, he kept a steady pace, but his thrusts became harder, grinding deep into her until she felt the rise of her release clutch him in a never-ending orgasm. She was spent, too far gone to think clearly, his name leaving her lips in a whispery awe as he released himself inside of her. Jake held her against him, their hearts beating as one, their bodies shuddering.

"Samantha." His voice was gravelly, raw.

She marveled at the intensity of what happened between them, the awe in his voice matching her own sense of wonderment.

Lifting her from him, he set her down, taking her face in his hands. "You are too good for me."

"No. We are perfect for each other."

He smiled, the smile she loved, the one that made her belly flutter the first night they met. "That was amazing."

"I know," she said.

"I would offer you a towel, but we don't have any," he said. Samantha giggled. She forgot about that small detail. "I guess Tobin will need to make a delivery, but until then..." His lips caressed hers in a sensual kiss, making her forget about the towels and everything else.

Samantha woke the following morning, sprawled out on the king-sized bed. Hearing Jake's footsteps, she opened one eye, rolling to her side. Seeing him in only his boxers made her remember their entire evening making love in almost every room of the apartment. Actually, it was sex—pure, wild, unadulterated sex that had started in the shower. Afterward, Jake made a call to Tobin, and a bag containing towels, overnight necessities, and a change of clothes was delivered. A second call to Monica's, and dinner was delivered. After dinner, they talked and cuddled over a bottle of wine, reveling in the next step in their lives, the time together drawing them closer, both of them needing to be near each other, touching, caressing, kissing.

"How are you feeling this morning?"

Samantha felt a slight burn between her thighs, then the cramping in her abdomen. *Ugh! Not this weekend!* She cursed to herself, but then smiled when he bent over her, his chest muscles twitching when she reached up to touch him. He was beautiful in every way, and he was all hers. She licked her lips. "Mmm."

"You." He kissed her on the lips. "Are insatiable."

"You make me that way."

"I had Tobin pick up breakfast."

She lay back down and stretched out on the bed. "I'm quite famished for sex. How about you?" She reached her hand out, trying to pull him back to the bed. He laughed and pulled his hand away. "What are we having?"

"Waffles." He kissed her and snagged his T-shirt.

She rolled off from the bed and threw on his button-down shirt from the previous night. After using the bathroom and brushing her teeth, she padded out to the kitchen, coming up behind him and embracing him. "It smells delicious." She lowered her hand to the waistline of his boxers, dipping her fingers inside.

Jake chuckled, removing her hand. "What am I going to do with you?"

"I can think of a few things."

"I think you need to replenish your energy. Eat." He pointed toward the stool on the other side of the counter. She groaned, sitting down and taking the Styrofoam container and plastic utensils from him. She spread butter on her waffles, dousing them in syrup, and taking a big bite. "You see? You're hungry."

"Aren't you working today?"

"I thought we could start moving some of our things in and figure out what we need for this place and maybe do some shopping."

Samantha heard a litany of text message beeps going off and pulled her phone from her purse sitting on the counter.

"Something wrong?"

"I don't know, looks like Richard and Charlie, but I can't figure out what's going on."

"You might want to just call him."

"Why? He's on vacation. He's never taken a vacation in all the time I've known him. I don't want to ruin it."

"Trust me, you should call him."

"I guess I could. He did text me."

"Yep, you should call him."

"Why do I get the sense you have more information than I do?"

"Because my mother called me."

"Ooh, wait." She swiped the screen on her phone. "What? Married?" Jake started laughing, nodding his head. "You knew?"

"Richard told me what his plans were before they left on the cruise. I thought they would wait to marry until they returned, but I'm not surprised either."

"Why didn't he tell me?"

Jake cut his waffles with his fork, took a bite, and shrugged his shoulders. "I suppose he figured you might try to find a way to be there, but he was aware of the plans I had, so I'm guessing he thought it was best not to tell you."

"I would have." After everything Richard had done for her, she wanted to be there to support him. He deserved to fall in love, to find someone he could spend his retirement years with, and he couldn't have found anyone more special than Monica.

Jake chuckled. "I know."

Samantha eyed the phone still in her hand when it dinged again, staring at the message from Kyle. She quickly locked it and threw it in her purse. She rubbed the tension forming at the back of her neck, wondering why he was texting her, but she'd have to read it later.

"Let's plan a party for them!" she said excitedly.

"For Richard and Mom?"

"Yeah, why not. They both have tons of friends, and it would be fun, and I bet neither one of them would expect it."

Jake lifted his thumb to wipe syrup from the corner of her mouth. "When will you find the time? I seem to recall a certain discussion in which I convinced you to marry me soon, which means there is some wedding planning to do." Samantha licked her lips, the simple stroke of his thumb causing her body to heat with desire. Jake chuckled, continuing to tease her with his thumb. "You should put that thought away until later."

She groaned. "And so it begins." She blew out a frustrated sigh and giggled at his laughter. She rifled through her purse, taking out two aspirin and downing them with a bottle of apple juice Jake had set in front of her.

"Headache?"

"Yeah. Probably PMS. I feel a little crampy this morning."

"Is insatiability a PMS thing?"

Samantha set the bottle down, turning to him, her mouth agape. "Are we seriously having a conversation about PMS?"

"You brought it up."

"Just to tell you it was PMS! Not to talk about it. Who does that?"

He chuckled and put his hands up defensively. "Hey, I was only asking the question. We are getting married; I'm not sure why it has to be a taboo subject."

She turned away from him, rubbing her temples. "It's not taboo. I'm sorry I yelled at you."

Rubbing her back, he turned her stool back to him. "Come here." Hopping off her stool, she straddled his lap. "We don't need to talk about it if you don't want to. I thought since you brought it up, it was OK. I didn't mean to upset you."

"Ugh! I'm not upset, I'm just moody, and I certainly didn't want the damn thing this weekend."

"I don't care about that, but your headaches concern me. Did the doctor call you back?"

"No, but it's only been a day." After recovering from her gunshot wounds ten years ago, she was determined to always keep herself healthy and fit. She tried to eat right and exercise. While she'd had a headache every once in a while, none had ever lasted for any length of time or been this incessant. Closing her eyes, she rested her chin against Jake's shoulder, remembering the headaches her mother had before she was diagnosed with cancer. Her doctor said she would call if there was anything concerning, and she hadn't yet called. She mentally crossed her fingers, hoping no news was good news.

Chapter 11

*I*t was nearing noon on Monday, Samantha's first day of work at Morgan Industries, and she was overwhelmed with paperwork and trying to remember the names of employees she'd been introduced to earlier. Exiting the Human Resources Department, she took the stairs up to her office floor, pausing to examine the photos displayed in the hallway. The first was of George Morgan, Jake's grandfather and the founder of Morgan Industries. She remembered Jake expressing his desire for her to tell his story, and as she read the inscription below his photo, she already began formulating a plan to do just that. The next photo was of Jake, Cal, Ammo, Shorty, and Max standing in front of the first club he opened. It was so like him not to display a photo of himself, but of his team, the people he referred to as brothers, the ones he had served with and now worked with.

She'd heard countless examples from other employees about what a great man Jake was. Though she didn't need anyone to tell her, hearing it from others made her smile and realize there was a side of him that he didn't often share with her, like the donation he made to an employee when he and his family lost their home in a fire, or creating a job for the sister of one of his employees when she couldn't find a job after taking time off to tend to their sick mother, or dressing up as Santa Claus for one employee's son who was in the hospital over Christmas. While he could be so strong and protective, he had a softer side, one he never talked about, but she had to find a way to tell his story too.

Jake's mood had continued improving after last Wednesday night. Though he took constant phone calls, he hadn't gone into the office on Thursday or Friday. Instead, they'd spent the time moving their things, shopping, and decorating. She smiled, remembering the two of them at the store, attempting to pick out linens. She hadn't realized the amount of thought that goes into picking out something as simple as a towel. She'd always selected them based on how they felt. Jake was more concerned about size and absorbency. They had laughed, and bantered about colors, until finally they found a set meeting both of their wants and needs. By Saturday afternoon, they were settled into their new apartment, spending much-needed quality time together. Jake had confided more to her about Kyle, including the night he saw him holding a gun to Shannon's head, attempting to rob his grandfather's restaurant. He also told her about how he blamed Kyle for Cuddy's death and the guilty feelings he has lived with since the day Cuddy died.

The door about Kyle was open, but she was still conflicted, unsure if it was her place to tell him about his brother dying, or that he had a daughter. She hated that Kyle hadn't told Jake himself, but she could also understand that when Jake got angry, there was no reasoning with him. Kyle's text message on Thursday morning had actually been Sofia. When she'd called Kyle back, he said Sofia must have snuck out of bed when he was in the shower and used his phone. He apologized profusely, and she had such a hard time imagining he'd done the things Jake said he did. When she was speaking to him, she wanted to tell him she knew about his illness, but she wasn't sure she was supposed to know. So many secrets…it all felt so…wrong.

"There you are," Jake said, coming around the corner near her office. "You're not smiling. Is that a bad sign?"

"What? Um…no. Actually, it's good to be back at work," she said, pulling her lost gaze from the photos to Jake, trying to smile, not wanting to ruin the five-day streak of a good mood.

"You may very well be the only employee I ever heard say that. How's your headache?"

"Gone, though after all the information that was just thrown at me, I'm surprised it didn't come back."

Jake chuckled. "Sorry. Shorty is working on that process."

"Do you realize that last week, I vowed my life to you, and today I signed my life over to your company."

"That means you're all mine then." Jake gave her a smug smile.

Samantha inched her brow up, taking in the beautiful man that would soon be her husband. She didn't have his name yet, but she was his, in every way. He owned her heart and her body, and most days he took over her thoughts. Just a few months ago, the idea of getting married to someone had never entered her mind. She had her family back and every dream she'd ever had was coming true, all because of him. He deserved so much more than anything she could ever give him. He deserved so much more than her keeping things from him. Jake put his hands in his pockets, looking at her with a smile on his face. "What?" she asked.

"Nothing. It's good to see you smile. Come on. Max has been waiting for you in your office, so we better get there before someone else finds you and whisks you off again."

"You seem to be the only one doing any whisking."

Jake chuckled. "If I was whisking, I would be whisking you upstairs to my office, where there is an apartment." He pulled her to his side and placed his arm around her torso, leaning into her ear. "Then I might whisk that blouse and skirt right off you, and once you were standing there with just your panties and bra, I think I may just whisk—"

"Jake!"

"What? I was just saying—"

"Stop it! You're getting me all flustered, and we are in the office."

"Are you flustered?" He rubbed her back, his hand sliding lower.

"Yes, and you shouldn't be touching me that way while we are at work."

"I don't give a shit what people think. But this flustered thing is something I should hear more about. Do you mean flustered as in wet?"

"Jake!"

"What?"

The innocent look on his face made her smile. "I don't want people surmising you gave me a job because I'm your girl—"

"Fiancée, and don't worry about what anyone else thinks. I've seen what you can do, and I would have hired you even if you weren't my fiancée." Jake kissed the top of her head. "But I'll stop making you feel uncomfortable." He dropped his hand from her waist. "Did they take you on a tour?"

"Yes, I was given a tour and introduced to everyone, except whoever was in the conference room with you."

"Excellent! Did they give you a key card?"

Samantha held up the key card with her picture on it. "Right here."

"That will give you access to any floor. All guests and visitors need to sign in and be issued a pass."

"I was already informed about the policy. They were very thorough about that. No one gets in without a badge unless cleared by you."

"Correct." He pulled a key from his pocket. "And this is the key to your office, which only Cam, Manny, Cal, and I have."

Samantha took the key from him. "This is the southeast corner, right?"

"Yes. Why are you laughing?"

"I'm one floor down and in the opposite corner from you. I'm just surprised you didn't find an office closer so you can monitor who's coming and going."

"I figured you would want a little space, but I'll still know who's coming and going."

"Of course, you will."

Still smiling, Jake led Samantha to her new office. It was smaller than Jake's office, but bigger than any work space she'd ever had. The contrasting colors of forest green and cream covered the walls. The sunshine permeated the room through three windows on the south and east. She ran her hand along the Cherrywood desk, jumping back when Max stuck his head up from underneath it.

"Sorry, almost finished."

"Hi, Max."

"What do you think?" Jake asked.

"It's way more than I need, but it's beautiful in here."

"It was painted last week, and we added a small conference table, some white boards, and the video equipment. If this room isn't big enough, there is a conference room on all three floors you can use until we figure something else out."

"It's perfect." She rose to her tiptoes, kissing his cheek.

"And the best part is you have state-of-the-art technology," Max said. "Give me a sec, and I'll show you how this works."

"And that's my cue." Jake turned to leave. "I'll be back in thirty minutes to take you to lunch."

"That sounds great. I'm starving. Where are we going?"

Jake stopped and turned back, winking at her. "Perhaps we'll eat in."

Samantha stared after him, her mouth agape, her skin heating and turning a crimson red. She cleared her throat as Max stood from behind the desk.

"I assigned you a tablet, figuring you need something smaller for easier transport in case you have any off-site meetings." Max turned the tablet toward her. "It has all the same features as a laptop, but we use our own videoconferencing software to connect virtually, so you can use it for meetings or presentations, or if you just want a face-to-face conversation with someone in or out of the office. You are connected to those two flat screens mounted on the wall. We have those in all of the conference rooms, so you could present from the comfort of your office if you want to, or you could record it for viewing at a later date. I'm just warning you though, anything recorded stays in the system until you record over it. If the red button between those two screens is on, you are being recorded."

For another twenty minutes, Samantha listened as Max rambled on about the technology in her office. Most of it went over her head, and she was thankful when he finally left, allowing her a few minutes to try to understand it. After staring at the remote for ten minutes and fiddling with the buttons, she threw it on her desk. "How will I ever figure this out?"

Jake was the reason she wouldn't figure any of it out. She could still see him winking at her, a silent promise for more to come. And he was right about her being wet. A mere touch from him, and a fire in her belly had been ignited, increasing the ache between her thighs, which was now palpable from just thinking about him. Closing her eyes, she anticipated what her lunch hour might entail. He would first tease her with his hands, rubbing them along her swollen folds before inserting them inside of her. Then his mouth would cover hers, or he might kiss her neck, or her collarbone, or her breasts. His lips were magical, holding some sort of potent powers putting her under his spell. The very thought him taking her breasts into his mouth made them heavy with desire.

She sat down at her desk, crossing her legs to ease the ache, sending him a quick message. She waited for a response that never came. Sighing, she dropped her phone on her desk, disappointed that he was probably in a meeting for this or that and she'd end up having lunch on her own. Picking up the paper Max had left with her with her usernames and passwords, she began logging on to her tablet, just as Jake appeared at her door.

Samantha licked her lips, a heated flush washing over her at the mere presence of him. Hot and sexy, two words popping into her head. He positioned himself against the doorjamb with his hands tucked in the pockets of his trousers, his biceps bulging through his white dress shirt. The blue tie he wore had a silver hue to it, matching the amusement in the beautiful blue orbs staring back at her. Removing his phone from his pocket, he held it up. "You sent me a text."

"I…ahem…I did."

He closed her door and locked it, stalking toward her. "Say it."

Her insides pulsated, her body craving him, more than one might think is healthy, but her steady diet of him always made her want more. She stood, holding on to the desk, afraid her weakened knees would have her tumbling to the floor. "Boon."

He sauntered to her side of the desk, and she turned just as he reached out to close her tablet. "Say the words, Samantha."

She groped for the desk, needing it to steady herself. "Say it," he said again, leaning in, his lips touching her neck, the intimate gesture causing her to moan. Lifting her head, she tilted it back, giving him unrestricted access. He took full advantage, trailing seductive kisses up to her ear. "Say the words," he whispered.

"Bring on orgasm now." She hated the desperation in her voice, but lately she couldn't seem to get enough of him.

"What are you wearing under the skirt?"

"Aah…um…my white panties."

He palmed her breast, rubbing his thumb over the taut peak of her nipple now protruding through the thin material of her blouse. He skimmed his hand down her abdomen to the hem of her skirt, inching it upward. "Mmm. The satin ones. And they're wet."

"You seem to be able to make me that way just by looking at me."

"So what happens when I do this?" He shoved her panties aside, his fingers dancing along her folds, spreading her arousal.

"Oh, God!" Samantha gasped for a breath as he thrust one finger inside of her.

With his other hand, he grabbed her head, bringing his lips within an inch of hers. "I need you, baby."

"Then take me." She barely got the words out before his lips crashed over hers in a frenzied kiss. She moaned into his mouth when he curled his finger, the tingling sensation spreading through her veins, awakening every nerve in her body.

He pulled back, smiling at her before dropping to his knees, sliding her panties down her legs. When he stood, she reached for the belt of his pants, just as a loud knock on the door sounded, halting her movement and bringing her back to reality. "Shit!"

Jake smiled. "To be continued." He straightened her skirt and headed toward the door.

"Jake!" She held on to the desk to steady herself. "My panties."

Jake held them up to her. "These?" he asked with a chuckle before shoving them in his pocket.

"Jake!"

He laughed louder, and she crossed her arms, biting her bottom lip to stifle her own laughter.

"Sorry to interrupt, but it's bad, JT," Cal said, his eyes darting to Samantha.

Jake regarded Samantha for a moment, his jaw clenched, uncertainty etched across his brow. "Samantha is my fiancée. She's also a member of our leadership team now. Whatever it is, you can say it in front of her. There are no secrets between us."

"OK," Cal said, still looking at her, gesturing with a slight nod. She hoped that meant her secret was safe and not that he was about to tell him everything they knew about Kyle. "It's Kansas City again. This is going way beyond vandalism, Jake. This is personal."

Samantha breathed a sigh of relief, but it was short lived as she observed Jake's reaction. "When?"

"Last night sometime."

"It's almost noon, and we are just learning about this now?" Jake questioned.

"That's my fault. Late night, and don't ask. They finally got ahold of Ammo, who tracked me down." Cal walked past Jake to Samantha's desk, snatching the remote control and punching a few buttons. They all watched the screen as the vandalism photos appeared.

One look at the photos, and Samantha raced to Jake's side. She didn't need anyone to tell her what this was going to do to him, but she was too late. His body was already rigid, bristling as he stared at the photos. She rubbed his back, trying to offer whatever comfort she could.

"Turn it off!" Jake shouted.

Cal shut it off, tossing the remote back on her desk.

Samantha didn't want him to leave, but she understood he had to. This was his company, and right now someone was trying to destroy it, and if they succeeded, it would destroy him. "You need to go." She held her finger to his lips when he was about to speak. "If it's as bad as Cal says, you need to be there. I have Tobin, Cam, and Manny, and Charlie if I need him, plus Max and Shorty are here."

"I'll wait downstairs," Cal said, leaving them alone.

"I don't want to leave you."

"We'll talk every day, but you need to go," she said, hating she was encouraging him. She should be there with him, to help him through this. "I'll give your assistant, Elise, my schedule, and I'll carry my phone, and I will answer it too." Her attempt to make him smile didn't work.

"If I'm a target, Samantha, so are you."

Samantha nodded. He'd already told her that, though she'd kept it tucked away in her mind, she understood the risk of being with him. "That's why you hired Cam and Manny, and if it makes you feel better, I'll ask Tess, Jen, or Dana to stay with me."

Jake took her face in his hands. "I love you, baby. I'm sorry."

"I love you too, but don't be sorry. This is your grandfather's company, your company. You need to go take care of it."

Samantha shut her door when he left, racing back to the remote control and pushing the same buttons she had watched Cal push. Staring at the screen, the photos began to appear. She took a step back, falling into the chair at the small conference table, unable to peel her eyes from the screen. She was a photographer, and while pictures may never show the full story, these did. This was personal, and Jake was right in the midst of it all.

Chapter 12

The dreary morning clouds reflected Jake's current mood as Cal took the final turn toward the Kansas City nightclub. He didn't understand any of this, or why anyone would be trying to destroy his clubs.

"You OK?" Cal asked.

He wasn't OK. He wanted someone to blame, and up until Cal showed him the surveillance video on the plane, he'd thought Kyle had done this. He wanted it to be Kyle, but the person appearing in the video definitely was not Kyle.

"Jesus Christ!" Cal slowed down to turn into the parking lot.

Jake looked up, his heart sinking at the sight in front of him. He and Cal exited the vehicle, and Jake placed his hands in his pockets, grabbing on to Samantha's panties he'd shoved in his pocket earlier, praying they could somehow calm him. Jake slowed his steps as he neared the building, kicking at the glass and debris along the exterior. It was scattered five feet onto the sidewalk. Spray paint marred the retro design on the outside from the bottom to about six feet up.

"Jesus," Cal said, standing a short distance away from him, a look of disgust on his face. "It didn't look this bad in the photos Dean sent."

Jake stared helplessly at the building in front of him, trying to figure out who in the hell would do this. He and Cal had viewed the video, seeing the gun-toting vandal shoot her way through the glass doors. Yes, *her*. It was definitely a her.

Dean, the club manager, came out of the plywood-clad doors. "I got here as soon as the alarms went off, but the damage was already done."

"They started out here," Cal said, walking around the building. "They knew we had alarms, and they knew they wouldn't go off until they were inside."

"How bad is it inside?" Jake almost choked on the words; part of him didn't want to know.

Dean waved at them to follow him. "The cameras were shot out, so you didn't see the worst of it."

The prominent smell of liquor greeted Jake as he walked across the wet, sticky floor, the broken glass crunching with every step. The neon lights that had once electrified the dance floor now lay shattered, forming a sea of cataclysmic colors throughout. Tables and chairs were askew, some turned upside down, others lying on their sides covered in glass. Bullet holes plastered the walls from top to bottom. A small section of the bar had been marred with more spray paint, leaving another cryptic message behind.

"Who has been in here since this happened?" Jake asked.

"Just the police investigators you see here now collecting evidence."

"Did you talk to the police?"

"No, sir. Cal said you were coming and would handle it."

"Did the police take anything else?"

"You can ask him." Dean pointed toward a man entering through the plywood. "He's the detective."

"I'm Detective Grady." The stout gentleman held his hand out to Jake.

"Jake Morgan." Jake took his hand.

Detective Grady looked around and let out a heavy sigh. "I remember when this place was built. You dedicated it to a friend of yours who was killed in action, right?"

Jake nodded. "Lance Cudhoff."

"Ah, yes. I remember now." Detective Grady pulled out a small notepad from his chest pocket. "Seems like this is becoming a regular occurrence here. You have video surveillance, correct?"

"Yes," Cal said. "The intruder appears to be female with an automatic rifle and a nine-millimeter pistol. She took out the cameras first, then shot off several rounds."

"How do you know it was a female?" the detective asked.

"Tight black leggings, top and ski mask. She appeared to be about five eight and thin."

Detective Grady eyed Cal carefully. "You own other clubs too, correct?"

"Yes," Jake said.

"Have you had any incidents at your other locations?"

"Yes," Cal said. "I can send you the details. Everything has been reported to the local police departments."

"Thanks." Detective Grady handed Cal his card. "I'll need all the details."

"I'll send it right over."

"Any reason why anyone would want to do this?"

"Not that I'm aware," Jake said.

"We'll need a full listing of your employees."

"I can send you a list. We do background checks on all of them."

"Interesting. Do all restaurants and clubs do that?"

Cal shrugged. "They have access to the property and assets, handle money and customer credit cards, and sign for purchases. We need to make sure anyone working for us is trustworthy."

"So you trust all of them?"

"Damn straight," Dean chimed in.

"Do any employees have connections to the other cities that had vandalism?"

"We looked at that angle when the vandalism first started happening," Jake answered. "We never found a connection."

"Any recent employee complaints or terminations?"

"No, sir. Our crew is solid. They've all been with us for over a year, and only one employee left. He'd just finished college and moved down to Texas," Dean said.

"How about previously, say in the last year?"

"A couple. We mostly hire college kids, a few older than that who want part-time work."

"Include the names of those that left in the last year."

"Anything else?" Jake asked.

"How about you personally? Any threats? Business transactions gone bad? Spousal trouble?"

"No, nothing."

"Not married?"

"No."

"Girlfriends? Exes you might have pissed off?"

"None." Jake was taking a chance by not mentioning Samantha, but he didn't want her involved in any of this.

"You understand if there is anything you're hiding, I'll find out, right?"

Jake's hand twitched by his side. "Do what you need to do."

"How about your family?"

"I ask you to respect my wishes and leave them out of this."

"I can't do that. We need to look at all possibilities."

"With all due respect, detective," Cal spoke up. "His sister lives in New York, and his mother is on a cruise."

"I see."

"Detective Grady," Jake ran a hand through his hair, his frustration more outwardly apparent than he wanted it to be. "You can look into my family if you must, but do not tell them about this. I haven't told them anything about the vandalism, and I don't want to give them any reason to think they may be in danger."

Detective Grady nodded. "All right." He handed Jake his card. "Give me a call if you think of anything."

Jake couldn't stand to look at the place any longer. Shaking his head in disgust, he walked back to the manager's office with Cal right behind him.

"This is the same person, JT."

"But who the hell is it?" Jake hung his head, taking a deep breath and counting to ten...twenty...thirty. "Let's start with Greg Cudhoff. This has to end."

He and Cal walked back into the club, and Dean handed Jake a piece of paper. "The press called. They want a statement."

Jake figured it wouldn't take long for the press to get wind of this with the high-visibility area. "Thanks. Refer all future phone calls to Cal."

"These are good employees," Dean said. "Most of them survive with this job. I'm sure they wouldn't mind helping clean up. They lost time after the last incident, and now this."

"No." Jake shook his head. "Hire a professional crew to clean up. Submit pay for all of the employees assuming this place is open. I'll pay each an extra thousand if they don't resign over this. We should be open in two weeks."

"Two weeks? That's faster than the last time, and this is worse," Cal said.

"Two weeks. I'll pay whatever it takes."

"Jake Morgan. How the hell are you?" Greg Cudhoff held out his hand with a wide grin.

Every time Jake saw Lance's brother, he was reminded of the friend he lost, Lance Cudhoff, or Cuddy, the name they had given him in the army, often teasing him over his cuddly bear hugs. He was the newest member of the team... just a good-natured kid, young and full of life.

"I'm good, Greg. How are you?" Jake asked, finding Greg's resemblance to Cuddy a little unsettling. The broad shoulders, toothy grin, square jaw, dimples in both cheeks, and hazel eyes that glimmered with mischief gave Jake insight into what Cuddy may have looked like today.

"I'm great! And Calvin, it's nice to see you again." Greg shook Cal's hand. "I'm glad you called. Come on back to my office. Would you like some coffee or water?"

"No, thanks; we're fine," Jake said. "Vice president now?" Jake fingered the sign on Greg's office door. Cuddy had told him his brother had worked at this bank since going to college, starting off as a part-time teller.

"Yep. Promoted a year ago, but let's be honest, half of the employees that work in a bank are vice presidents. Hey, thanks for the baby gift by the way."

"You're welcome." Jake nodded to the picture on his desk. "He resembles his dad and uncle."

Greg raised the photo and stared at it. "Yep. We named him Lance too." He placed the photo back on the desk. "So, what brings you to town?"

"The Bear's Den was vandalized last night. I'm sure it will be on the news tonight or in tomorrow's paper," Jake said.

"I'm sorry to hear that. It must be bad if you're here. Any leads on what's going on?"

"Not yet. The police are working on it," Cal said.

Jake shifted uncomfortably in his chair, preparing for the difficult conversation ahead of him. Though he trusted Cal to ask the right questions, this was something he needed to do. "We dedicated this club to Cuddy, and the day we opened, there was quite a bit of media attention. The paper ran a large feature on it, and the local news did a spotlight segment for their newscast."

"I remember. A lot of people came out for it."

"This latest incident isn't the only time the club was vandalized," Jake explained. "The police have been brought in, but we seem to be hitting a dead end. We've looked at every employee past and present, business transactions and partners, and geez, Greg, I really hate to say this, but we suspect possibly this is about Cuddy, or about revenge against me because of what happened to him."

"Whoa! I didn't see that coming," Greg said. "You think this has to do with Lance? We don't blame you for what happened, Jake. Lance made the decision to enlist, not you."

Jake cringed at the dumbfounded look on Greg's face. "I appreciate that, Greg. What about before Lance joined. Did he have any enemies?"

"You think someone had a beef with Lance?" Greg dropped the pen he was holding on the desk and sat back in his chair, his brow creased with concern. "My little brother was a teddy bear. He may have been a big man, but he had a soft heart. He didn't have any enemies."

"I had to ask, Greg."

Greg nodded. "You know, I understand why you named the place The Bear's Den, but you should have named it The King of Hearts."

Jake scratched the back of his neck. "Why do you say that?"

"One of Cuddy's favorite pastimes was playing cards. Whether it was poker, solitaire or go fish, he could always be seen carrying a deck of cards. When you opened that nightclub here, the reason you had so much exposure was because Cuddy was known as the King of Hearts around here, but not for his card playing."

Cal and Jake exchanged a glance. Jake had known Cuddy played cards. Every time they were on a base, in a makeshift bunker, or sleeping under the stars, Cuddy would bring out a deck of cards at any time of the day or night to pass the time. If Jake had known that Cuddy was known as the King of Hearts, he certainly would have considered a different name for the club. "If not for his card playing, then what?"

"Because he was generous. That last year, his charitable contributions outweighed the amount he could deduct from his taxes. He volunteered his time too, both before he left for the army and every time he came home on leave. After he passed, I was the executor of his will, and he left a hefty sum to the local animal shelter and a women's shelter. One would think that would be enough, but he also named nine other charities, giving them all a smaller, but quite significant, contribution."

"That would explain all those pleas to each of us to adopt a pet," Cal said.

Greg nodded. "You wouldn't be the first. He advocated for those homeless pets for hours. He even threatened to sneak one through airport security so he could take it with him. He thought having a dog might be good for your unit."

Jake smiled, remembering the many times Cuddy would walk around the barracks and show pictures from his Facebook page of animals needing a home. "That's the Cuddy I remember."

"Me too. But to be honest, there was something different about him that last time he was home. We all knew it was going to be his last tour and the next time he would be home, it would be to stay."

"I know," Jake leaned forward and clasped his hands together. Cuddy did come home to stay; it was just in a box draped with a flag. It was an ending none of them wanted, but it was always a possibility. "I know."

"He loved the unit. He called you his second family."

"And he was ours," Jake said.

"What did Cuddy do the last time he was home?" Cal asked.

"Kim and I scheduled our wedding around his leave." Greg closed his eyes. "When I think back on it now, I think he knew he wouldn't be coming home again."

"What do you mean?"

"I don't know. When you lose someone, you wonder about things, like did he do that or not do that because he knew he wasn't coming home."

"What kind of things?"

Greg stared at something on his desk. "It was sort of our thing that every time he came home on leave, I would pick him up, and our first stop was the Sonic drive-thru to buy Lance his favorite root beer float. Then we would drive around for a couple of hours and catch up before I'd drop him off at home. But the last time he came home, he insisted on renting a car. There were other things too, like how he was late for the wedding pictures, and he's never late for anything, or how he was going to meet me and Kim for dinner the night before we left on our honeymoon, but he said he couldn't make it and he'd see us off at the airport since he was leaving around the same time, but he never showed. I wasn't sure if he actually made his flight or not, so I called Mom when we landed, and she told me he did, but she was worried about him."

"Why was she worried?" Cal asked.

"She said the two days before he shipped out, she only saw him once, which is so unlike him. The day he left, she said he looked tired, like he'd been out partying all night."

Jake and Cal exchanged another glance, concern on both of their faces. "Lance didn't drink," Jake said. "He liked to have a clear head."

"We know. She couldn't smell anything on him, but he seemed a bit off. Mom thought he was struggling with getting out of the unit, or maybe he knew he wouldn't be coming home again and he didn't know how to say good-bye."

"Did he act differently before those two days?"

Greg shook his head, still staring at his desk. "Yes and no. I mean he seemed happy, like always, but the wedding stuff kept me busy, and he told me to do what I needed to do and not to worry about him. He said he had things to do, and at the time I figured he was going shopping for a wedding gift."

"At the time? Did something make you change your mind about what he was doing?" Jake asked.

"Lance didn't drink, but he knows I appreciate a good whiskey. Our gift was a personalized decanter set with our names and wedding date. He must have ordered it long before the wedding because the charge on his credit card statement was three weeks before he came home."

"Is it possible he needed to pick it up and didn't want you to see it?" Jake asked.

"No. It was from a company in Oklahoma that specializes in barware."

"How did it get here?"

Greg finally peeled his eyes from the desk, a perplexed expression on his face as he looked at both of them. He began rocking in his chair. "I…I guess I'm not sure. Kim and I were living with my parents at the time because we were building a house and the lease was up on our apartment. There were boxes all over. If it was shipped to the house, I didn't notice it."

"Do you remember the name of the company?"

"I don't, but maybe Kim does." Greg forced out a laugh. "Do you know what really bothers me, though?"

"What?" Jake was desperate for any information that might give them any insight into Cuddy's last days at home.

"What bothers me is that I had no idea just how kind-hearted my brother was until after he was gone," Greg said. "I mean, I knew he was a giving person and he volunteered his time, but sympathy cards came from everywhere. I wasn't even aware some of these charities existed, and here I'm upset because he was late for the wedding pictures when he'd been playing big brother to one of the kids in some foster program. It makes me feel like a schmuck."

Jake thought about his friend Cuddy, imagining him playing catch with a young boy, or teaching him card tricks. He would have made a great dad because he was such a kid himself. "Could that be why he looked so tired? Maybe he was trying to fit everything in?"

Greg scratched his head. "I don't know. You don't think all this club non-sense has anything to do with him, do you? After all this time?"

"I hope not, but we don't want to leave any stone unturned. It was pretty bad this time. I have a hunch the detective is going to track down every lead, including Cuddy. It was the first thing he mentioned."

"I better give Mom and Dad a heads-up then."

"We appreciate your time, Greg. If you think of anything else that could help, please give me a call." Jake stood from his chair.

Greg tapped his pen on the desk. "Come to think of it…there is something I've been meaning to ask you. Which one of you did he owe money to?"

Jake creased his brow. "Cuddy didn't owe us any money."

"Are you sure? Because the day he left, he took ten thousand dollars out of his savings account."

"Maybe he gave the money to the charities," Cal said.

"That's what I thought at first too, but he made those contributions with a check. And he wouldn't have had time anyway. Lance liked to be at the airport at least two hours before his flight in case there was a gate or terminal change. That transaction happened shortly after one in the afternoon, and his flight was at two thirty."

"He was running late for the airport but stopped to take money out of his account?" Jake didn't understand any of it. None of what Greg was saying sounded like Cuddy.

"It's not just that. As his power of attorney, I had access to everything. Most of his transactions were money coming in, his direct deposits from the army. He didn't have any debt, and the transactions coming out of his account were always in check form, or an ATM withdrawal of a hundred or two hundred dollars. He could have come in the bank at any time while he was home on leave, but he did it that last day, after I was gone. I figured he didn't want me to know he owed anyone. You know how he liked to gamble."

"Yes, but he never gambled with real money when he was in the unit. It was too much of a risk to break the team up if someone lost a lot of money."

"Besides, we were usually on the base a day, sometimes two, before we were taken off the radar again," Cal added. "And the army paid for just about everything, so he would have no reason to borrow that much money."

"He didn't have any cash in his personal belongings. Could he have done something with it here? Maybe a down payment on something? Or paying back a debt?"

"We would've heard about something like that by now. We hired an attorney to handle all of the estate, so notices were placed everywhere. Everything went through the courts, and no one contested a thing or brought anything up. Besides, he couldn't have done it that quickly, not with only an hour and a half to get to the airport." Greg checked his watch and glanced at the door.

"We appreciate you making time for us, Greg. We don't want to hold up your customers." Jake shook Greg's hand.

Leaving the bank in silence, Jake and Cal slid into the rented SUV. Starting it up, Jake looked over at Cal. "Ten grand? What the hell would he need ten grand for?"

"I don't know, but can I just say, for the record, if I were Cuddy's brother, I sure as hell would have been asking more questions about it six years ago. What a dumbass!"

"Now that he knows the money wasn't because of gambling, I'm sure he's kicking himself for not asking questions before now."

"We need to find out what he did with that money. I suspect it has something to do with what's happening right now."

Chapter 13

Edward pulled up to the curb outside The Hub and put the vehicle in park. "Text me when you're ready for a ride."

"Thanks, Edward. Are you coming in, Charlie?"

"Not tonight," he said, shaking his head. "I'll hang out with Edward, but those two goons are waiting by the door for you."

Samantha groaned, exiting the vehicle. After mentioning to Charlie about Jake going to Kansas City, he insisted she come out to Larchmont so she was with him, and Cam and Manny had been parked outside of Richard's place since then, staying the night and following her to work today. As much as she hated them being there, with the recent incident at Kansas City, she wasn't going to argue about it, but she also wasn't going to let them keep her from her brother or her friends. She loved spending more time with Charlie. The years apart hadn't broken the strong bond between them, and sometimes it felt like no time had passed at all. Catching sight of her friend, Jen, at the bar, Samantha maneuvered through the crowd toward her, hoping to put some distance between her and Cam and Manny.

"Hey!" Jen jumped off the barstool, embracing Samantha. "I'm so glad you could make it!"

"Me too. I've missed you."

Jen pulled away and grabbed Samantha's hand, fingering her engagement ring. "Wow! The picture you sent all of us does not do this ring justice! Just… wow!"

"Thanks, Jen."

"He's so perfect for you. Look at you all glowing and happy." Jen dropped Samantha's hand and hopped back on her bar stool. "Sometimes it makes me sick how perfect your life is now."

Samantha joined Jen at the bar. She promised Charlie she wouldn't stay long, but Jen sounded like she needed a friend. "'Now' being the key word in that sentence."

"Sorry, it's just the green-eyed monster talking. She usually rears her ugly head when the alcohol starts flowing."

"You don't have to apologize. Is anyone else coming?"

"Tess will be here a little later, but Dana is out of town," Jen said.

Dana was Samantha's first friend in New York. During their first year of college, they met Tess and Jen and the four had remained friends since then. "I knew this day would come. We get older, busy with our lives, and never see each other anymore."

"Yeah, and I have to work nights all of next week, so I'm so glad you made it back from Vegas so we could catch up. How was it?"

"Great. We've been back for almost a week, and we moved into a different apartment over on Furman Street."

"Wow," Jen said, her mouth slightly agape. "That was fast."

"Right?" Samantha waved at Bill, their favorite bartender, who smiled and nodded at her as he served a customer a drink. "Who's the girl behind the bar with Bill?"

"I'm assuming a new bartender. She makes a good drink—nothing like what Bill makes for us, but I can live with it."

Bill approached them. "Ready for another, Jen?"

"Fill me up!"

"Great to see you Samantha! I hear congratulations are in order."

Samantha raised her eyebrows. "Thanks. I guess I didn't realize the news had been announced."

"Technically, it hasn't. I overheard the manager talking to Cal on the phone," Bill said. "Would you like the usual?"

"Sure, that'd be great."

"And bring us each two shots of tequila," Jen called after him. "My treat."

"Oh God!" Having a drink was one thing, but Samantha didn't handle shots well, especially not on an empty stomach.

"Look at him," Jen said, twirling the straw in her drink and watching Bill. "He's so distraught over you and Jake getting married, he practically choked on the word congratulations."

Samantha followed her gaze. "Bill?"

"Yeah, Bill. He's like a lost puppy, following you around with his tongue wagging." Jen stuck out her tongue and panted.

"Jen, stop!" Samantha nudged her.

"He was drooling so bad when he was standing here, I thought I might have to ask for a bar rag."

"Jen!"

"It's true. He's always had a thing for you, and now look at him. He keeps glancing over his shoulder at you."

"I don't think so. It looks like he and the female bartender maybe have something going on."

"Oh please, he's just flirting with her."

"Shh," Samantha stifled her giggle, grabbing Jen's arm. "He's coming back."

Bill delivered their drinks, and Samantha snatched one from his hand. "Thanks, Bill. Who's the new girl?" Samantha nodded toward the female bartender, who had an easy smile but looked tired. Her deep-set brown eyes were dull, sad almost.

"Her name is Rebecca, and she isn't new. She's worked here a little over three months. She usually just works the weekend but had to change her schedule this week."

"Is she your girlfriend?" Jen asked.

Samantha kicked Jen under the bar, chastising her for being so nosy. "Sorry, Bill, she had an early start."

Bill wrinkled his nose and set four shot glasses on the bar in front of them, filling each one with tequila. Knowing how Jen liked her shots, he set four lemons and the salt shaker on the bar next to them. "We go out for drinks once in a while," Bill said.

"Oh, come on," Jen said, rolling her eyes. "Give us the scoop."

"No scoop," he said. "She's not from around here so she doesn't know many people. We hang out sometimes, and I've introduced her to my friends. That's about it." He placed his palms on the bar and leaned forward. "These are on the house, but don't tell the house."

Jen leaned in close to him. "I won't tell, but I know you've been in Rebecca's panties."

"Jen!" Samantha covered Jen's mouth, giving Bill an apologetic look, but judging from the look on his face and the color matching a ripe tomato, she had an inkling there was more going on between Bill and Rebecca than he was letting on.

Bill shrugged and walked away, and Samantha removed her hand from Jen's mouth. "I can't believe you said that! He probably won't wait on us again."

Jen shrugged. "What? You know damn well there's something going on between them."

Samantha didn't want to believe it. Bill was one of the good guys, and though she'd always known he had a thing for her, she was never interested, but Rebecca didn't seem like his type. She was too quiet, not outgoing at all like he was. "So, what's going on with you?" Samantha asked, changing the subject.

Jen slid a shot glass over to Samantha and handed her a lemon. After licking her hand, she dashed a bit of salt and licked again before downing her first shot of tequila in one gulp. Samantha followed the same motions as Jen, grimacing at the taste of the tequila and immediately reaching for both the lemon and her drink to dull the taste. She could feel the alcohol burning its way through her veins. Jen raised the second shot, and Samantha reluctantly joined her, clinking her glass before they both downed the second shot.

"So?"

"So, what?"

"Come on, Jen. In the last eight years, I can't remember you ever calling me on a Tuesday and asking me out for a drink. Tell me what's going on with you. How's the new place? Your job? Your mom and dad?"

Jen laughed, waving at Bill and Rebecca and holding up her almost empty glass. "The new place is fine, and commuting is actually easier than I thought it would be. My job is great. I'm going to try the night shift next week. And Mom and Dad, well…you can't pick your family, I guess."

"Meaning what?"

"I finally got around to announcing my breakup with Brad."

"Jen! It's been over three months, and you just now told them?"

"What was there to say? I thought Brad would have told Dad considering he's still working for him."

"I bet he's not now."

Jen snorted. She twirled the straw in her drink for several moments as she seemed to drift off somewhere. "Dad thinks I am the reason Brad wanted out of the relationship. He says I'm too high maintenance, and he was surprised it took Brad so long to figure it out."

"He said that?" It was one thing for Jen's parents to be upset with her decision when she switched her college major from political science to nursing, but it was quite another to blame your own child for a failed relationship. It was inconceivable to Samantha how a parent could say such a thing.

"Yep, and Mom didn't even defend me and instead walked away, saying nothing to defy the 'almighty senator.'"

Samantha downed the rest of her drink, gulping past the lump. "So let me get this straight. Brad cheats on you, gets this other girl pregnant, and your dad somehow thinks this is your fault?"

"Yep, which is why Brad is still working for him."

"Seriously?"

"Dad is his pathway to a senate seat, and Dad is shaping his protégé, making sure to establish a lifelong connection to the Senate for Brad." Jen sighed, waving her hand, attempting to dismiss the absurdity of the situation. "I never wanted any part of that life, and now it's a lot easier to stay away."

"You mentioned you are commuting to work now. Does that mean you no longer have a driver?"

"Apparently there's no reason to have one, and it's a waste of Dad's hard-earned money. I'm to take the train like everyone else, and since he was in such a generous mood, he also told me my monthly allowance was cut off."

Jen chewed on a piece of ice from her drink. "So, there you have it. Brad gets everything he wants, including my family."

"Oh my God, Jen, I'm so sorry. Do you need anything?"

"Actually, Sam, this is all a good thing. It was time for me to find my own way and do my own thing instead of relying on my parents or Brad for everything. My nursing job pays well, and I can afford to live on my own," she said with a shrug. "Besides, when I was spending Daddy's money and Brad's money, I was saving my own. I think somewhere in the back of my mind, I knew Brad was using me to get to my father. I was his conduit to bigger and better things: the affluence, the connections, the power that goes with that type of lifestyle. As far as I'm concerned, he and my father deserve each other."

"What about Paige?" Samantha asked, referring to Jen's younger sister.

"Dad never liked any of her boyfriends either. If they aren't in politics or sitting in some high-ranking position at a major corporation, they are of little value to him. Paige will graduate from college in December, but she's moving in with me before fall semester."

"And you still have us."

"Yep, and I guess it's true what they say: time heals all wounds."

In some ways Jen was right, time did heal, but some wounds are so deep that even time doesn't take away the pain. Her mind drifted again to what Jake told her about Kyle, a perfect example of how time doesn't heal everything.

Rebecca delivered more drinks. "Bill made these for you. He told me to tell you these are on the house."

"Thanks." Jen clinked Samantha's glass again, winking at her. "Going out with you has its perks."

Samantha giggled, then remembered Rebecca. "Hey," Samantha called after her as she started to walk away. "I'm sorry, what was your name?"

"Rebecca. Give me a shout if you need anything else."

"Can I see that tattoo on your wrist?"

Rebecca looked down at her arm, fingering the tattoo on the inside of her left wrist. "Let me know if you need anything," she said, then turned and walked away.

"OK, that was weird," Jen said.

"Right? Was that rude of me to ask to about her tattoo?"

"No. If it was on her chest, or ass maybe, but it was on her wrist. Who puts a tattoo on their wrist but doesn't want to show anyone?"

"I don't know. Maybe it was the name of an old boyfriend, and she regrets it now because she has Bill, who by the way is avoiding us."

Jen giggled. "I know, but it's cute, isn't it?"

"No, it's not cute. He's probably mad, and he probably thinks I'll go running to Jake and tell him he's banging the new bartender."

Jen covered her mouth, trying to swallow the liquid she'd sipped. "Oh God, I think I forgot how much fun you were. I'm so glad you came out."

"I'm not telling Jake. I may ask about it, but I'm not going to be the tattle tale. But it's weird she wouldn't show me the tattoo."

"I think it was a picture of something, but hey, maybe she's being so secretive because she's living a secret life." Jen choked a bit on her drink as she started laughing.

"Ha, ha. Very funny."

"Come on. I remember when we all got those tattoos, and you wouldn't tell us what those tulips meant. It's not like it's impossible to imagine someone else having a similar issue."

"Yeah, I suppose not." Samantha squinted in Rebecca's direction just as she dipped her head closer to Bill, who was saying something. She raised a brow, eyeing Samantha carefully.

"Bill probably just told her you were Jake's fiancée, and now she regrets being mean to you."

Samantha cocked her head to the side, staring at Rebecca. Her brown eyes narrowed at Samantha before she spun around and headed in the opposite direction. "That was not a look of regret."

"No," Jen agreed. "That was definitely the green-eyed monster."

"It reminded me of Brittany."

"Aah, the evil wench. Here I thought maybe she was afraid she'd be fired because you know about her and Bill, but it appears you may have another ex-lover to deal with."

"Just great."

Chapter 14

The noise coming from her tablet interrupted Samantha's concerted efforts. She'd been working diligently all week to rebuild the Morgan Industries website, tell Jake's grandfather's story, and create the perfect brochure for The Orchid. She glimpsed over at her screen, her annoyance quickly fading when she saw Jake's picture appear. She excitedly clicked the icon and answered. "Hey! Shouldn't you be on a plane on the way home?" She brought her hand to the screen, rubbing her finger over his beautiful lips. He'd been gone for three nights…three very long nights.

"About that."

Her heart sank. "You're not coming home."

"I'm sorry, baby. I have some business in Las Vegas."

Samantha was afraid of what his words meant. She'd talked to Ammo yesterday, and so far, there had been no mention of Kyle, but now that he was going back to Vegas, she wondered if it was to fire him. "I want you to join me."

"Where? In Vegas?"

"You don't work Fridays anyway. Carver called a buddy of his, and a charter plane is fueled and ready to go. Tobin is waiting for you in the parking garage."

"How did you know I would say yes?" She tried to keep a straight face, but it was impossible when he tried to act so innocent.

"I was hoping." He dangled her panties in front of the screen. "I need to return these to you."

Samantha giggled when he peeked from behind them. "I have more."

"Then maybe I can exchange these for a new pair."

"You never quite play fair, Morgan." She shook her head, smiling at him. She thought about everything she had to do. She could work from anywhere.

Charlie would certainly understand her wanting to go, so the only thing holding her back was Dana. "How many meetings do you have?"

"A few, but you will have all my nights. We'll return home on Sunday." He flashed her his best smile.

"With all those meetings, I might need to bring a friend along."

"Charlie?"

"No, Dana. I still need to find that dress!"

"I'll book her a room. Clay will be on the plane too."

Samantha gripped the arms of the chair, her knuckles turning white. "Clay? Why is Clay coming?"

"I have some legal matters I need his help with."

Samantha feared for Kyle and what his future held and what that might mean for Sofia. She had to do something, if nothing else, she would try to talk him out of it. "Then I'll see you in a few hours." She blew him a kiss and ended the call.

After several hasty phone calls, one stop at her apartment to pack a bag, and another stop at the new lingerie store she'd been dying to visit, she relaxed in the back seat as Tobin drove to Dana's apartment. She had never been on a trip with Dana before, and she was just as excited about that as she was about seeing Jake…and Sofia. When she told Kyle she was coming to visit again, his reaction was silence and an audible sigh. With an understanding Jake was going to be there, he probably figured he was going to be fired. She folded her hands together, saying a silent prayer, asking for strength, something she was going to need when she told Jake the truth about Kyle and Sofia.

After landing at the airstrip in Vegas, Samantha, along with Dana, Clay, Cam, and Manny piled into a waiting limo. Samantha wiped her palms on her shorts, her nervousness beginning to show, and it didn't help how Clay was looking at her. He glanced at Cam and Manny before leaning toward Samantha.

"When are you going to tell Jake about Kyle?"

Samantha gasped. "You know?"

"Shit," Dana said. "Did we talk loud?"

Samantha had told Dana everything on the plane. She trusted Dana, but more than that, she was going to need her this weekend, and better to have an ally when she tells Jake the truth.

"Well?"

"How did you find out?"

"Jake told me about him, and then I heard you talking."

"Obviously, the whispering wasn't a big enough hint it was a private conversation," Dana said.

Clay quirked a brow. "Never occurred to me. With two three-year-old boys who like to get into things they shouldn't, I guess I have a trained ear when it comes to whispering and conniving."

"We aren't three, nor are we conniving," Samantha said. "To answer your question, I don't know. He hasn't exactly been around this last week. Why did he ask you to be here?"

"He has some business he needs my help with. And he wants to fire Kyle."

"You can't do that, Clay! If you overheard our conversation, then you understand what's going on. He's sick, and he has a daughter."

"I heard, which is why I'm wondering when you are going to tell him."

"Are you going to tell Shannon?" Samantha asked.

"Not over the phone."

"You can't let him do it, Clay. You have to talk some sense into him."

"I doubt he'll listen to me, but he asked me here, knowing he was putting me in a bad position with Shannon, but he needed someone he could trust and not some attorney he doesn't know."

Dana joined their small huddle. "Maybe you should meet him before you decide to help Jake fire him. I mean, you must have some ethical obligations."

"I do. To my client, which at the moment is Jake Morgan, the CEO of Morgan Industries."

"But what about your family?" Dana asked.

"I'm in a tough spot. I guess I'll have a few drinks and try to forget what I heard."

"Sometimes doing the right thing isn't always easy. Just remember that, Clay, when you are sitting in a room with a dying man who has a three-year-old daughter. What if it was Shannon and she was a single parent?"

"Don't do that, Samantha. I have legal obligations."

"Pfft!" Samantha rolled her eyes at him.

"Do you really think he's going to flip out when he finds out you went to see Kyle?" Dana asked.

"Yes," Samantha and Clay said at the same time.

"Not to mention the fact I have kept it from him for almost two weeks."

"How long have you known about Kyle?" Dana asked Clay.

"A couple of days," he said.

"What's your excuse for not telling Shannon?"

"The American Bar Association. They issue my license to practice law."

"You could disappear. If you aren't around, he won't fire him without you."

"So he flies me down here, and I disappear?"

"Why not? It is Vegas!" Dana said. "Maybe that will give Samantha time to tell him."

"As long as she tells him," Clay said.

"We promised no more secrets, and here I am, two weeks into our engagement and already keeping them." She glanced up as the driver pulled up in front of The Orchid. "But I have no plans of enlightening him with that information tonight." She nodded toward the entrance where Jake stood with a bouquet of tulips.

"Damn," Dana said. "If only I could find a man like that."

Samantha didn't wait for the driver to open her door. She jumped out, racing toward Jake. He caught her in his arms, lifting her off the ground.

"God, you feel good." He buried his face in her hair.

Closing her eyes, she inhaled the familiar woodsy scent. He was her everything, and she missed him more every minute they were apart—his touch, his kiss, his body protectively spooning her at night. She held him tighter, wishing away the secrets she was keeping, hoping like hell when he finds out, they wouldn't drive him away. He set her down and kissed her.

"I missed you," she said, breaking the kiss and looking up at him.

He pulled her into his chest. "I missed you more, and I'm sorry to make you travel again. Are you ill?"

"Just a little headache, but I took something for it. I'm starving, though."

"Then we should eat, but these are for you." He handed her the bouquet.

"How do you do that? These are a spring flower, and yet you always seem to find them somewhere."

"I would fly around the world if it would make you smile like that." He stepped around her. "Hey, Dana, Clay."

"Thanks for letting me tag along, your highness," Dana said, attempting a half-hearted curtsy. Samantha laughed out loud, and Jake rolled his eyes. Dana was always good for a little comic relief. Whatever she was going through to cause her to lose weight, act fidgety, and not care about her appearance certainly didn't affect her sarcasm or quick wit.

"Here are the key cards to your rooms. Why don't you settle in, and we'll meet you downstairs in an hour for dinner?"

Once Cal and Dana exited the elevator on their floor and Samantha was alone with Jake, she turned to him, studying him carefully. He looked tired and a bit defeated, though he tried to hide it by smiling at her. "What happened in Kansas City? You were pretty vague on the phone."

"I don't want you to concern yourself with Kansas City, at least not tonight."

"I saw the news reports. It was bad, Jake."

"I know. I was there. Can we please not talk about this tonight?"

Samantha nodded, taking his outstretched hand as he led her to the hotel suite. "I feel like I was just here." She placed the bouquet on the table, turning back to him, just as he swept her into his arms again.

"I'm so happy you said yes, and I know you're hungry, so I'll wait here while you get ready."

Samantha started to walk toward the bedroom, but stopped. "Before I forget again, I've been meaning to ask you about that new bartender at The Hub; Rebecca is her name. When Jen and I were there on Tuesday night, I met her. Do you know her?"

"No. Why?"

"I don't know...she seemed a little off...jealous, maybe."

"I imagine most women are jealous of you."

Samantha placed her hands on her hips. "You're changing the subject. Did you two date?"

Jake shook his head. "I've told you before: I never really dated, and I've never met her, Samantha, nor do I know who she is or what she looks like. And before you ask, I don't remember ever being with a woman named Rebecca."

"You're sure?"

"Positive."

Samantha bit the inside of her cheek. She shouldn't be questioning him, but she couldn't shake the image of Rebecca glaring at her. Jake walked over to her, taking her face in his hands. "Can we not argue? I honestly don't know her, Samantha, and I want this weekend to be about us, not Kansas City or Rebecca, or anything else."

Samantha wanted the same thing. "I'm sorry. I just had to ask, but it's already forgotten."

"Good." He kissed her, letting his lips linger on hers too long, leaving her wanting more when he pulled away. "You better get that beautiful ass in there and change or I may cancel our dinner plans."

She smiled and nodded. "I'll be out in ten minutes."

Samantha pulled on her new lace panties, looking at herself in the mirror. With not being able to run or do much exercise the last couple of weeks, she had gained a little weight. Though she started exercising as soon as her stitches were removed, it would take a while to get into a routine again. Jake probably wouldn't notice, but he would definitely notice the gift she bought for him. After putting on the matching bra, she slipped into her skirt and blouse and stepped into her sandals.

"I'm ready," she announced, coming out of the bedroom and grabbing her purse.

"Wow, that was quick. Beautiful as ever." Jake took her hand, leading her out the door.

"Can we make a quick stop on the rooftop before we join the others?"

Jake drew his brows together. "Now? You just said you were starving."

"Yes, now." She smiled when he pushed the button to the rooftop. She pulled a card from her purse. "I have no idea what to give someone like you for your birthday so, for now, I have this card and me."

"My birthday isn't for another week, so how about if I skip the card and just take you?"

Laughing at his playful comment and an unspoken promise of his intentions, she stepped onto the rooftop and instantly knew this place would be perfect regardless of the time of day. The sun had set, and the neon lights lit up the night sky. The traffic noises below were dulled by the background music in the hotel, and the strings of white lights still adorned the small pergola. "I love it up here." She handed him the card, watching him open the envelope and pull out the glossy trifold brochure she had created for The Orchid.

He moved closer to the light, reading the card first, then the brochure. "You did this?"

Samantha nodded, pleased by the smile on his face.

He turned to the final page, raising his brows. "The Rooftop Rendezvous?" He continued reading it, studying the pictures. "A wedding chapel on the rooftop?"

Samantha clasped her hands together in excitement. Ever since the night they were engaged and made love on the rooftop, she has wanted to do this. She designed it in her head, and if Jake said yes, it could actually happen.

"How did you get these pictures?"

"Charlie and I staged some of it while you were working the last time we were here. The rest is just a lot of editing and photoshopping."

Jake folded the brochure, setting it on a nearby table. "Hmm…this is exactly why I hired you, but—"

"You don't like it?"

"No, I love it. It's perfect and just what this place needs to be competitive here, but—"

"But you've only owned the hotel for a couple of weeks, and there are other priorities." Her disappointment oozed from every pore of her body.

Jake chuckled. "Let me finish." Taking her hand, he pulled her close, dancing her around the rooftop. "I have been trying to say we are the first."

"The first to what?"

"Get married here. It's our hotel, our rooftop, and you were the one to give it the name after our amazing night up here." He twirled her around, pulling her back to him. "It's only fitting we should be the first." He pressed himself against her, his steel shaft palpitating against her belly. "So, the deal is, if you want your Rooftop Rendezvous, you'll have to abide by my one condition."

His tone was laced with a seductive challenge. She licked her lips. She envisioned his mother wanting a big wedding, but the only thing that mattered to her was pledging her love for him in front of family and friends, and there was no better place to do it than right here. "You're negotiating marriage?"

"You already said yes; it's only the venue we're negotiating. And since you want the Rooftop Rendezvous up and running by the first of September as you announced in your brochure, you don't have much of a choice."

"Well..." She struggled for words, unable to take her eyes off from him as he gyrated against her. "I just inserted a date. I have no idea how long it will take to remodel it."

"I do recall you saying yes to marrying me in a month."

Samantha nodded. "You were very convincing."

"I can be when I need to be."

"Yes, you can," she repeated.

Jake stopped moving, his predatory gaze intent on her, rendering her helpless to think straight. "What's it gonna be, baby?"

She was hungry earlier, but the only thing she craved now was him. "I think I should show you your birthday present."

"You gave me the card, but you didn't answer the question."

"There's an early birthday present waiting for you under my clothes." She slid her top to the side, revealing a red lace strap. "It matches this."

"You are wearing my birthday present?" Jake asked, reaching out his finger to follow the strap of her bra, his tantalizing touch eliciting a satisfied moan. "You were planning to seduce me all along."

Samantha licked her lips, entranced by the beautiful man in front of her. "I'm not very good at it, remember?"

His hands drifted lower to her chest as his slow smile built to a magnanimous grin. He unhooked the first button of her blouse, then the second. "You are better than you think." He continued to unbutton her shirt. Rubbing his hand against her bare abdomen, he slid her blouse to the side, revealing the red lace bra scantily covering her breasts. "I need an answer, baby."

His lips parted when she gazed in his eyes, glossed over with desire. Samantha's body ached with the need for him to touch her. Her breath quickened amid the fluttering of her heart, appreciating how this man loved her despite her past and her scars. She felt her knees weaken, feeling almost light headed under his alluring trance. When his thumb rubbed over her nipple through the lace bra, every nerve ending in her body stirred to life. She opened her mouth, licking her lips, and instead of words, she moaned when he cupped her breast in his hand.

"OK, next month," she breathed out through another moan.

Jake smiled. "That's only three or four weeks."

"Yeah, something like that."

He pushed down the cup of her bra, leaving her breast exposed. "You're stealing my line."

"You're stealing my breath."

"Oh, baby." His lips neared hers. "We are going to be late for dinner because I haven't even started."

Chapter 15

On Sunday morning, Samantha stood in the lobby in front of the guest services counter, tapping her pen, waiting for Dana, who was a little sluggish this morning after a late night. Cam and Manny were with her, one on her left and one on her right. The checkout line was roped off as several guests stood with key cards in hand prepared to leave. If only she could stay another few days, not only to see Sofia again, but to have Jake all to herself. He had done explicitly as he promised, spending every night with her and part of yesterday, making up for the last week without each other. She had no idea how she survived that long without him. *Never again.* She thought to herself.

Dana had been the best travel companion too. Understanding Samantha wanted time with Jake, she hung out with Clay and Ammo and some of the staff, starting casual conversations about Kyle and filling Samantha in the next day. Dana had also been the one who told Jake that shopping for a wedding dress is private and having Cam and Manny with them would ruin the experience. Tired of arguing with Dana, Jake had relented, offering a compromise to have Ammo accompany them. Samantha had quickly accepted the terms of Jake's offer, trusting Ammo to keep her safe, and to not question her decision to spend time with Kyle and Sofia instead of shopping. But that choice had left Samantha with a dilemma: she still didn't have a dress.

Holding up her phone, she looked at the picture of her and Sofia. Dana had snapped the photo without her realizing it, making it authentic with both of them laughing. She remembers that moment on the playground outside of their apartment when Sofia had captured Samantha's face with her hands, touching her nose to hers, her cute little smile covering her face.

When Samantha told Kyle about her photography business, he told her about his illness, insisting she not tell Jake about it, or about Sofia. When she pleaded with Kyle to try to work things out with Jake, he simply shook his head and changed the subject by asking her to take photos of him and Sofia. He didn't have to tell her why he wanted them. She knew he didn't want Sofia to forget him or how much he loved her. Samantha willingly took hundreds of pictures of the two of them together, trying not to think about Kyle's illness, how much time he may have left, or what might happen to Sofia. *No way!* There was no way she could let that little girl go to someone other than family. She had to tell Jake, and she had to do it today.

"Hey, beautiful." Jake came up behind Samantha, kissing her neck. Startled, Samantha held her phone to her chest, quickly locking the screen. She turned to him, snuggling against his chest so he wouldn't see her tears. "Hey, what's wrong?"

"Nothing, I thought you were going to be in meetings again."

"I was, but my brother-in-law appears to have overslept, so I'm waiting for him. He's supposed to meet me here in the lobby any minute now."

The only thing Clay mentioned to Samantha was a business meeting off site he attended with Jake on Saturday morning, and she knew it didn't involve Kyle because she and Dana were with Kyle. "That doesn't sound like Clay."

"No, I'm afraid Dana may have had a little influence on him. They headed straight for the poker table after dinner last night. What are you doing down here anyway?"

"I'm trying to figure out rooms for our wedding. I don't think there are enough available for everyone. So, do I pair them up?"

"I have a better idea. You give me a list of your friends and family and when they can be here, and I'll handle the travel arrangements for everyone: plane tickets, hotel rooms. Don't worry about anything."

"Are you sure?"

"Yes. What else can I help with?"

Samantha chewed on her bottom lip. "Let's go outside. I need some air."

"Are you feeling all right?"

"Yeah, but I have to talk to you." Taking his hand, she led him out the front doors, directing him off to the side of the building. She had to tell him about

Kyle. "Um…I…um," Samantha stammered, searching for the right words. She looked away, silently praying for the strength to tell him.

"Samantha? You look worried. Are you sure you feel OK?"

"Yeah…um, who do you think should walk me down the aisle? Richard? Chase or Charlie?" Samantha internally berated herself, but she was torn between her vow to Jake to not have secrets between them and her promise to Kyle she wouldn't tell him about his illness.

"That's what your worrying your pretty little head about? You know I can't help you with that."

"I talked to Pastor—er, Uncle Daniel, and he said he would have no problem finding someone to cover for him, so he'll be the officiant. Richard seems the logical choice, but do you think Chase and Charlie would be offended?"

"I can't speak for them, but I doubt it."

Samantha nodded, crossing her arms in front of her, preparing herself for what she had to do. She closed her eyes, swallowing past the dryness in her mouth.

Jake chuckled and put his arm around her. "They will understand if you choose Richard. You are all family."

"Jake, I need to—"

"Morning!" Dana shouted, interrupting her midsentence.

Samantha turned, finding Clay and Dana walking toward them. Dana's jovial mood was evident by the smile on her face.

"Late night?" Jake asked.

"You could say that," Clay said. "Damn, that sun is bright. Why are you out here?"

"Just talking," Jake said.

Clay looked at Samantha, inching his brow upward. She shook her head, silently admitting defeat. She'd been so close to telling him everything, but just when she was about to, Clay and Dana had appeared from nowhere.

"The sun is beautiful!" Dana elbowed Clay. "You're just crabby because I beat your ass in poker. But, Jake, I have to thank you. Not only did your casino pay for all of my shopping sprees this weekend, but it's also going to pay my bills for the next two months."

"Yay! You won!" Samantha gave Dana a high five.

"Yeah, and what she won, I lost," Clay said.

"So the house is even." Jake squeezed Samantha's shoulder, looking down at her with a smile.

Clay rolled his eyes. "Spoken like a true casino operator, but what I'm curious about is where the hell you learned to play poker?" he asked, looking at Dana.

"I'll never tell," she said, smiling at Samantha.

"Auntie Sam, Auntie Sam!" Samantha froze, her heart pounding out of her chest, lodging in her throat at the sound of Sofia's voice. *What the hell is she doing here?* She glanced up at Jake, silently asking for forgiveness as she took a step away from him.

Samantha held out her arms as Sofia launched herself into them. She hugged Sofia close to her, afraid of what would come next, but needing to protect Sofia from whatever it might be. Samantha loosened her hold as Sofia struggled in her arms, shoving a coloring book page into her chest. "Look, I finished it. The one we were coloring yesterday." Sofia's excitement poured from her. Samantha moved Sofia to her hip, clutching the page in her hand as she gave a quick look in Jake's direction. His head was cocked to the side, his eyes questioning her. Sofia followed her gaze, her eyes getting big before she turned back to Samantha, squealing and bouncing up and down. "That's Uncle Jake!"

"Um, yeah." Samantha flashed her eyes to Dana and Clay, pleading for help. Dana was trying not to laugh, and Clay merely shrugged. "Would you like to say hi?"

Sofia nodded, holding her arms out to Jake. Samantha lifted her, forcing her into Jake's arms, so he had no choice but to take her. Sofia hugged him, and he clenched his jaw, the confusion evident.

"What's going on?" Jake asked.

"Sofia!" Kyle called out to her.

Samantha turned, spotting Kyle running toward them. She glanced back at Jake, the unnerving glare he gave her, making her cringe.

"Daddy! Look, it's Uncle Jake!" Sofia squealed.

"Daddy?" Jake questioned.

"She's my daughter." Kyle came to a stop in front of him. "Her name is Sofia."

The color drained from Jake's face, his entire body tensing. Sofia let her arms fall from Jake's neck. "I love you, Uncle Jake!" Her little hands covered his cheeks, and she placed a big wet kiss on his lips. She giggled, her excitement obvious from the way she smiled and bounced in his arms, but she was oblivious to what was about to happen. The tears burned behind Samantha's lids, seeing how much the little girl loved Jake, and praying he didn't hurt her feelings.

Clenching his jaw, Jake hoisted Sofia from his torso, setting her on the ground. He glared at Samantha, and she narrowed her eyes back at him, motioning to Sofia, who appeared as though she was about to cry.

"Care to explain, Samantha?" Jake asked, his accusatory tone making her wish she could disappear.

Samantha opened her mouth, then snapped it shut. This wasn't supposed to happen, and for the life of her, she couldn't figure out why Kyle would risk coming here with Sofia if he didn't want Jake to know about her.

"Do you want to see the picture I made for Auntie Sam?" Sofia's voice was the meekest Samantha had ever heard it. The excitement that had been there mere moments before was gone. "It's from the new coloring book she gave me, and I used the new crayons too."

Jake tore his eyes from Samantha, looking down at Sofia. She was looking up at him, her big blue eyes now watery, her bottom lip quivering. Jake bent down. "I'm sorry, Sofia. Something has come up, and I need to go."

A tear fell on to her cheek. "When will I see you again?"

"I'm not sure."

"Don't you like me?"

Jake's jaw clenched. Samantha wanted to say something...anything. She should grab Sofia and get her away from Jake and Kyle, but she couldn't move. She was frozen as the very secret she tried to keep from Jake unfolded in front of her.

Dana lifted Sofia up, positioning her on her hip. "I think I have some coins in my purse. Would you like to throw them in the fountain?"

"Can we, Daddy?"

Samantha held her hand to her chest, relieved that the excitement had returned in Sofia's voice.

"Yeah, go ahead," Kyle said.

Jake stood, watching Dana carry Sofia toward the fountain on the side of the hotel. Clay ran a hand through his hair, following them, not saying a word. As much as Samantha wanted to follow them and let Jake and Kyle duke it out, this was her fault. She had to fix this.

"Jake, I can explain."

"I bet you can," he said, taking a step back from her and Kyle. He stared at both of them, his eyes becoming darker with each second that passed. He took another step back, then another until he turned, disappearing inside the hotel.

"Oh God!" Samantha fought for a breath.

"I'm sorry, Samantha. I thought you said he would be in meetings. Go after him."

"Why are you here?"

"You forgot your camera." He handed it to her. "I thought I could give it to someone in the security office and have them get it to you, and Sofia was going to leave the picture for you, but she saw you the second we turned the corner and took off running." Kyle put his hands on his hips, shaking his head. "Why are you standing there crying? Go after him."

"And what am I supposed to tell him?"

"I put you in a bad spot. I'm sorry, Samantha. Just go. Tell him whatever you need to, just make it right for both of you."

Samantha couldn't speak. Her heart was pounding. She had to make this right with Jake, but for the first time, she was scared to face him. Taking a deep breath, she raced toward the door, yanking it open and bolting toward the elevator with Cam and Manny on her heels. "This is private!" She scolded them.

"We got that. Once we know where you are going, you won't see us," Manny said, slipping inside the elevator next to her.

The elevator stopped at the floor to their hotel suite. Samantha jumped out, running toward the door and inserting her key card. "Jake!" She was sure he would come here, but the only response was silence. *Where could he be?*

Running back to the bedroom, she pushed the door open, finding him packing his clothes. He brushed past her, stomping into the bathroom, grabbing his items from the counter. "Jake. I'm so sorry. I didn't want you to find out this way. I didn't know they would be here." Her voice was trembling as much as her hands. She set her camera down, following him to the bathroom. "Please talk to me. Let me explain."

Shoving past her again, he threw his bag on the bed and turned to her, the anger reflecting in his black eyes, burning a hole through her like a heated laser. "You think you can explain to me why the hell my brother has a daughter that you apparently spent time with yesterday?"

"Jake—"

"Why the hell didn't you tell me? Or for that matter, why the hell didn't he?" Jake seethed.

"Because you didn't let him! You only saw the Kyle that hurt you! You didn't see him for who he is today!"

"Christ! What the hell happened to no more secrets, Samantha? Why would you keep this from me?"

"Because I knew you would react just the way you are now, and I was waiting for the right time!"

"Is now a good time? Jesus Christ!" Jake ran a hand through his hair and turned from her again, grabbing his bag. "It's obvious you have spent time with Kyle and his daughter. I suppose you told Shannon and my mother too!"

Samantha raced through the living room, bounding in front of him, standing between him and the door, refusing to let him walk out on her. "I didn't tell them!"

"Like I'm supposed to fucking believe you? How did you know he had a daughter?" He demanded.

Samantha took a deep breath, gripping the door knob for support. She knew she had to answer him, and she knew what his reaction would be. Her heart was throbbing so fast, she could feel it pulsating in her neck. She licked her lips, swallowing hard. "This is what I wanted to tell you outside before Clay and Dana showed up. I went to see Kyle."

"Jesus!" Jake threw his bag on the floor, releasing a heavy sigh of exasperation. He pointed at her. "I specifically told you I did not want him in our life! Not only do you defy my wishes, but you keep it from me!"

Closing her eyes, she took another breath, realizing she needed to be the calm one because yelling was getting them nowhere. "You don't get to decide who is in my life and who isn't. I didn't know he had a daughter until I was there. Once I found out, I couldn't walk away from them."

"When did you go see him?"

"Two weeks, ago," she said, opening her eyes. "Right after you told me."

"Jesus! Did you even let me finish telling you about him before you ran off behind my back?"

"I—"

"After everything we have been through, the promise of no more secrets, and you blatantly ignore everything I told you about Kyle and go see him anyway!"

"He's dying, Jake."

"Oh, Christ! He's fucking brainwashed you!" Jake threw his hands up. "Here we go! Poor Kyle! It's the 'woe is me' all over again, and you're naïve enough to believe him!"

Samantha cocked her head to the side, biting back the words on the tip of her tongue. "You're upset, so I'm going to choose to ignore that comment. Your brother is dying. He has—"

"I don't fucking want to hear it, Samantha!" He took a step closer to her. "Don't you get that? I want nothing to do with Kyle or whatever story he might have come up with this time to get more money for his fucking addiction!"

"He hasn't used drugs in four years!"

"Bullshit!" Jake ran a hand through his hair. "I should have fired him the goddamn first day I owned this place; then none of this would be happening!"

"You can't fire him. He has a daughter, your niece. He needs a job with health insurance."

"That's not my fucking problem! None of this is my fucking problem!"

"My God, Jake, what the hell is wrong with you?" Samantha moved away from the door, placing a gentle hand on his arm. "This is your family we're talking about."

He jerked his arm away from her. "What's wrong with me?" Jake laughed and threw his head back.

Unsettled by his cynical laughter, Samantha crossed her arms over her chest, wondering how such a giving and caring man could create a job for someone he doesn't even know, or visit a sick child in the hospital dressed in a Santa Claus suit, but be so obstinate and uncompassionate when it came to his own brother.

"I'll tell you what's wrong with me." Jake lowered his voice, his dark eyes piercing through her. "I trusted the wrong person."

"Like I did when I told you about my past only to have you go traipsing off to California to meet with my brother?" she snapped back.

"That was different, and you know it!"

"You're right!" She had heard enough. He had pushed her to her breaking point and now she was fuming. "The situation was different, but the reason was the same! You did it to bring my family together again. I wanted to do the same for you, so yes, I went to meet Kyle; I spent time with Sofia. I took her shopping and bought her some new crayons, and we went to the spa and got our nails painted. She's a three-and-a-half-year-old girl who will soon be without the only person who has ever cared for her. A little girl who will be placed in the system if her family doesn't step up and do something!"

"It's a fucking sob story, Samantha! Why can't you fucking see that?"

Samantha shook her head at him, backing away, a sense of uneasiness tying her stomach in knots. She didn't know this uncaring, unforgiving man. "I thought I was going to marry a man who would do anything for his family, to love them and protect them. But now a helpless little girl needs her uncle, a dying man needs his brother, and here you are, blinded by your anger at Kyle for what happened in the past. You're blinded by the pain he caused you when he chose drugs over his family. I know you are hurting, but I can't let that little girl be placed with strangers when her family is right here. Just give him a chance, Jake."

Jake pointed a shaky finger at her again, his face red, his eyes dark. Samantha took two more steps back. "That'll never fucking happen!"

Samantha glared back at him, shaking her head. The man she loved had slipped away from her. The suffering he endured in the past was driving his anger. It was controlling him and she was powerless to stop it. "Then you're not the man I thought you were." She took a deep breath and turned, walking out the door.

Chapter 16

Jake sat at the conference table in the executive offices suite, staring at the laptop in front of him. He had told Samantha what a miserable asshole Kyle was, how he had chosen drugs over his family, and how he was no longer a part of their family. He had told her he didn't want Kyle in their lives, and yet there she was, sitting in the hotel lobby, right next to Kyle, listening to him spew more lies, believing every word he said.

But Jake knew Kyle, and he didn't believe a word of what Samantha told him. *Dying?* He should have been dead a long time ago after how he abused his body with drugs. As far as Jake was concerned, he was already dead. He was only looking for money, someone to help him fund his next high. He even doubted the little girl was his. Knowing Kyle, he would use any underhanded tactic to gain the sympathy of Samantha. Kyle wasn't responsible enough to be a father. Hell, he wasn't responsible enough to be a brother.

Jake lifted the glass of whiskey from the table, bringing it to his lips and tossing the entire contents back. Now that Samantha had gone to see Kyle behind his back, he was going to be watching her every move, just like he was doing now. Setting the glass back on the table, he squeezed it hard, but it did little to ease the anger coursing through him. He filled the glass again and zoomed the screen in on the little girl. He didn't want to believe Sofia was Kyle's daughter, but as he took in the dark curly hair, the wide blue eyes, the button nose that reminded him of Timmy's and Tommy's noses, and the dimpled smile that was a family trademark, he couldn't deny she looked like a Morgan. But if that's true, then where is the mother, and why would she be placed in the system if Kyle were to die? Sofia looked up at Samantha then, the pink clip in her hair catching on Samantha's blouse. Removing the clip, Samantha gathered Sofia's hair on top of her head and placed the clip back in it. There was no sound coming from his screen, but it was obvious Sofia was laughing.

He moved the screen, zooming in on Kyle. He didn't let Samantha finish her sentence about what he was supposedly dying from, but Jake could guess it had something to do with his drug use. *Why am I even entertaining the thought he is dying?* Kyle was a user, of both drugs and people. He could never change, not after all the times Jake and his family had tried to get him help.

Picking up his drink, he swallowed it in one gulp, then moved the screen to Samantha. Of course, she would have to throw her head back in laughter at the same time he zoomed in on her. Damn her for being so fucking beautiful both inside and out. It was why he loved her as much as he did. He never thought he would be capable of loving anyone. His anger controlled him, made him incapable of it, but Samantha had defied the odds, broken through the anger and calmed the storm raging inside of him. Until now—now she was the reason for it, sitting there with Kyle, chatting him up when she should be with him.

Jake glanced up when Ammo entered the room. "What now?"

"I thought maybe you would like to talk," Ammo said.

"You thought wrong." Jake waved him away.

"Then you listen, and I'll talk."

Jake raised his eyebrows at the determination in Ammo's voice. Ammo was quiet, but when he had something to say, he made himself heard, and now was one of those times. Jake slammed his laptop shut, reclining in the chair, lacing his hands behind his head. "So talk."

"I'm the reason Samantha has been able to spend time with Kyle and Sofia. We made up the story about checking out the competition in the area so she could spend time with them until she figured out how to tell you everything."

"Jesus, Ammo! First my grandfather buys into Kyle's lies, then the Valentes, then Samantha, and now you too?" Jake pushed out of his chair and placed his palms on the table, grinding his teeth together. "Why is everyone keeping things from me?" Lifting his head, he focused on Ammo. "Tell me, Ammo! Why?"

Ammo pulled out a chair and sat. "You solve nothing by being angry. If you would stop and listen—"

"I won't fucking listen to more of his bullshit!"

Leaning back in his chair, Ammo crossed one leg over the other, his eyes scrutinizing Jake, making him uncomfortable. This was Ammo's tactic. He would sit here all day and not say a word until a civil conversation could be had. He refused to raise his voice, ever. When his father died, Jake thought he might blow, but he didn't.

Jake eyed the door. He could leave right now, and the conversation would never occur, but when he looked back at Ammo, he gestured toward the door with a shrug, challenging him to go ahead and walk out. But if Jake did that, he would turn his back on his brother. Jake pushed off the table. Hoisting up one of the chairs, he flung it toward the wall. It landed on its side, the wheels still spinning. He sat, taking a deep breath and running a hand through his hair.

"I have never told anyone about my father, except that he died in a car accident earlier this year, but I think it's time to share my story," Ammo began. "For the first sixteen years of my life, my father was a drunk, and the more he drank, the meaner he became. When my mother hid his booze, or dumped it down the sink, he would lash out at her, or me. Whoever was the closest to him would take the brunt of the mental and physical abuse."

The coil of Jake's anger holding his gut taut began to loosen. Ammo had never said anything about his father being an alcoholic. After all the years they served together, he had ample opportunity to tell him. *Why is he telling me this now?*

"I was in counseling by the time I was ten. Between the ages of ten and sixteen, we tried to commit him to a rehab center. Would you like to know how many times we tried?"

"How many?" Jake asked, now understanding where this story may be going.

"Fourteen."

"What changed?"

"I'm not sure, but I think when he learned my mother was pregnant, he maybe thought he had another shot at being a better father the second time." Ammo tapped his fingers on a file folder he brought with him. "The point, JT, is that he found a reason to change, just like Kyle had a reason to change when he learned his girlfriend was pregnant with Sofia."

"And where is this so-called girlfriend?" Jake's cynicism was evident.

"She died during childbirth, leaving him to raise Sofia on his own."

"So that's his story, huh?" Jake was still angry, but tried to calm his voice. He poured himself another drink, and after emptying the contents, he filled the glass again.

Ammo slid the file across the table. It bumped up against Jake's laptop, coming to a stop within his reach. "Cal, Max, Shorty, and I took the liberty of getting you all the information we knew you would want. Everything you need to know is in that file."

"All of you knew about this?" When Ammo nodded, Jake became more upset than he had been.

"Those are all certified documents we obtained from the county: birth certificates, death certificates, drug test results. Don't even think he tried to manipulate any of us, or Samantha, or your grandfather. He's telling the truth: he's been clean for over four years."

"So he says."

"Do you know what he did when Samantha went to see him?"

Jake didn't respond. He imagined their meeting to be similar to what he witnessed on the security camera.

"He told her to leave. Think about that a minute, JT."

Ammo gave Jake a full minute to wrestle with his thoughts. It was obvious to Jake that whatever Kyle may have said didn't work, because Samantha went back again, taking the little girl shopping, coloring with her, going to the spa together, and who knows what else.

"How easy would it have been for Kyle to try to swindle money from Samantha?" Ammo asked. "How easy would it have been to just go back to a life of drugs, rather than be a father who is responsible for a child? How easy would it have been for him to go to your mother and ask for money? He didn't do any of that, JT. He lives by simple means, barely making rent each month, buying used furniture. He pays for Sofia's babysitting by doing things for his neighbors. Sofia's clothes are from garage sales."

Ammo stood, carefully positioning his chair next to the table. "Believe what you want; push your fiancée away, your friends, the rest of your family; but if you take a look in the file, you'll see that for the past four years, Kyle has tested clean. After the first year of Sofia's life, there was no requirement to continue with the tests, but he did, because he wanted to hold himself accountable. We are all capable of change, JT, even you." Ammo walked toward the door, grabbing the knob, then turned back to Jake. "Samantha wanted me to tell you she will be packing her things, and she, Dana, and Clay are returning on the flight as scheduled."

Ammo left him there, alone with the file. "Aaargh!" He collapsed back in his chair, bending over and holding his head in his hands. In his mind, Kyle was dead; he was no longer part of his family, but Samantha had gone and befriended him, and his daughter. Prior to the meeting he had planned with Kyle today, his team tried to convince him to keep Kyle, saying he was a model employee. They had all argued with him, and now that he understood they all knew about Kyle and about Samantha going to see him, he was infuriated.

With Clay heading home, he needed to tell his mother and sister about Kyle. The thought burned a hole in his gut, and if Samantha thought she was doing them all a favor by bringing their family together, she was wrong. She was wrong on so many levels. He poured another drink. *Samantha.* He rubbed at his chest, the pain of watching her walk out the door was almost too much to bear. He never thought she would actually leave. He should have run after her, but as upset as he was, he was also coherent, realizing he didn't trust himself to not hurt her more than he had.

He stared at the file lying on the table. It was taunting him. Begging him to pick it up. He looked away, opening his laptop again. "Fucking perfect!" he said to no one but himself when he saw the image in front of him with Samantha, Kyle, and Sofia in a group hug. Samantha waved at them when they walked out the front door. "Damn her!" He slammed his laptop closed and picked up the file, but he couldn't bring himself to open it.

His phone vibrated and he peered at the screen. "Just great!" he said, shaking his head, but answering it anyway.

"Shannon," he said by way of a greeting.

"Hey, little man, how's the wedding planning going?"

"What do you want, Shannon?"

"Who pissed in your cereal this morning?"

Jake sighed. Shannon could be the perfect professional—tactful, never letting her hair down—but then something unexpected would come out of her mouth. Jake usually laughed, but he wasn't laughing now. "Superman," he answered, holding the bridge of his nose.

"He should have left some kryptonite behind to blast that piss-poor attitude of yours."

"Enough with the bullshit, Shannon. Superman wasn't *my* favorite superhero."

"True. You always liked the Hulk, and Jake, I know all about Superman. Clay called and told me everything…I know about him, his daughter, and how pissed off you are at Samantha for not telling you."

"She didn't tell you either."

"No, she didn't, but let's not forget, neither did you."

"Because he would only bring heartache to our family again."

"You don't know that! Are you just going to ignore the fact he has a daughter, our niece? Clay said he's not using. He's clean Jake."

"And let me guess, you believe it too?"

"I believe my husband, and I believe Samantha."

"Of course, you do." Jake snorted, disgusted with Shannon's response.

"Are you drunk?"

"Well on my way." Jake poured himself another drink.

Shannon groaned. "Like alcohol is going to help this situation."

"It has before."

"Did Kyle look like he was using?"

"He may have changed physically with gaining a hundred pounds and wearing his hair in a ponytail, but he would never give up drugs."

"That's not what I asked. Did he look like he was using?"

Jake sighed. "No."

"Then I'm coming out there!"

"Like hell you are! You are staying right where you are until we figure out if we tell Mom or not."

"Of course, we tell her! She and Richard arrived home yesterday."

"Let's discuss this when I get home."

"We'll discuss it when I get there tomorrow. I just booked my flight. I'll text you with the details so you can pick me up at the airport."

Jake threw his phone. *Am I the only one sane enough not to fall for Kyle's bullshit?*

Chapter 17

*S*amantha sat down on the dock on Monday evening, petting Buster, who sat beside her. She had waited in the hotel room yesterday for Jake to return, but he didn't. At the airport, she asked Carver to wait five minutes, then another five minutes, but he told her he had to either fly or cancel the flight. When they landed in New York, Charlie and Edward had met her at the airport. After dropping off Clay and Dana, she told Charlie everything, and that's when the tears had started.

Today, she'd gotten up, gone to work, and tried to act like there was nothing wrong, but everything was wrong. As much as she tried to bury herself in her work, she couldn't focus. She'd been calling and texting Jake since last night, but the lack of response made her tears worse. Ammo told her Jake asked not to be disturbed. As far as he knew, he was still in the hotel suite.

She should have stayed. She never should have walked out. She wiped the tears from her eyes, wondering if he would ever forgive her. She thought she could make a difference and help Jake and his brother reconcile. She didn't learn about what Kyle had done to Shannon until after she met him, but even so, he was under the influence of drugs. He didn't know what he was doing.

Listening to the waves rushing toward the shore and the occasional squawk from the sea ernes, Samantha looked out at the water, thinking back to the first time Jake came out here to Larchmont with her. They barely knew each other, but even then, there was something about him...the way he looked at her, the way he made her feel, that told her they were meant to be together. She had thought he was the most giving person she had ever met, one with a big heart, but hearts forgive...and Jake couldn't forgive Kyle.

"Need some company?" Charlie didn't bother waiting for a response, but sat down next to her, opening a can of beer. He downed it in a few seconds, crushing it with his hand and tossing it on the dock. "Maybe once he digests everything, he'll calm down."

"Maybe."

"At least you aren't still crying over him." Charlie plucked another beer from the six pack he brought with him, opened it, and guzzled it down. "Clay called while you were at work today. He said Shannon flew out to Vegas."

Samantha looked over at Charlie. "She did?"

"Yep," he said, crushing the second can and tossing it next to the first. "You'd think if she can forgive Kyle, Jake could too."

"You'd think," she said.

"Aren't you just a bundle of joy today. The world hasn't ended; it's still spinning as far as I know."

"Maybe you don't know everything."

Charlie chuckled. "Now we're getting warmer. You know, I remember a time when you used to get mad at me and would say you hated me. Damn, you could get pissed. I want you to do that now—yell, scream, anything!"

"I only did that because you were in my business most of the time."

Charlie shrugged, opening another can of beer. "When your favorite brother joined the navy, someone had to watch out for you."

"I appreciate you being here, Charlie, but you know damn well I don't have a favorite." Samantha drew her knees to her chest, wrapping her arms around them. "I just wish I knew why relationships have to be so complicated."

"Yeah, I'm gonna have to defer that question to someone else."

Samantha snorted. "You mean to tell me in all these years, you never had more than a couple of dates with someone?"

"A couple might be stretching it."

"You took my friend Patty out more than once."

"Before we go down that road, we should define what that means, because I may not have taken them out on an actual date, but I may have been with them more than once," Charlie said, winking at her. "Besides, I had to decipher all that girl code shit so I knew who was going to be where."

Samantha gasped. "What? How did you know about that?"

"Brothers are supposed to know these things, but it's not like you hid it very well."

"Did you snoop through my room?" Samantha narrowed her eyes at him.

"Aah, there she is." Charlie playfully punched her in the shoulder. "The snarky little sister is back."

Samantha tried to smile. If nothing else, Charlie was taking her mind off Jake. "So, did you snoop through my room?"

"Nope, never had to."

"Patty gave up our code to you?"

"Patty gave up more than your code," Charlie said, puffing out his chest, rubbing it proudly.

"Oh God! Like I needed to hear that! What did she tell you?"

Charlie laughed. "Not much, but it didn't matter. I always knew what you were up to."

"How many times were you with Patty?"

"A few. But of all your friends, I liked Stacy the best."

"Stacy?" Samantha gaped at him. "My best friend, Stacy? How did I miss that?"

"Jesus, that girl could shimmy out of a pair of jeans faster than I could say please."

"You are pathetic."

"Probably, but back then I was just a hormonal teenager."

"You are lucky you don't have twenty kids running around the state of California right now."

"I always used protection."

"You know that's not a hundred percent effective, right?"

"Oh, I think I would know by now if there were any juniors running around," he said with a smug laugh.

Samantha shook her head, looking back out to the water. "Do you ever think about going back to San Diego?"

"Not really. The only thing there is that ugly brother of ours. You?"

"I used to, but now with you and Chase in my life again, I don't think about it anymore. My life is here."

"With Jake?"

"I hope so, but I don't know if he will forgive me."

"Has he called or responded to your text messages?"

"Yep, he called, but he was drunk. I could barely understand his slurred speech, especially when he was yelling at me."

"He yelled at you?"

"He said I betrayed him." Samantha bit her bottom lip, fighting back the stinging tears, remembering the sheer power of his voice and his harsh words.

"Are you going to answer that?" Charlie asked, nodding to her phone vibrating on the dock.

Samantha looked at her phone, seeing Jake's image appear on the screen. "No. Maybe once he's had a chance to sober up."

"Do you want me to fly out there and talk to him?"

Samantha shook her head. "No."

"Kick his ass?"

Samantha shook her head. "As much as I appreciate the offer, I don't think it will do any good. He thinks I betrayed him, and he's right." She sighed, dropping her head to her knees. "What the hell am I supposed to do now?"

Charlie put his arm around her. "You could always go out and have fun with your friends. A little fun might take your mind off things."

"And what am I supposed to tell them? Jake isn't even talking to me, and I don't feel like answering twenty questions."

"I'm sure Dana has filled them in, and so what if they know?"

"I'll just be a downer."

"You're a downer now."

"Gee, thanks." Samantha lifted her head, knowing she had to get out of the funk she was in. She believed in her heart Jake would forgive her, she just needed to give him some time to sober up and remember everything they had together. "I just don't feel like going out."

"I guess I can endure your pleasantry for a while longer then," Charlie said. Samantha stuck her tongue out at him, making him laugh. "I'm kidding, but you should know Richard called just before I came out here. He and Monica are staying at her place, but he wanted me to tell you they know about Kyle, so I don't think you have to worry about little Sofia."

Samantha breathed a sigh of relief, but it was short lived. Now that Jake's mother and Shannon both knew about Kyle, Jake would be furious.

"Do you still love him?"

Samantha nodded. "I do. When I first came here with Richard, I was miserable. I was in a strange house in a strange city with a man I was supposed to trust, but had never met until he showed up at the hospital. I didn't know what you or Chase were doing, where you were, or what you were thinking. A year passed, and then another. With every year that went by, I felt like I was forgetting both of you. I lived my life the best I could. I tried to be happy with my career and my friends, and God, I prayed all the time, hoping all of it would be over and I could be with you and Chase again.

"Then I met Jake, and everything changed. For the first time in ten years, my heart was beating again. I tried so hard to hide my past from him. We were so happy and had so much fun together. I was so afraid when he found out the truth he was going to leave me, but he didn't. He still loved me, despite my physical and emotional scars. There aren't many people in this world that would do what he did for me. He put his life, and that of his friends, on the line to save me."

"Do you love him because he saved you?"

"I love him for who he is, Charlie. He's kind and generous, playful, yet serious. He's passionate about his family and his friends, and doing right by his grandfather. He's the first person I think about when I wake up in the morning, or if I wake during the night. And when he looks at me, I still get this little flutter in my heart."

"His anger doesn't bother you?"

"It hurts me to see him like this. When he's hurting, I'm hurting," she said. "He has a lot going on right now with the vandalism and now his brother, and he still has a business to run."

"Sounds like you're making excuses for him. Remember what Dad always said about excuses?"

"It's better to offer no excuse than a bad one," Samantha repeated the words her father had said more times than she could count. "But I'm not making excuses for him, Charlie. He's hurting because of all of this, and I did this to him. I made a promise to Kyle that I wouldn't tell Jake about Sofia or about his illness, but I had no right to do that. I put him before Jake, and that was wrong...I was so wrong, Charlie, and I don't know how to fix it."

Chapter 18

Sensing someone watching him, Jake stirred from his sprawled position on the sofa. Opening one eye, the sun beamed a merciless ray right through him, awakening every aching inch of his body, but somehow the angle of that ray didn't seem right. Squeezing his eyes closed, he wished away the throbbing ache in his head, making him wonder if someone had taken an axe to it, slicing it open, leaving a gaping hole and filling it with pins and needles. He licked his dry lips, swallowing past the cotton in his mouth.

"Glad to see you are conscious," a voice sounded.

Jake recognized the voice, but it couldn't be. He had to be in some sort of dream. With his eyes shut, and using an inordinate amount of effort, he pushed himself to a seated position, unable to remember a time when sitting up had ever zapped so much energy from him. He scrubbed his hands down his face, wishing away the unpleasant feeling in his stomach burning an acidic hole right through his skin. He inhaled, opening one eye, and a blurred image of Chase and someone else came into view. "Shouldn't you be in court or something?"

"We need to talk."

Jake winced, Chase's words piercing his eardrum with yet another needle. Chase and the female next to him both laughed. Jake opened both eyes, recognizing Shannon's laughter. He tried to nod his heavy head toward her, but it was useless. Every movement made the pins and needles rattle around in every direction, poking holes where there shouldn't be any. He inhaled, holding his hands over his ears in preparation for Shannon's voice as she scooted forward.

"Yes, we definitely need to talk," Shannon said.

"About what?" he dared to ask amid the deafening voices.

"Drink this." Chase opened a can of something, but it sounded more like a goddamn weapon being fired.

"What is it?"

"Kombucha, it's a—"

Jake waved him off, unable to take the noise. "I know what it is." He held his nose, worried the smell alone would make him hurl the bottle of whiskey he had polished off. When the cool liquid hit his tongue, he forced himself to swallow, needing the nasty concoction to take away every pain in his body.

"While that works its way through your system, why don't you go shower? You smell like a goddamn bottle of whiskey," Chase said. "But I guess when you drink all the contents of one, or maybe two, that's what happens."

Jake ignored his comment as he struggled to stand, swaying a bit when his feet hit the floor. Shannon started to rise, but Chase held her back, probably figuring he deserved to fall over. His heavy feet lumbered back to the bathroom in the hotel suite. He walked by the bed, unable to look at it. He tried to sleep there, but he couldn't get Samantha out of his head. Her body, her smell, and her taste had haunted him, making him believe he was spooning behind her, nuzzling her neck, his hand caressing her hip. Running a hand through his hair, he entered the bathroom, disgusted with the reflection in the mirror. He was unshaven, with bloodshot eyes and a puffiness around his cheeks. He dug in his overnight kit for aspirin, popping four in his mouth, downing them with a glass of tap water. Taking off his watch, he noted the time: just after five in the evening. He squinted at it, thinking that it couldn't be right. He felt in his pockets, locating his phone. He viewed the screen, throwing it down on the counter. Once he started drinking, he lost all track of time.

After brushing his teeth, he stepped in the shower, holding on to the wall. The water flowed over him, swirling down the drain and disappearing, much like the last two days had disappeared in his drunken stupor. This was precisely the reason he limited himself to one or two drinks. He hated losing his head, blacking out, having no recollection of the past forty-eight hours. He had only been trying to numb the pain of seeing Kyle, cognizant of the fact he had a daughter and he was dying. Yet, he couldn't forgive him.

His presence brought back memories he'd rather forget, and after examining the contents of the file Ammo had given him, the guilt of wanting him dead overwhelmed him. Kyle had been clean for four years, just like he said. Every single test result was accounted for. He read the notes from the doctor about Kyle's illness. Apparently, Kyle had been diagnosed with liver disease over a year ago, but hadn't shown any major signs or symptoms until recently. There were also the pictures of Kyle and Sofia, his residence, and even the old car he drove with balding tires.

Then there was Samantha. He remembered her voice over the phone, but for the life of him, he couldn't remember the conversation. The angry part of him wanted to hurt her the way she hurt him. He felt betrayed by the woman he loved, but he never wanted her to walk away from him. Jake thought back to their heated exchange, knowing she had tried to talk to him. It was his own obstinate behavior that forced her to leave. He wished she were with him now, to take away his misery with her caring words, soothe his anger with her gentle touch, and heal his broken heart with her soft kisses.

After a long, hot shower, Jake sat on the bed in a pair of jeans and a T-shirt. Picking up his phone, he searched for new text messages from Samantha. He had wanted to read the words "I love you" with the cute emoji smiley face and a heart she sent him every day, but there was nothing. His fingers hovered over the keyboard on his phone, but a text message couldn't fix this. He locked his phone and, with a heavy sigh, pushed himself off the bed, feeling better than he had when he first woke. Exiting the bedroom, he felt more prepared to face Samantha's brother and his sister. He looked at both of them, apprehension overwhelming him under their scrutinizing gazes.

"Eat this." Chase slid a plate in front of him.

Unable to remember when he had eaten last, he picked up the fork and dug in. He chewed slowly, eying Chase carefully, trying to read his thoughts, anticipate what he might say, but Chase's stoic stare left Jake clueless. The first time he met Chase, he had worn his navy dress suit, but today, he sat across from Jake in a pair of distressed jeans and a short-sleeved, black T-shirt with the word NAVY on it. He shifted, crossing his ankle over his opposite knee, revealing a pair of loafers sans socks. He studied Chase, noticing the edge of a tattoo peeking out from the sleeve of his shirt, one he didn't remember him having when he was shirtless at the cabin.

Jake took another bite of his food, glancing at his sister. Her pouty lips indicated she was less than pleased with him. Her legs were crossed, the top one bouncing nonstop on the other. She too was in a pair of jeans paired with a blouse and her staple heels. She was to arrive yesterday and he wondered if she had seen Kyle yet.

Neither one of them spoke, but they watched him finish a plate of bacon, eggs, and toast. He had expected the verbal tirade to begin the moment he stepped out of the bedroom, and he started to feel restless and uneasy with the silence. He finished his meal, pushing the plate away and gulping down a bottle of water.

He knew why Shannon flew in from New York, but with Chase here, none of what was about to ensue in this hotel room could be good. "What's this about?"

"Charlie called me," Chase said. "Since I was closer, he said I needed to come here and kick your ass."

Jake nodded. No doubt he deserved it. Chase was smart, fighting court battles with his mind rather than his fists, but judging from the bulging bicep muscles and what he remembered from the cabin, Chase was just as strong, if not stronger, than Charlie.

"Being an attorney, I'm fully aware there are two sides to every story. So, before I kick your ass, I want to hear your side."

"I didn't mean to hurt Samantha. I was angry."

Chase tilted his head, crossing his arms over his chest. "Angry about what?"

"Is this a therapy session?"

Chase ground his jaw in a rhythmic motion as he stared Jake down. The minutes ticked by. He remembered the silence from the first time they met. This was Chase's tactic; he was a man of few words, using the silence to control the conversation.

Jake sighed. "Look, Chase, I'm sorry. I didn't mean to hurt Samantha. I told her about my brother Kyle, and she went to see him behind my back."

"In my line of work, we use the term double standard. Do you know what that means?"

Jake nodded. "Yes."

"While not a legal term, when situations arise, we look at the standards with which the law was applied in a given case." Chase stood, pacing around the room. "If I were arguing this case in court, do you know what standard I might refer to, Morgan?"

Jake shook his head. "I don't know, but this is anything but a court case."

"Bear with me," he said, resting his arms on the side of the sofa, leaning in toward Jake, his face showing no emotion. "I'd look at the standard you set when you came to see me." He pushed off the sofa and started pacing again. "One, you didn't tell her you were coming to meet with me; ergo, you set the standard that it was perfectly all right for her to go meet your brother without telling you. Two, the circumstances surrounding your visit had much higher stakes with lives at risk, but that didn't stop you, thereby creating another standard, so when the risk was lower, it was an easy decision for her."

Jake rolled his eyes. "I get it."

"I'm not done, Morgan. It should be noted for the jury that my sister confided in you. She told you everything about her past, and even after hearing that, you made the decision to come and see me. On the other hand, she had little information to go on because you didn't tell her everything that happened between you and your brother until after she had gone to see him. Is that correct?"

Jake sighed. "Yes, but even after—"

"And finally," Chase said, cutting him off. "Let me remind the members of the jury that my sister forgave you because she somehow is in love with your sorry, drunk ass, but what did you do? You yelled at her, drowned yourself in a bottle of whiskey, and then you drunk dialed her, yelling at her again."

Chase was an attorney, apparently a brilliant one. He'd made his opening arguments, and if they were in court and if the jury Chase was referencing actually existed, Jake would be found guilty because Chase had made his case. Jake was an ass, and he knew it. He had double standards when it came to what he thought was best for Samantha, but Chase didn't know the whole story. "Do you want to know why I was upset she went to see him?"

"You were afraid your brother was using, and you didn't want him in your life or hers. But he isn't using. In fact, the evidence Ammo presented you is crystal clear. Then add in the fact he's just a nice guy, and it occurs to me you are missing out on a hell of a lot by drowning in your own self-pity."

Jake stood, crossing his arms in front of him. "How do you know he's a nice guy?"

"When we couldn't wake your drunk ass, your sister and I went to see him. That little Sofia, she's going to be a heartbreaker one day, but I guess you may never know that if you aren't a part of their lives."

Jake stared at Shannon, his anger beginning to coil in his gut again. "You too?" he asked Shannon. She nodded and smiled without saying a word, seemingly enjoying how Chase was pointing out Jake's shortcomings. "After everything he did?"

"Get over yourself, Morgan. He was on drugs, completely out of it. You should know what that's like!"

"I never used drugs."

"Maybe not, but you sure as hell resemble that bottle of Jack Daniels: all belly and neck and no head."

Jake brought his hands to the back of his neck, staring up at the ceiling. He couldn't argue with Chase. He was here because of his concern for Samantha, and he'd do the same if someone treated Shannon the way he had treated Samantha. "I'm sorry, Chase."

"Seems you should be saying that to someone else."

"Yes, and I will."

"Oh, you will all right, but first, whatever this thing is between you and your brother, it ends today."

Oh hell no! Jake shook his head and started to walk away, his gut tightening. He tried to shove past Chase, but found his groggy reflexes were no match for Chase's precision movements. Grabbing ahold of his arms, Chase shoved him, planting his face against the wall. With a tight grip on Jake's wrists, Chase pulled them behind his back.

"I'm disappointed you made that so easy. Liquor slows your reflexes, relaxes your mind. Maybe next time you'll think twice about downing an entire bottle." He kept ahold of Jake's wrists, but loosened his grip. "Here's how this is going to go down. I'm going to walk out that door and get your brother and bring him in here. Then you two are going to work this out. Understand?"

"Like hell that's going to happen!"

"Hell has arrived, my friend, because it's going to happen."

"You have no fucking idea what I had to deal with because of him!"

Chase tightened his grip, shoving Jake's face into the wall again. "You think you're the only one on this damn planet who has suffered one way or another? How about losing a parent to cancer, then losing the other one and your sister to some madman a year later and for ten years never understanding what the fuck happened to them? How about losing your home and everything in it, coming home to a pile of ashes because someone hated my father that much? How about dealing with insurance agents, cleanup, media inquiries, while barely hanging on to your sanity long enough to get through school and training? How about suffering alone because your parents and sister are buried in a shallow grave and your brother is off on some suicide mission again because he has a fucking death wish and would rather die than face his own goddamn reality. Consider yourself lucky you have a family that loves you and a fiancée that would do absolutely anything for you because we all have our share of shit, Morgan, and most of us get out of bed every day and put one foot in front of the other. Some people can't, but I'm here to tell you I do, every fucking day, and if I can do it, then you can too—and you will!"

Chase's words delivered a powerful punch, leaving Jake speechless.

"He's dying, Jake," Shannon finally spoke. She stood and walked over to him. "I was at his doctor appointment with him today. I know everything, and I know that little girl loves her daddy, and she talks about you and Samantha constantly. Give him ten minutes. We don't know how much time he has, and I don't want you to regret any of it because you didn't listen or find it in your heart to forgive him."

The image of Sofia's face flashed back into Jake's mind. He had watched her closely on the security footage, seeing her smile and laugh, watching her hug Kyle. He remembered when Samantha forced her into his arms and how his gut tightened when he heard Kyle was her daddy. But his anger subsided for a second when her tiny little hands grabbed his cheeks, and he felt a little pitter patter in his heart when she placed a wet kiss on his lips, followed by a heart-melting giggle. Cursing under his breath, Jake opened his eyes and pulled his head from the wall. "Let me go, Chase. I'll listen. He has ten minutes." Chase released him, and Jake's body tensed, his palms fisting by his side as Chase walked out the door.

"Damn," Shannon said, fanning her face with her hand. "I must have a thing for attorneys, or handsome, sexy ones anyway."

Jake ignored her comment. He was fuming at being told what he had to do. "Dammit, Shannon, how could you let this happen?"

"*Let* this happen? Do I need to remind you that you were supposed to pick me up at the airport, but you didn't show? Ammo picked me up, and imagine my surprise when Chase was with him, looking all hot and sexy in a pair of jeans that should be outlawed."

They both turned toward the door when Chase entered, followed by Kyle. Jake glared at Kyle, who took two steps inside the room and stopped.

"When we were kids, you looked up to me," Kyle said, holding up his hand when Jake wanted to speak. "Just hear me out. There are things I need to say." He took a deep breath and blew it out. "I let you down, and for that I'm sorry, but there are some things I need to tell you." Kyle propped himself against the wall.

"After Dad was gone, I had difficulty adjusting. I went to a party one night and smoked my first joint. I was only ten. I tried it again, off and on for those first couple of years, and then I couldn't get enough of it. I could never seem to reach the high I had that first time. I wanted something stronger to take away all the pain of having to look at myself in the mirror every day. I hated myself, Jake, not only for what I did, but because of how I let you down. You tried to help me, more than you should have, but I couldn't look at you, and I didn't want you looking at me to see the awful person there."

Jake wanted to respond, to lash out at him, agree with everything he was saying, but Chase gave him a stern look, and he backed down.

"When I left New York, I headed west, to Utah. That's where I met Ronnie, Sofia's mother. At the time, we had one thing in common—we both wanted to get high on crack. She was abused by her father and I...well, I just wanted to forget," Kyle said with a shrug. "When we realized she was pregnant, she was four months along, and she'd been using during that time." Kyle took a deep breath. "I wasn't sure what to do. The only thing I knew for certain was I didn't want my child to pay for my sins. My child deserved a chance to live and thrive and not make the same mistakes I made. She's the reason I wanted to change.

"I called Grandfather, and he was here the next day. He helped us get the treatment we needed, but the withdrawals were hard on Ronnie and Sofia. Ronnie went into labor during her seventh month, and Sofia was born six weeks early, but she pulled through. Ronnie didn't. Her heart gave out two minutes after Sofia was born."

Jake's resolve slipped for a second as he listened to Kyle's story. If it were any other man, Jake would be offering his condolences, but this was Kyle, the man who held a gun to their sister's head, a man who put drugs before his family. His story wasn't enough for him to forgive the past.

"I didn't realize how much I loved Ronnie until after she was gone. I figured I deserved it after what I did, but that was all in the past. The only thing I cared about was Sofia. Grandfather paid for the medical bills and Ronnie's funeral. He helped us find a place I could afford by working at the hotel. He promised to come back, and even though his health was failing, I never imagined that would be the last time I would see him."

Jake snorted. "So, Grandfather does all of that for you, and you don't have the decency to show up at his funeral?"

"Morgan," Chase warned. "Let him finish."

"It's fine, Chase. He's right; I should have been there. Sofia was too small to travel and on medication, and I couldn't put that burden on someone else. Putting that aside, I wasn't ready to face all of you. My support system was here with Mike and Vanessa, my social worker, and the hospital."

"Grandfather understood," Shannon said.

Jake had heard enough. This is how it always goes: Kyle gets off, everyone forgets, then he goes back to his old ways again. He was done with it. He started to walk away, toward the bedroom, but Chase stepped into his path. "Don't you have anything to say?"

Jake pursed his lips together and shook his head. "Nope. I'm good. I listened, and now I'm done."

"Jake," Kyle said.

The tight coil in Jake's gut twisted. Every memory of Kyle from his childhood up until the day Cuddy died filtered through his mind. He turned to Kyle, pointing at him. "Don't, Kyle! I'm tired of this bullshit. Every time you waltz back into our lives, you have some kind of sob story. You manage to get everyone to believe your little charade until you disappear off the face of the earth again! I'm done!" Jake turned back toward the bedroom, shoving Chase with his shoulder. Then he stopped and turned back to Chase. "He tried to kill Shannon. I guess maybe you didn't have all the facts, did you?"

"I did," Kyle said, not giving Chase a chance to respond to Jake. "I was strung out, under the influence of drugs. I loved you both, and I never meant to hurt either one of you."

"And he apologized to me," Shannon said. "I forgave him, so the question is, can you?"

"Why the hell couldn't you have fucking stayed in rehab?" Jake spit out.

Kyle wiped the tears from his eyes. "I couldn't face you."

"Why didn't you step up and be the big brother I needed back then? Why did you have to start using? Our father walked out on us and then you did!" Jake stared at Kyle, watching his face grimace. Jake crossed his arms, shaking his head in disgust.

"He didn't walk out. I killed him." Kyle's voice cracked.

Jake froze, unsure he heard Kyle correctly.

"I killed him, Jake. That's why I couldn't face you!"

Jake saw Chase walk toward him. He felt his hand on his shoulder, but it was like he was in another place, transported back in time to when he was a child and none of this was real.

"After he left that night, I followed him down to the pier and found him getting ready to take Grandpa's boat out. He was stumbling and I knew he was drunk. All I could see was you, how he'd hurled your little body across the room, and I couldn't let him do that again. I had it all planned in my head how I was going to do it, but he saw me before I could, and the last thing I remember is him running after me. When I woke, my head was throbbing. I could taste the blood in my mouth and my vision was blurred from my swollen eye, but I could see the lights of the city in the distance and I could feel the boat bobbing up and down. He must have hit me so hard I passed out, and then he dragged me into the boat. I was so scared." Kyle pressed his thumb and forefinger to the bridge of his nose, squeezing his eyes closed. His bottom lip quivered, and he took another deep breath.

"Dad was leaning against the side of the boat. I called out his name, and he didn't respond. When I got closer to him, he had his fishing rod in his hand, and he was passed out. I remember thinking what a loser he was, not caring about his child and getting so drunk he couldn't drive me back to shore. Grandfather had only let me drive the boat once, so I didn't know what I was doing. I started the engine, and it must have woken Dad. He yelled at me and started coming toward me. I pulled down the throttle and the boat lurched upward. God, I thought it was going to flip over backward. By the time I backed off and she settled back in the water, we had moved a few feet. I was shaking and yelling for Dad, but he never came. I turned around to see what he was doing, but he was gone." Kyle began crying. "I killed the engine...but it was so dark...I...I couldn't see him in the water. I have no idea how long I sat there...just staring at the water, hoping he would appear, but I knew if he did and he was alive, I wouldn't live another day." Kyle composed himself, swiping at his eyes. "I stayed there all night, until the sun came up in the morning, and he still wasn't there. The next thing I knew, Grandpa pulled up with another man and got on the boat. I told him everything, but the guilt over taking his life weighed on me. The only way I could forget was to get high. I'm so sorry, Jake, for everything."

For all these years, Jake thought his father had walked out and never looked back. Though he had only been four, he remembered how mean the man was, how he'd hurt his mother, Shannon, Kyle, and Jake. All this time, Kyle had never said a word about it. And his grandfather...Jake now understood how his grandfather had always stood up for Kyle. He held his hand to his eyes, squeezing them shut. Something inside him snapped and broke free, maybe his guilty conscience for believing he drove his father away, or maybe it was the fact that

Kyle had tried to protect his family, and by doing so, he'd suffered more than any of them had.

The silence in the room was deafening. For the first time in his life, Jake had no idea what to say or do. He didn't have any words, he didn't have a plan, and he didn't dare move, afraid his legs would give out. His chest began to pound, every beat pulsating through his entire body, causing the room to begin to spin. The walls were closing in on him. He needed to get out of there.

Chapter 19

Jake was thankful for Cal's call Wednesday morning, offering him an excuse to leave Las Vegas and not have to face Kyle or Shannon. Cal pulled along the curb outside of a single-family home on the north side of Kansas City. Though dusk was settling in, it was clear the blue siding wrapping around the front of the home was the only element different from the rest of the cookie-cutter houses on the small lots. Even the lawns looked the same, with only a few patches of green blades—evidence of the summer heat taking its toll.

"It doesn't look like anyone is home. Are you sure this is where the package was delivered?"

"This is the address Max gave me," Cal said. "The house hasn't exchanged hands for over ten years. We'll wait it out a few minutes."

Jake nodded. "Can I ask you something?"

"You want me to be your best man?"

Jake tried to smile, knowing he had many apologies to make, starting with Samantha. "Yes, if she'll still marry me."

"She will."

"I was going to ask you why didn't you tell me about Kyle."

Cal held the steering wheel, drumming his thumb, deep in thought. "He asked all of us not to, including Samantha. He didn't want your forgiveness if it was misguided sympathy. He wanted to tell you about his illness, and about Sofia. He thought maybe you would forgive him since he'd been clean for so long, but since you wouldn't listen, he gave up and decided it was maybe better you didn't know."

"Do you believe him?"

"It doesn't matter what I believe; it matters what you believe." Cal continued drumming his thumb, then sighed. "JT, we've known each other since we were teenagers. I followed you into the army, and now I'm working for you. I've seen your anger, and honestly, I thought you had it under control, but when Samantha disappeared last month, you lost it. Yeah, I know you've been going to counseling, but now with Kyle...man, I haven't seen you this riled up since the day you got out of the hospital after Cuddy died."

Jake remembered the day well. "I guess I don't have it under control."

"I suspected something may have triggered it, and I think I know what it is."

"Do tell," Jake said, resisting the urge to roll his eyes when he looked at Cal.

"Cuddy. Everything about that situation with Samantha brought back memories of the day Cuddy died. You thought you were going to lose her."

Jake dropped his head on the seat behind him. The emptiness in the pit of his stomach wasn't from hunger, but from the conversation he had avoided for too long. In less than a week, this was the second time he was faced with that day, and he was emotionally drained, unprepared to deal with the past. But, if he wanted any chance of resolving whatever issues he was holding on to, he had to face it, and there wasn't anyone he trusted more than Cal. "Maybe," Jake said. "But let me ask you, Cal, did I make the right call, or should I have ignored the order and pulled us out?"

Cal snapped his head toward Jake. "What?"

"That night...we had our orders, but I was responsible for giving the command to go in. I could have stopped it."

"Jake, what the hell? Ammo said you had a lot to drink, but did you lose a few brain cells?"

Cal never called him Jake, and having him do it now and question him was confusing. He furrowed his brows, waiting for Cal to say something.

"You didn't give the command, nor did you have time to stop it. Cuddy went in before you could. Jesus! Have you been blaming yourself and hanging on to this all these years?"

"No, I gave the order."

Cal chuckled, shaking his head. "No, you didn't. Every day we were given the rules of engagement. We all had our orders. They fired first. Cuddy fired back."

Jake shook his head. None of what Cal said was how he remembered it. "I thought—"

"Whatever you thought was wrong. Yes, we had bad intel, but we had a job to do and we did it. It sucks that Cuddy was killed. Hell, we all loved him, but you can't blame yourself. The only thing to blame is the war."

Jake reached for the memory, the sound of voices, the footsteps, the enemy on the other side of the wall, the gunshots. It was all there, but he couldn't remember Cuddy firing.

"It all happened so fast, JT. I should have let you complete your own after-action report. Maybe then you would have remembered."

"I did complete it."

"No, you signed it. I filled it out for you. You were still in the hospital, maybe a little drugged up, so don't tell anyone about that. I thought I was helping."

"So I didn't give the order?"

"No, you didn't." Cal inhaled deeply, blowing it out. "We had just assumed our positions. We heard footsteps and voices too close to the wall, and before you could give an order one way or another, they fired at us. When Cuddy stuck his head around the corner and fired a shot at them, he was hit."

"But I was responsible to get him out alive."

"You got the rest of us out alive. You led us to higher ground, and how you knew which direction to go to avoid falling into enemy hands, I'll never know. How you carried Cuddy on your shoulders and gave Max the coordinates for our extraction without stopping was nothing less than heroic." Cal took a deep breath. "I'm sorry, JT. I thought you knew."

Jake rubbed both hands down his face, a futile effort to recall the events of that day as Cal had said them, but nothing came to him. "Why can't I remember?"

"Maybe because you're too focused on wanting to blame someone for what happened. Kyle maybe?"

Jake could feel the tight twinge in his stomach. Cal knew him better than he knew himself. "He's always been a pain in the ass. He was a distraction that day, and you know it as well as I do."

"Can you honestly tell me that you didn't think about Kyle the night before? Or the morning before? You think because your mother calls to tell you he walked away from treatment it changed the course of that day? You were a damn good leader, and you led us the same on that mission as you have any other. Your brother didn't have a damn thing to do with it."

Jake turned away. He had thought about Kyle often, almost every day, wondering why the brother he once looked up to had turned to drugs. He didn't have to wonder anymore. Now he understood the depth of Kyle's pain, the guilt he carried, the secret he never shared with anyone except their grandfather—all in an effort to protect those he loved.

"Now let me ask you something," Cal said. "Would Shorty, Ammo, Max, or I be working for you now if we didn't think you were a great leader? Or if we blamed you for Cuddy's death?"

Jake struggled with what Cal was asking, unsure how to answer. Though they were all good friends, he was walking on pins and needles, waiting for the day when one of them would ask him why he gave the order.

Cal's phone rang, lighting up the dashboard with Max's face. "Saved by Max," Cal said, pressing the green phone icon on the screen. "You're on speaker, Max. JT's with me."

"Hey!" Max said. "I'm here with Shorty. I thought you both should know I'm a fricking genius."

Jake and Cal exchanged a glance, both of them smirking. "I always knew that about you Max," Jake said. "What makes today any different?"

"Before he goes on his little tirade, I have something interesting," Shorty said. "You both remember my sister, right?"

Jake didn't realize his groan was audible until Cal started laughing. Shorty's sister was some sort of wannabe psychic, into all sorts of card and palm reading. Whenever Shorty went home on leave, he would return with some new psychic theory about this or that. "What about her?" Jake finally asked.

"When you told us what Cuddy's brother said about the King of Hearts, I was curious and thought she might have some insight. It turns out, King of Hearts people are kind and friendly and give of themselves effortlessly, responding to anyone needing help. It's in giving that they receive."

Both Jake and Cal perked up, and Jake hoped this had something to do with solving who was behind the vandalism. "King of Hearts people? What does that even mean?"

"Every person is associated with a card based on astrological signs and birthdays," Shorty explained. "A significant birthday for this card is October the twenty-second."

"That date sounds familiar," Jake said.

"It's Cuddy's birthday," Max said. "Weird, huh?"

"Very," Cal said.

"As I was saying before blondie here interrupted me, I'm a genius," Max said. "At every scene we found the clues, the combination of letters and numbers, sometimes written backward to throw us off, but there were other things too, like the various shapes—hearts and diamonds, circles, squares, and then the two rectangles. I have been trying to decode this shit for longer than I care to think about. I tried cryptograms, Morse code, binary code, dice, ciphers, transposition, and even other languages. I can't tell you how many hours I spent staring at a worksheet or drawing out those damn symbols on a piece of paper, or researching shape meanings, and still nothing. I may be smart, but at some point, I realized it was going to take a damn genius to figure this shit out! Ergo, I'm a genius."

"You solved it, Max?" Jake asked.

"There were times when I thought I had it all figured out, and I thought it might have something to do with Cuddy, but I didn't want to get your hopes up because there were too many letters that didn't fit, and those damn crazy-ass shapes were puzzle pieces I couldn't fit together with anything else. Now that I know Cuddy was known as the King of Hearts, it's the missing piece I needed. It all makes sense."

"And?" Jake's patience was wearing thin.

"Look at your new text message."

Jake picked up his phone, tapping on the photo. "A crown? I don't understand."

"That's not just any crown," Max said. "It's one of kind, drawn by yours truly, except I'm sure whoever left those shapes behind has drawn it too, and you know what the scary part is? Every straight edge, circle—whatever shape it was—is symmetrical, every fucking one of them: the same size, width. I mean it's kinda freaky when you think someone is that damn precise when they just vandalized one of our clubs."

"So our fucking suspect is a goddamn artist?"

"Deranged artist," Cal said, mimicking his frustration. "Basically, what you are saying is when you put all the shapes from all the scenes together, you get a crown. Is that correct?"

"You make it sound like it was easy. We are not talking about a simple clip-art or drawing here. This is complex, like the Imperial Crown of England."

"The Imperial Crown of England?" Cal asked, rolling his eyes. "Really?"

"It's just an example," Max said, clearly frustrated. "I wanted you to understand how intricate the details were and the amount of thought and effort that went into putting this puzzle together."

"And what does this have to do with Cuddy?" Jake asked.

"Oh, just everything," Max said. "When I remove all but one of the shapes from the equation to make the crown, then add in the letters for the phrase 'King of Hearts,' the message is clear."

Jake creased his brow, more in agitation and exhaustion with Max. "Jesus, Max! What is it?"

"The last letters in Kansas City filled in the blanks. The only shapes that didn't fit the crown puzzle were the two rectangles—the same shape as dog tags. The message is Cuddy's name, rank, social security number, birthday, religion, and blood type, along with the addition of the phrase—"

"King of Hearts," Cal said, interrupting him.

"Jesus!" Jake said, running a hand through his hair. "This is all about him?"

"It seems that way."

"Who would have his dog tags?" Jake asked.

"It's possible they may not," Shorty said. "But more than likely, it's someone who knows exactly what was on it, but it's not his parents or brother or sister-in-law. We've ruled them out based on descriptions and whereabouts."

"I did get a copy of Cuddy's last will and testament," Max said. "I'll email it over to you. Maybe someone at one of those charities knows something we don't."

"Thanks, Max." Cal ended the call. "Our homeowner has arrived."

"What do you make of this, Cal? Who knows what information is on our dog tags other than the army, someone in it, or someone who is up close and personal?"

"Based on the person we saw on the video, I'm going with the up close and personal and guessing he had a girlfriend, but I'm surprised he never said anything to us."

"After what I learned about him today, I'm not. He wasn't the type to talk about anything too personal. But if he did have a girlfriend, and she's the one responsible, she wants revenge."

"By the way you say that, you mean she wants to make you suffer as much as she has."

"Yes."

"Meaning Samantha."

"I always thought she was more of a secondary target, not the first."

"You don't know for sure that she is. Whatever you do, JT, don't let this woman keep you from living your life. That's not how we roll."

"Those are Cuddy's words. He always used to say that."

"Yep. Let's go see what our homeowner has to say."

The two of them walked up the short driveway and up three stairs to the main entrance. Jake raised his hand to knock on the door, but it opened before he could.

"Who the hell are you?" the man asked. He was about the same age as Jake and Cal, maybe a couple of years younger. He had a stocky build and balding head and was dressed in a pair of khaki shorts and a polo shirt. He held a golf club in his hand. "I saw you parked out front. You selling that religious crap? If you are, get the hell off my property!"

"No, sir," Jake said. "We aren't selling anything. We were hoping you could answer a few questions for us."

"You a cop?"

"No, we just have some questions about a friend of ours, Lance Cudhoff."

"Lance? Why?"

"You know him."

"I *knew* him. If you knew anything about him, then you would know he isn't here."

"Let me start over. My name is Jake Morgan, and this is Cal Mitchell. We served with Lance in the army."

"Yeah? How do I know you are who you say you are, and how do I know you served with Lance? I don't remember you from the funeral."

"We were there," Cal said, removing his wallet from his pocket, showing the man his driver's license. Jake did the same.

"New York. What the hell are you doing here?"

"I own the Bear's Den," Jake said.

"I know it well. It was dedicated to Lance."

"Six years ago, before Lance left for his last tour, he had a box delivered to this address. All we want to know is what your connection is to Lance and anything else you can tell us about how he spent his last days here."

The man stared at the two of them, rubbing his jaw, presumably contemplating whether to tell them anything, call the police, or beat them away with the nine iron. "My name is Trevor." He set down the golf club. "We can talk out here." Trevor sat on the steps, Jake rested against the house, and Cal perched against a steel railing along the steps. "I was just grilling you back there. Lance talked about you two quite a bit."

"What can you tell us about Lance? Why was the package delivered here?" Cal asked.

"It was a gift for his brother, Greg, for his wedding. Greg and his fiancée were living at his parents' house, and he didn't want it delivered there, so we offered to have him deliver it here."

"We?" Cal questioned.

"Me and my brother, Trey. We went to the same high school, and my brother graduated with Lance. Damn shame what happened to him." Trevor folded his hands, resting his elbows on his knees. "The good Lord got a good one there."

"He sure did," Jake said.

"So did you see Lance quite a bit when he was back on leave?" Cal asked.

"Every time he came home, we usually got together. Hell, he's the reason Trey isn't here anymore. He introduced Trey to Angela. They got married about eight years ago, but they moved away from here earlier this year."

"How did Lance know Angela? Did she go to the same high school?" Cal asked.

"No, no. He met her and her crazy sister when he was volunteering at the shelter. Their mother had died, and their father was abusing them. Gheesh, he was a mean motherfucker. Anyway, the girls were too old for foster care, so they took refuge in the shelter. The shelter needed new front steps, so Lance talked me and Trey into helping him, and one look at Angela and Trey was a goner." Trevor chuckled. "The rest is history."

"You mentioned a crazy sister," Cal said. "What can you tell us about her?"

Trevor shook his head, scrubbing a hand down his face. "That's not altogether accurate. It wasn't until after...she changed." Trevor shook his head. "You know, I think maybe I've said enough." He stood, effectively ending the questioning. "If you want more information, you should talk to my brother. It's not my business."

"Where can we find your brother?" Jake fisted his palms by his side. He wanted to throw Trevor against the wall and pound information out of him, but that wouldn't get them anywhere.

"Trey Baxter. He lives in Atlanta."

Back inside the vehicle, Cal pulled out his phone, typing a text message. "He knows more than what he's saying," Cal said.

"I know."

"It's interesting his brother lives in Atlanta, but I can't connect the dots. If Angela is married, why would she risk traveling to Boston and New York and back here to Kansas? We're missing something."

"Maybe it's not Angela. Maybe it's the crazy sister."

"Let's go see what information we can get from the shelter," Cal said.

"If Samantha is the target, you don't think Kansas was a distraction, do you?"

"No, I don't. But I'm a little concerned. These incidents have been escalating each time and if Max has solved the puzzle, what else is there? What comes next? A fire? Another part of a message?"

"I can't let anything happen to Samantha, Cal."

"I know, man. We've got this. I'll get everyone on it."

Chapter 20

*S*amantha couldn't stop her hands from trembling. Once she received the phone call from Dr. Carlisle just before lunch asking her to come back to the clinic, everything was a blur. She was nervous and scared, and she needed Jake. When Dr. Carlisle removed her stitches, she had ordered lab tests, hoping to find the cause of Samantha's headaches. She said she would only call if it was serious—and she called.

Samantha watched Charlie pace in the waiting area. He was on his phone, his face contorting in strange ways. After a few minutes, he ended the call, parking himself in the chair next to her, taking her hand in his. "Do you want me to come back there with you?"

Samantha shook her head, unable to form a coherent sentence. What she honestly wanted was to be holding Jake's hand, but she had been so stubborn, waiting for him to call her when she should have just tried to call him again, but she didn't want to be the groveling fiancée, bowing at his feet and begging for forgiveness. If he couldn't understand why she did what she did, or if he couldn't see how great of a father Kyle was to Sofia or how special that little girl was, then maybe they weren't meant for each other after all. She twirled the ring around on her finger, hating that she was even thinking about it. He was her soul mate, but she couldn't compete with his anger.

She wiped a tear from her cheek, unsure if it was because of Jake or the apprehension of the news about to be delivered. If she had cancer, she was in for a far bigger fight than the one she was having with Jake right now.

"Everything is going to be fine." Charlie tried to reassure her. Charlie came into the city to take her to lunch, waiting outside her door, though she hadn't known he was there listening to her conversation when she was speaking to Dr. Carlisle on the phone.

"Don't overthink it. It might be nothing. But if it is something, Chase and I are here for you. Don't forget that."

"Who were you talking to?"

Charlie scratched the back of his head. "Jake. His flight from Kansas City just landed."

"Kansas City? Why was he in Kansas City?"

"He didn't say, and I didn't ask."

"Why did he call you and not me?"

Charlie shrugged. "I'm not sure."

"He's still mad at me, isn't he? For going to see Kyle and walking out on him?"

"He didn't sound mad, more concerned."

"About?"

"You. Cam and Manny told him we were at the clinic. He was wondering why. He said you told him the doctor would only call you if it was serious."

"Oh God. You didn't tell him, did you?"

"Not exactly."

"Not exactly? What does that—" Samantha's question was interrupted when the nurse called her name. "You better not have told him anything." She took a deep breath, following the nurse back to the small examination room. After finishing a quick assessment of her vitals, the nurse handed her a gown that crunched like Rice Krispies. As she sat on the cold bed, she drifted back to the few months before her mother was diagnosed with cancer. She remembered the bad headaches her mother would get. They debilitated her, rendering her unable to get out of bed for a day, sometimes two. She was sick too, often throwing up whether she ate or not. After she was diagnosed and started the treatment, it was worse, and Samantha had been there, holding her hair back when she hurled in the toilet, rubbing her back when she was in too much agony to sleep, driving her to doctor appointments when her father was in court. She experienced everything with her mother, watching a strong woman go frail in only a few months.

A quick knock on the door, and Dr. Carlisle stepped inside. "Hello again! How are you?"

Samantha cleared her throat, trying to bring herself back to the present. "Fine."

Dr. Carlisle pulled aside the gown, fingering the scar on her leg. "Your scar is healing well. You must be heeding my orders."

"Yes, much to the detriment of my closet, though I did start exercising, so maybe I'll get back in shape soon."

Dr. Carlisle covered her legs with the gown, patting Samantha's legs. "A few weeks off from exercising doesn't make you out of shape. You look great. How are you feeling? Any headaches or nausea lately?"

Here it comes. Be strong. You can do this. "I feel great. I started running the day after you took the stitches out. Only short distances mixed with some walking, but Charlie and I ran a mile this morning. No headaches or nausea. It's been a good day."

Dr. Carlisle smiled. "Is your fiancé here with you?"

"Um…" Samantha gave her a questioning look. Dr. Carlisle had noticed the last time she was here that she was engaged. She must think she needs someone here when she delivers the bad news, but she didn't need anyone. She had been strong and independent for ten years. *I can do this!* "No, my brother came with me today. You said you would only call if it was anything serious. I checked my record online, and my test results weren't posted."

Dr. Carlisle nodded. "I asked them not to post them on line because yes, I wanted to see you in person."

Samantha gasped, holding her breath, her heart beating rapidly as her thoughts transcended to the worst possible scenario. "So, it's bad then?"

"Well, I—" Dr. Carlisle started to say.

"It's cancer, isn't it? The same cancer my mother had? That's the reason for the incessant headaches and nausea. Oh God." Samantha covered her face with her hands. "I should have known. Mom was sick all the time too. She had awful headaches. Shit! This couldn't have come at a worse time."

"Samantha." Dr. Carlisle pulled her hands away from her face and wiped her tears. Samantha couldn't imagine going to any other doctor ever. Ten years ago, Dr. Carlisle had shown up in Larchmont at Richard's house, in the middle of night, seeing to her injuries. After that night, she visited her at least once a week for three months, then once a month for the next year. Dr. Carlisle referred her to specialists, grief counselors, and was there the day she took her first solo steps without the aid of a crutch. She was her trusted confidant, helping her with the female things she couldn't share with Richard. And now she was going to start out on this journey with her too. "Samantha, you don't have cancer."

Samantha stopped blubbering and wiped her eyes. "What? I don't?"

"No, you don't."

"Oh thank God." She made the sign of the cross and folded her hands in her lap. "Well, what is it then? Why am I getting headaches, and why am I nauseated? It must still be serious if you had me come in."

"Everyone is different. Hormones do crazy things to our bodies, but it's common for women to have headaches and feel nauseated from time to time during the first trimester."

"So it will go away?" she asked, her eyes widening. "Wait, what did you say?"

"Samantha, you're pregnant."

Samantha stared at Dr. Carlisle, her mouth dropping to the floor along with her stomach. "There must be a mistake." She shook her head, still not believing it. "I just had cramps last weekend...no, the weekend before."

"Did you have your period then?"

"Well...no, but..."

"There's no mistake, and a little bit of cramping is normal too. I checked the results myself, Samantha. You're going to have a baby!"

"No! No, no, no, no, no, no. It's too soon. I'm not married."

Dr. Carlisle laughed, then patted her hands. "You don't have to be married to have a baby, but you're engaged to a wonderful man."

"You said the pill was effective, that this couldn't happen."

"Ninety-nine percent of the time it is. You're in the one percent."

Samantha gaped at her. "Did my brother put you up to this? Is this some kind of a joke?"

Dr. Carlisle laughed again. "No sweetie, it's not a joke, and I haven't seen or talked to your brother since he was here with you the last time." Dr. Carlisle turned to the screen on her desk, her fingers flying across the keyboard. "If I remember correctly, we put you on birth control five years ago because you stopped having your period. According to my notes, the pill has helped, but they are very light. Do you remember when you had your last one?"

"Three weeks ago?" She was beginning to question herself. "I think."

"How long did it last?"

"Oh God!" Everything was becoming clear. "It didn't."

"It was probably light spotting. That happens sometimes in the first trimester too. It may be nothing, but we should still do a vaginal ultrasound."

With her heart pounding wildly, Samantha blindly followed the arrows on the carpet toward the clinic lobby. *Seven weeks!* It had to be the night of her birthday party at his mother's house. It was the first time she opened up about her father and the first night she told Jake she loved him. Their lovemaking was intense but beautiful, and now she understood why, but she should have known, not only then, but because the signs were there—the nausea, the headaches, sensitive breasts, moodiness, weight gain, and the interminable crying. She reasoned it all away with the flying, the stress, and her injury, trying not to think about what it could be, but she never thought it would be this…

"Well?" Charlie asked, coming up behind her.

"Uh…" Samantha stammered, quickly shoving the ultrasound picture into her purse as she tried to remember everything Dr. Carlisle told her: *There are two of you now, so listen to the little one. Running is fine, walking is better, exercise is good for both of you, eat three square meals a day. Your blood sugar levels may be causing the headaches, so snack often, but call if they get worse.* Dr. Carlisle had calmed her down when she fretted about the injection in her leg and how much she had drunk over the past seven weeks, and the stress she went through when her father's cousin tried to kill her. She was told to come back in two weeks to make sure things are progressing fine.

"You look a little pale. You sure?"

"Nope, not a bit," she said, bolting toward the exit doors.

Charlie caught up to her, heaving her into his chest. "What did she say? Is it cancer?" He rubbed her back. "I'll call Chase."

"No! Don't. I don't have cancer."

Charlie pulled her off his chest, holding her shoulders. "Then why are you crying?"

Samantha shrugged. "I don't know. I think I'm relieved."

Charlie shook his head. "Your doctor has you come all the way back up here to Larchmont to tell you that you don't have cancer?"

"Yep, pretty much. She knew I was worried and wanted to reassure me in person."

He stared at her for far too long. "I don't buy it. You can't look me in the eye. Are you trying to protect me and Chase? Is that what this is about?" Charlie dropped his hands from her.

"No. I swear I would tell you if it was."

"Are you going to tell me what the doctor said, or do I need to march right back in there and find out myself?"

"Don't, Charlie. Please don't. It's nothing. I'm fine. Really, I'm perfectly fine."

"If you are perfectly fine, then why are you pale, and why are you still crying?"

"What did you tell Jake?"

"You should be more worried about your health than what I told him!"

"You were on the phone a long time. What did you talk about?"

"You."

"What about me?"

"Christ!"

"What about me, Charlie? Is he breaking up with me?" She held her hand to her chest, swallowing hard.

"No!" Charlie took a step away, pacing around her. "He wants to see you."

"That's it?"

"That's it."

"Now who's not telling the truth?"

"It's not my place to tell you."

"Then this conversation is over."

Chapter 21

Knowing Samantha was safe at Richard's Larchmont estate with Charlie, Bauer, and his mother, Jake needed to make one more stop before going to see her. He looked up at the building Tobin had parked in front of—a building so foreign to him, yet one he thought may have some answers he needed. After Cal told him the events as he remembered them, Jake called every single one of his team, and he received the same information. Their account of the events at the compound were all the same, and none of them had known he was holding on to a false memory. But he was holding on—too tight—and it had provoked an onslaught of nightmares, causing him to wake in a cold sweat at least three times the night before.

Having just left his session with Dr. Kinzie, which went over his allotted time, he should be mentally exhausted, but he felt renewed, in a strange sort of way. Maybe validated was a better word, at least because of the explanation Dr. Kinzie gave him about suppressed memories. Apparently, he wasn't the only soldier coming home from war who suppressed memories about what they'd seen or been exposed to. It was a symptom of post-traumatic stress disorder, or PTSD, as it's more commonly known. Now that he and his good doctor knew the root of the problem, he could work on getting better, and then he could fix everything else in his life.

His thoughts turned to Samantha. When he called Charlie, he filled him in on what he knew about Kansas City. He trusted Charlie to keep her safe, but he had hoped Charlie would reciprocate and share with him why Samantha was at the clinic. Yet Charlie had skirted the subject, telling him he would let him know if it was anything serious. If he hadn't been such an ass, he would have been at her doctor appointment with her. Whatever the doctor told her, he would be there for her, however she needed him. If it was serious, he would find the best doctors and do anything he could to get her better, even if she didn't want him anymore. The thought of her being in pain and dealing with an illness made him shudder. But he knew he needed to get himself right in the head so he could be strong for her.

With uncertainty, Jake opened the door to Pastor Murphy's church. He was immediately greeted by the scent of incense mixed with other smells he couldn't name. Not seeing Pastor Murphy, he looked down at the two cups of steaming liquid he'd purchased from the coffee shop. He set both cups down in the last pew and checked his watch, counting down the minutes until he could drive out to Larchmont to see Samantha. Putting his hands in his pockets, he walked to the side of the church, staring at the depiction of Christ carrying a cross, wearing a crown of thorns, falling to his knees, blood dripping from his head and his body.

No longer able to look at the image, he walked away, his mind more than chaotic when he thought back to the past two weeks. One minute he was thinking of Samantha, then Kyle, then little Sofia, then the vandalism. He wished he could reset the clock back to the night he proposed to Samantha. Everything had been perfect up until that damn phone call that changed everything, but he couldn't reset the clock, because then he never would have learned the truth about why Kyle turned to drugs, and he never would have had the conversation with his friends about the night Cuddy was killed in action. He couldn't change the past, but he could move forward, and he was desperate to move forward— precisely the reason he was here.

"Jake."

Jake jumped at the sound of Pastor Murphy's voice. He'd been lost in his own thoughts. He could usually sense people nearing him, but Pastor Murphy had walked right up to him. That thought alone made him anxious.

"Pastor Murphy." Jake reached for his outstretched hand.

"You can call me Daniel, or Pastor Dan, if you like."

"I…uh…I brought you coffee." Jake walked over to the last pew, picking up both cups. He had always been nervous around any type of church authority, and today was no different.

"You must not be a fan of church coffee either."

"Not particularly."

"I hear congratulations are in order. Are you here to talk about the ceremony?"

Inching a brow upward, Jake tried to discern whether or not Pastor Murphy was serious. Surely Samantha had told him what happened this week, that the last time they saw each other didn't end well. He handed Pastor Murphy one of the cups. "I wasn't sure how you liked your coffee. It's black, no cream or sugar."

"Sounds perfect." He took a large drink. "Oh wow, that's good coffee. I'm so used to drinking coffee at the church that I forget how good the real stuff is."

Jake stared at his own cup, unsure of what to say. He started to regret his decision to call Pastor Murphy, but he was so far out of his element, he didn't know how to excuse himself.

Pastor Murphy studied him for a few minutes, turning his cup in his hand. "Would you like to sit? As you can see, the church is empty. The choice of seating is yours."

"I'll follow you then."

Pastor Murphy nodded, leading Jake up the center aisle to the front pew. He said he'd follow, but if it were his choice, he would be in the back, or maybe outside where he didn't feel so confined.

"You seem nervous."

"Maybe a little."

"Not much of a churchgoer?"

"Not really." Jake looked around the church, staring up at the cross, the ceiling, the altar—anywhere but at Pastor Murphy, who sat next to him.

"You are still marrying my niece, aren't you?"

Jake flinched at his words. Images of Samantha flashed through his mind. From the first time he met her, there was a spark between them, setting off rampant volts of strange sensations he had never felt before. She made him smile and laugh—two things he rarely did before she was in his life. Whether he was touching her, kissing her, or just looking at her, his heart felt full. They were meant to be melded together as one. He rubbed his chest; the dull ache from knowing she was going through a difficult time with her medical issues made him want to be with her this very instant. He should have gone to see her before he came here, but the emptiness he felt without her made him want to come here. To move forward, he had to let go of the anger so he never hurt her again.

"It's complicated."

"It doesn't have to be. Do you love her?"

"Yes, but——"

Pastor Murphy waved him off. "It's either a yes or a no. If you love her, what's keeping you from picking up your phone and calling her?"

"So you know everything?"

"Yes, I know. Samantha and Charlie were at the youth center two nights this week. Charlie mentioned that you and he had a good talk."

"Yeah. I don't know if it helped or not."

"It did, and he appreciated it," Pastor Murphy said. "Tell me what you are thinking about."

Jake scrubbed a hand down his face. He'd just spent the better part of two hours pouring out his feelings, and he was still subjecting himself to the painful process. "The night I asked Samantha to marry me, we promised no more secrets between us, and the very next day, she's off to see my brother after I explicitly told her not to."

Pastor Murphy took another drink from his coffee and relaxed back in the pew. "You know, I remember when Samantha came to me. You two had only been seeing each other for about a month, but she knew she loved you then. She was upset because you kept something from her."

Jake nodded, remembering the chain of events that led up to her walking out of the bar that night, and what he thought might be out of his life. The same gut-wrenching response he had then returned.

"She kept her past from you too, with good reason. Letting go of things isn't easy for anyone. After what Samantha had been through, she didn't trust easily, much less trust someone who had withheld some serious information from her. But she loves you, so not only did she forgive you for withholding information from her, but she opened up to you by sharing her past. Then you went to see Chase, and she forgave you for that too."

"I know," Jake said. "Chase showed up in Vegas and reminded me."

Pastor Murphy chuckled. "Samantha's father always said her brothers would make it nearly impossible for her to marry anyone. I think surviving the last ten years without her, not knowing where she was, or if she was alive, has made them more protective of her."

Jake took a drink of his coffee, welcoming the strong flavor on his tongue. "Yeah, I got that part."

"Are you here because of the fight you two had?"

"I'm not exactly sure why I'm here."

"From what I hear, it sounds like you haven't forgiven your brother for all the pain he caused you years ago."

"I always hated him for turning to drugs in the first place."

"Do you know what it means to forgive, Jake?"

"Burying the hatchet, I suppose. But I guess I may need some help doing that."

"Burying the hatchet," Pastor Murphy repeated his words softly. "Does that mean you keep a map of where you buried it and go dig it up the next time he wrongs you?"

Jake looked at Pastor Murphy, furrowing his brows. *Is that what I've been doing?*

"Did Samantha tell you about my past?" Pastor Murphy asked.

"Yes."

"Then you know how angry I was at my mother. It's why I acted the way I did, but you see, Jake, forgiving isn't so much about them as it is about you. If you stop resenting someone and put aside your anger because of something they did or something you perceived they did, your mind is free. We can't control what other people do, and we don't always understand the reasons they do it, but we can control our own response, and we can try to be empathetic to their situation. Once I gave myself permission to accept what my mother did, I can't tell you what a difference that made in my life, to put aside all of those negative emotions."

"I tried to help him so many times, and now that I know why he turned to drugs, I feel guilty for all of these thoughts and feelings I had for years."

Pastor Murphy placed his hand on Jake's shoulder. "At some time in our lives, we are all tested by evil. Sometimes it may be our actions, and other times it may be how we think. It doesn't define who we are. God challenges us every day, and sometimes we wrestle with our faith, or think we are losing it, and that's what makes us stronger."

"I'm not sure I ever had any faith."

"Don't be so hard on yourself, Jake. Faith is ingrained in all of us. Sometimes we don't always recognize it, but it's there. Think about you and Samantha and everything you two have been through. You can't tell me you got through that night at the cabin without having a little faith."

"I suppose you're right."

"Sometimes you need to hand things over to God and let go. You will be surprised how much your life can change."

Jake slid into the car just as his phone vibrated in his pocket. "Cal. Did you find them?" He had sent Cal to Atlanta, hoping to find Tyler and Angela. Max may have solved the puzzling message about Cuddy, but it was too sketchy for his liking. They were missing something.

"Yep. Landed in New York about twenty minutes ago. I'm on my way to the office. I tried to call you before I left Atlanta, but it went straight to voicemail. Tobin said you were in some meetings."

"Yeah," Jake said, wiping his brow. "It's been a busy day. So did you talk to them?"

"I spoke to both Tyler and Angela, and you aren't fucking going to believe this. Jesus Christ!"

"Well? What is it?"

"Angela Steinway Baxter is her full name. She and her sister, Aimee, were at the shelter we visited in Kansas City for a couple of years. That's how they met Cuddy and, soon after, Tyler. From what Angela said, Cuddy had proposed to Aimee the last time he was home. They were planning to marry when he returned."

"You're kidding me!"

"Nope. Angela said since Lance's brother was getting married, he didn't want to announce it to his family until he returned home for good."

"And he never returned," Jake said, pinching the bridge of his nose.

"The day before Cuddy was scheduled to ship out again, Angela and Aimee's father showed up at Tyler's house. They were both there, and according to Angela, he threatened both of them, holding a knife to Aimee and taking her out of the house. Angela called Cuddy right away, and he went after her. Neither one of them came home that night. The next morning, Cuddy dropped Aimee off at the house. About an hour before Cuddy's flight, he called Tyler, asking him to meet him at the airport. According to Tyler, Cuddy didn't look like he'd slept. He gave Tyler an envelope filled with cash, asking him to make sure Aimee went to see a counselor. When Tyler asked him why, he wouldn't say. Tyler asked him why he didn't give it to Aimee so he could at least say good-bye to her one more time, and he said he didn't want to make things more difficult for her. Tyler wasn't sure what he meant at the time, but the next day Angela received a call from the Kansas Police Department telling her their father had been murdered."

"Murdered how?"

"He was stabbed once in the lower back and once in the stomach. They found him when they received an anonymous tip that morning."

"Do you think Cuddy killed him?"

"It doesn't fit, and after what Greg told us, I don't see it."

"What does Tyler think?"

"He said Aimee and Angela's father was a drunk and owed a lot of people money, so it wouldn't surprise him if it was someone else, but when he walked me out to my car later, he told me Lance never would have killed Aimee's father. He said he thinks Aimee killed him and Lance found her, which is why he wanted her to get help."

"Jesus! What happened to Aimee? Where is she now?"

"She went off the deep end when she found out Cuddy was killed in action. She was also pregnant."

"Oh Christ! With Cuddy's child?"

"Yep. Angela tried to help her. She tried to make her go to counseling, but she wouldn't. Angela said she did what she could to help by finding her a place to live, going to Lamaze classes with her, helping her find a job, and getting her enrolled in school. Once the baby was born, Aimee became obsessed with the child she named Lance. She never left the house, was living in filth, and the baby was suffering from malnutrition. Angela and Tyler were married, and by this time, they had a child of their own, but she and Tyler took the baby while Aimee tried to get her life together. Angela said she would do fine for a month or so, but then she would disappear for months at a time, then show up again, wanting her baby. When Angela refused to give her the child, Aimee got worse and started terrorizing their family. Tyler and Angela had seen enough and started the process of legally adopting Lance. Since they had basically raised him as their own for five years, the court granted them full custody with no visitation rights for Aimee."

"Jesus, Cal!" Jake ran a hand through his hair. "Do they know for sure if the child is Cuddy's?"

"I don't know; I didn't ask, but I met all of their kids. There's no question in my mind; he looks like Lance."

"But they never told Cuddy's family about the baby?" Jake asked.

"No. Angela started crying at that point. Aimee was paranoid Cuddy's family might try to take him from her, so she listed the father as unknown. Angela knows it was wrong not to tell them when they filed for custody, but she'd been caring for Lance since he was a baby, and he's her child. She was worried about the same thing Aimee was."

"They have a right to know."

"Not our place, JT." Cal released an audible sigh. "Do you remember our first vandalism incident?"

"What about it?"

"It was one week after Tyler and Angela were awarded full custody."

"So it is the crazy sister then?"

"I wanted to be sure, so I asked if Aimee was an artist, and Angela said Cuddy had always encouraged her to go to art school, so during her pregnancy, she attended some classes. Angela showed me one of Aimee's drawings from school. She was saving it for Lance to show him when he's older. I have to be honest, JT: that was the first time in a long time when I almost lost my shit."

"Literally or figuratively?"

"Both. It was drawn in pencil, but imagine a King of Hearts playing card, except in the middle where the image of the king should be, it's a picture of Cuddy wearing a crown. He's sitting in a chair, holding a baby—no shirt, only his dog tags hanging from his neck, with every detail visible."

"Jesus!"

"After seeing that, I told Tyler and Angela about the vandalism. I showed them pictures and also the video. Though our perpetrator was wearing a mask, Angela is ninety-nine percent sure it's Aimee."

"Where do we find her?"

"That's just it. We can't find her. Aimee Steinway appears to have fallen off the face of the earth. She hasn't reported any wages under her social security number for two years. Tyler and Angela cut off all contact with her. Angela hasn't talked to her or seen her since that day in court, but for what it's worth, she apologized for her sister's actions."

"Did she go by any other name? Her middle name? Anything?"

"Max is searching for any information and hopefully a photo from the department of motor vehicles, but there is one more thing."

"I don't like your tone, Cal. What is it?"

"When the club in Kansas City opened, both Angela and Aimee were there. Angela said it was one of Aimee's good days. After you finished dedicating the establishment to Lance, Aimee sort of went into a trance. Angela said it wasn't the first time she was like that, I guess when she talked about Lance, she would often drift off. This time, she was talking to herself, and when Angela tried to get her attention, the only thing she said was a question about whether or not you would know how it feels to lose the love of your life. Angela just thought it was Aimee being Aimee. She would say strange things a lot."

Jake felt a twinge in his heart. He rubbed at his chest, trying to control his sudden rapid breathing. "Samantha."

"If she knows about her—which considering it was in the paper, or if she did any kind of research, she does…"

"How fast can you get all the security personnel to report in? We need to make a plan so someone is always with her."

"Already ahead of you. Every member of our security team will be in the conference room within the next ten minutes. Can you be there?"

"I'll be there."

"Where is Samantha now?"

"With Charlie, Bauer, and my mother," Jake said.

"Nothing to worry about now then," Cal said, chuckling. "But as your best man, I'm going to give you a little advice. You need to tell her. Don't keep this from her."

"I know. I plan to."

Chapter 22

After a long walk on the beach with Buster, Samantha showered and changed, feeling like she was in a much better place to do what she had to do. Though she didn't know where she and Jake stood, at least he was back in New York, so rather than waiting for him to come to her, she put aside her stubbornness. She couldn't deny that being pregnant added a whole new element to her life. Every decision she made from this point forward would be different. She had more than herself to consider now. Her relationship with Jake, if they still had one, would never be the same. She refused to force her pregnancy on him though. She wanted him to want her for her, not because of the baby, and if she sensed any hesitation on his part, she was prepared to walk away once and for all without divulging anything about the baby. She didn't need him to raise a child. She didn't need anyone; she was strong and independent. She could do this on her own.

"Are you still mad at me?" Charlie asked.

Samantha looked over at him as he walked next to her. Though the sun had set, she didn't miss him craning his head from side to side and behind them. "Are you looking for someone?"

"No one in particular. Just being observant, or distracted as you call it."

"You didn't need to come with me. I'm a big girl. I don't need a referee."

"I know. I just wish you would tell me what the doctor said."

"You've asked me that like thirty times. Just drop it."

"Fine. But how do you know Jake's even here?"

"I don't know for sure if he is, but I know Cam and Manny tell him everything, so I'm sure they have told him by now that I'm here, and if he's not...well then I guess I know exactly where we stand."

"He said he wants to see you, so if that's the case, I'm sure he's here. What are you going to say to him?"

"I don't know yet. Maybe I'll invite him to his mother and Richard's party we've been planning."

Charlie laughed. "I'm sure he'd appreciate the invite. It's at the Roosevelt, right?"

"Yep, Anna reserved a room for us. It's not a big party, just family and friends, and probably some of Richard's former coworkers."

"Anna. What was that thing between her and Chase that night at Monica's house? It was like they knew each other."

"Aren't you the one who told me there was lipstick on a glass in the hotel room?"

"Yeah…whoa! You think that was Anna? They didn't even talk to each other the whole night."

"You know, Charlie, this is why I worry about you." She stepped off the elevator, into the lobby of Morgan Industries. The quietness was such a contrast to the normal working hours, when it was abuzz with activity.

"Why do you worry about me?"

"Because for someone who seems to know everything, you know nothing."

"Meaning?"

"When we were in Vegas, you recited to me everything about the people in the pool area, yet you didn't notice that night at Monica's house that Chase and Anna had not only excused themselves within two minutes of each other, but also, when they returned, they totally couldn't take their eyes off each other."

"What? Are you serious? I must have had too much to drink. Did you ask her about it?"

"No, it's not my business," she said.

"But my liking Tess is?"

Samantha looked over at him and smiled. "So, you do like her?"

Charlie stopped, reaching out his hand to stop Samantha. "I hear voices. Is there a light somewhere?"

"I hear them too."

"Jake's office is that way, right?" he asked pointing in the opposite direction of the voices.

"Yeah, and the only thing down that hallway is the conference room."

"Maybe that's where he is."

"He might be in a meeting. I shouldn't interrupt him."

"Oh Christ, we came all this way, and like you said, Cam and Manny probably told him, so it's not like it will be a surprise."

Together, they approached the conference room, stopping outside the door. Samantha listened for only a few seconds before she heard Jake's voice.

"I asked you here because there is a situation. We decoded the messages left at the scenes of the vandalism, and we've been able to identify the person responsible. We know her real name, but we can't locate her. But one thing we do know is that this person is seeking revenge. I am the ultimate target, but she will get her revenge by taking something near and dear to me: Samantha," Jake said.

"Oh God!" Samantha covered her mouth.

"We'll be in teams of two, twelve-hour shifts around the clock. At no time is she to be left unattended. Ten feet, that's the farthest away from her you should be at any given time," Jake said.

Samantha backed away from the door, looking at Charlie, who had a guilty look on his face. She bolted toward the stairs, taking them two at a time, aware Charlie was right on her heels. Racing toward her office, she switched on the light, leaning against the wall and catching her breath. She'd come here to apologize, to let Jake know she was wrong to go see Kyle and let the chips fall where they may. She was prepared for the anger she might witness, the yelling and the screaming, but she was not prepared to learn she was the target of the vandalism. She didn't even know him when it first started.

She loved him. Being separated from him had been difficult, but she thought she was allowing him time to sort things out. She was planning to apologize, to tell him she was wrong and if he forgave her, then she was going to tell him about the baby, and they could live a happy life. But now none of it mattered. She opened her eyes when she heard Charlie sigh louder than he needed to. "You knew."

Charlie nodded. "He told me he suspected you were the target when I spoke to him earlier today. I'm sorry I didn't tell you."

Samantha pushed off the wall and walked over to the window, staring down at the city below. As dusk turned into night, the lights of the city began to come alive, lit up from one end of Manhattan to the other. "Why am I the target?"

Charlie started to walk toward her, but she turned, narrowing her eyes at him. He held his hands up defensively and ambled over to her desk, perching himself on top of it. "Truthfully, I don't know." He picked up the remote control, twirling it in his hands and pointing it toward the two screens, pressing buttons.

"What do you know?"

"That's all. He asked me to stick close to you until he could tell you himself."

"Why didn't he? Why didn't he come straight out to Larchmont to tell me?" She shook her head, upset Jake hadn't told her himself, but more than that, she knew she had an important decision to make. "Don't play with that, Charlie. I don't even know what it does."

Charlie dropped the remote control on her desk. "Why didn't you knock or go in there and find out why yourself?"

Samantha held up her left hand, staring down at the ring on her finger. "It doesn't matter."

"What doesn't matter?"

"I can't do this anymore. I can't be part of this. I can't think about only myself now. I can't lose my family because someone wants revenge against him." She started to slide the ring off.

"Whoa, whoa, whoa!" Charlie jumped off the desk, holding her hands to keep her from sliding the ring off. "Chase and I are not in any danger."

"You don't get it, Charlie."

Charlie studied her, the crease in his forehead deepening, his jaw grinding. She hated the way he was scrutinizing her. She looked away, trying to pry her hands from his, but he wouldn't let her go.

"You should really cut me some slack. Just because I didn't pick up on the Chase and Anna thing doesn't mean I don't know what's going on here."

Samantha looked down at their joined hands. "You have no idea." She tried to pull her hands away again, and this time he let her go. She backed away from him, needing to distance herself, feeling as if he were dissecting her under a microscope.

"I think I do."

Maybe she had underestimated Charlie, but he couldn't possibly know. "I don't even know where Jake and I stand, and I just got you and Chase back in my life, and now I'm a target because of Jake, which means by default so are you. I can't do this."

"This has nothing to do with me and Chase, but everything to do with your doctor appointment today."

"What?"

"Come on, you've been acting all weird since we left the clinic. You're—"

"Don't!" Samantha shouted at him, holding her hand up. "Don't say it!"

"So it's true?"

Samantha wiped the tears that had broken through the strong front she tried to put up. She couldn't say the word, still processing the news herself. She nodded to him, the silent admission making Charlie smile.

"So I'm gonna be an uncle?"

Samantha nodded again.

"Yes!" Charlie pumped his fists, then tried not to smile when he looked at Samantha. "Hey, come on. You always dreamed of getting married and having kids."

"Not like this. Not with Jake and me at odds and me having a target on my head."

"Were you coming here to tell him?"

"I was coming here to see if he still wanted me for me. I didn't want to tell him about it until I knew. The last thing I want is for him to take me back because of...of...this."

"You can say it, you know. You're pregnant."

"I can't. This wasn't supposed to happen, at least not yet."

"What did you tell me the other day?"

"Shut up! I know! Oh God, Charlie, what the hell am I going to do?"

"We'll figure it out, but right now I think you need some time to think about all this before you make any decisions."

"There's nothing to think about. I have to protect the baby."

"Don't you think Jake would want the same thing? He's already making plans to protect you and he doesn't even know about the baby. Don't make any rash decisions about taking that ring off your finger until you hear him out."

Chapter 23

ake raced up the stairs, needing to burn off his excess energy. He was running late due to the evening traffic, but he hoped everyone was still assembled in the conference room. As soon as this meeting was over, he was going to see Samantha, and he was going to tell her everything. He would not keep this from her. Reaching the conference room door, he paused, taking a deep breath before walking in. Cal, Max, and Shorty sat around the table. Jake counted the bodies in the room, twenty-four men and women. After his conversation with Cal, part of him wanted to head straight to Larchmont, but he needed to make sure these individuals were committed to protecting Samantha.

What Cal told him had almost been as big of a bombshell as seeing Kyle. He just couldn't fathom what Cuddy must have been going through when he returned to the unit. He had never said anything about Aimee, her father, or being a father. They had all been oblivious to the fact that he even had a girlfriend at all. Jake thought about the facts surrounding Aimee and Angela's father's death, wondering whether Cuddy could have been involved. But Jake knew Cal was right—it doesn't fit. Not only was it not in Cuddy's character, but Cuddy was trained in special ops tactics and techniques like the rest of them. They all knew how to use a knife to deliver a lethal stab to the enemy. If Cuddy had stabbed him, death would have been instantaneous. The second stab to the body was a clear indicator Cuddy was not responsible.

His thoughts were interrupted when Cal made everyone in the room state his or her name and position, and a brief bio in five sentences or less, probably wanting to assure Jake the team was ready and prepared to deal with Aimee whenever they found her.

"Ammo is on the phone," Cal said.

"Cam and Manny?"

"Since they are point, I called them before I left Atlanta. When we are done here, I'll fill them in on the details of our plan."

"Good. We don't have time to waste. Let's get started. Cal, do you have the teams assembled?"

"Sure do." Cal passed out a single sheet of paper.

"I asked you here because there is a situation. We decoded the messages left at the scenes of the vandalism, and we've been able to identify the person responsible. We know her real name, but we can't locate her. But one thing we do know is that this person is seeking revenge. I am the ultimate target, but she will get her revenge by taking something near and dear to me: Samantha," Jake said, scanning the room, memorizing the faces of every person.

"We'll be in teams of two, twelve-hour shifts around the clock. At no time is she to be left unattended. Ten feet, that's the farthest away from her you should be at any given time."

"All teams and shifts are noted on the sheet I passed out," Cal said. "Backup teams are also noted, so if for any reason you are sick or find that you can't ful-fill this assignment, your first call is to Tony, and a replacement team will be assigned. Does everyone understand?"

Jake focused on every single one of the people in the room, studying their reactions. None of them were shy about looking him in the eye and nodding their head. He didn't know them all that well, but he had to trust the people he put in place to hire them. "Cam and Manny are the point team. They will always be with her, and when they can't be, then either Cal, Shorty, Ammo, or I will be, but that doesn't relieve you of your duty for protection. Watch for any suspicious female matching the photo Max will be sending to your phones. Since Samantha works here, all employee IDs with card access will be automatically terminated, and a guard will sit at the front desk to check employees off the list as they come to work. Shorty will be sending an email notification to all employees, notifying them that the contractor we use for office cleaning is on temporary hold, asking everyone to pitch in and help keep the office clean. Keep your eyes and ears open for anything. We've seen the damage this woman can do to a building, and we can only suspect what she may do to a person."

"Any questions?" Cal asked, both he and Jake scanning the room, searching for any sign or body language that indicated the men and women assembled here weren't committed to protecting Samantha. Seeing the determined faces, Jake nodded his approval to Cal. "Then you're dismissed," Cal announced.

"Get Cam and Manny on the line," Jake said, waiting for the others to leave the room. "Where is Samantha now?" Jake asked them when they chimed in.

"She's at the office, sir. We thought you knew," Manny said.

"Here? As in Morgan Industries?" Jake shoved himself out of his chair.

"She entered the building fifteen minutes ago," Cam said. "But she and Charlie just walked out the front door. They're getting in Edward's vehicle now."

"Stay with them. I told Charlie what's going on. It won't surprise him you are following closely."

"Will do, sir."

"What the hell was she doing here?"

"Maybe she came to see you?" Ammo asked through the phone.

"Let's just hope she didn't come here to leave her resignation," Max said. "That would be bad."

Jake grimaced at the thought, but he would like to think Charlie would have given him a heads up if she planned to resign. Hell, for that matter, he should have given him a heads-up she was coming here. "Why wouldn't Charlie tell me?"

"Maybe he couldn't. If Samantha was with him, that would put him in a bad spot," Cal said.

"I don't like it. Max, back up the security cameras from the time they entered the building."

Max started chuckling. "Way, way, way ahead of you. I knew I went through that demonstration with her too quickly." Max pushed a few buttons, and Samantha and Charlie appeared on the screen.

Jake's pulse rate accelerated at seeing Samantha on the screen, reminding him of how much he missed her, and how much he needed her. She was so beautiful, and like always, she took his breath away. His body temperature rose, his nerve endings tingling as he envisioned the last time he touched her. He could still smell the jasmine and eucalyptus in her hair. His muscles twitched at the thought of her touch. Memories of her crashed into him like a tsunami: her smile, the way she threw her head back in laughter, the way they could banter for hours, their lovemaking, holding her at night, and just having her next to him, whether they were talking or walking or just sitting together. Jake forced her from his mind, acutely aware he had been lost in thoughts of her.

"I'm guessing Charlie accidentally turned on the 'record presentation' mode," Max said when Charlie threw the remote on Samantha's desk.

"How the hell does she know she's the target?" Jake asked.

"If the timing is right and she came to see you, she likely overheard us," Cal said.

"Jesus!" He'd wanted to be the one to tell her. He gasped, nearly choking on his own saliva when she started to take the ring off. His world stilled momentarily, his heart beating with a thunderous roar, echoing in his ears. He couldn't breathe. He couldn't move. He could only watch. The agonizing seconds ticked away, torturing him. He prayed, handing it over to God like Pastor Murphy told him to do.

He sighed with relief when she didn't remove it, struggling to regulate his breathing and settle his pulse to a normal rate. The defining moments that could have shaped the course of his future were a mere blip in time, rendering him helpless as he watched her almost slip away from him. He needed to apologize and get control of his reactions and not let the anger take over, and he needed to do it now before she changed her mind. Jake stood, ready to leave and do just that, but his heart leapt into his throat, constricting his ability to take a simple breath when he heard the next exchange of words. He felt for the wall, needing to support himself, afraid his weak legs would give out. *Samantha is pregnant?* He could feel all the eyes in the room on him, yet he couldn't peel his eyes from Samantha, his heart filling with emotions he couldn't begin to describe.

Samantha had been his dream come true, finding a way to love him despite all of his faults. And now she was carrying his child. A bead of sweat formed on his brow, the mere thought of anyone hurting either one of them nearly asphyxiating him. "I need to get to her. I promised I wouldn't let anything happen to her."

It was past ten by the time Jake reached Richard's estate in Larchmont. The gate opened automatically. They knew he was here, and he was about to find out if that was a good thing or not. He cursed when he saw his mother and Richard come out the front door.

"Welcome home," Jake said as he approached them. "Congratulations." He hugged his mother, and even with the dimly lit porch, he could see her unnerving glare. He shook Bauer's hand. "Where's Buster?"

"Samantha took him for a walk on the beach," Bauer said.

"At this hour? It's dark down there." Jake was about to take off when Bauer placed a hand on his chest.

"Charlie is with her. Your mother and I know everything, about Kyle and the vandalism, and about Samantha being a target. There will be no more secrets in this family. From this point forward, it's all out in the open."

Jake clenched his teeth together. It didn't surprise him that Shannon told them about Kyle, but Bauer had no right to tell his mother about the vandalism. Jake was irritated that Bauer said there would be "no more secrets" when they both knew full well what Bauer was hiding from Samantha and her brothers. But if he called him out now, there would be hell to pay and he didn't come here to battle with Bauer. He took a deep breath, nodding to Bauer.

"I understand you're planning to have increased security for Samantha." Bauer crossed his arms, taking an authoritative stance.

"Yes, sir."

"Jake, why didn't you tell me what was happening?" his mother asked.

Jake sighed, seeing Samantha would have to wait until he could get past his mother and Bauer. He stood there for ten minutes, telling them everything, the entire history about Cuddy, his apparent fiancée, and how she snapped after he was killed. Before his mother could bring it up, he even told her about his meeting with Kyle and his plan to go see him again.

"Chase showed up?" Bauer asked. "Hmm."

"Surprised me too." Jake was restless, his eyes darting toward the beach. "Is that all?"

"Jake Thomas," his mother said, reaching up and holding his face in her hands. "I'm so sorry. I'm your mother. I should have known something happened when you returned from the army. Was anyone else injured?"

Jake removed her hands from his face. "We all were, Mom, but the rest of us made it out of there alive."

"What happened?"

"Can we talk about this later, Mom? I really need to talk to Samantha."

"Yes, of course. Go get that girl."

Jake nodded, looking at Bauer.

Bauer gestured his head toward the beach. "Get your ass down there, but if you hurt her, you answer to me."

Jake took off, sprinting toward the water. A light from the dock and a half moon lit up a portion of the shoreline. Jake hurried his steps. "Samantha!" he called for her.

Buster began to bark and was the first to greet him, wagging his tail and jumping up on him. "Hey, boy." Jake scratched his ears. Buster put his paws down, and Jake saw two figures walking toward him. One stopped, but not the one he wanted to stop.

Charlie approached him. "Morgan, she knows she's a target, but I didn't tell her."

"I know."

"You know?"

"When you were playing with the remote control, you recorded the entire conversation."

Charlie gaped at him. "Fuck! Then you know she's—"

"Yeah. I heard."

Charlie nodded. "Then do the right thing."

"I plan to."

Charlie patted him on the shoulder, whistling for Buster to follow him. Jake walked toward Samantha. "I was afraid if you found out I was coming, you wouldn't be here."

"Your fears are confirmed."

"Can we talk?" She didn't respond, and he could barely see her in the moonlight. "Samantha, baby, I'm so sorry. I was a jerk."

"Pfft. That's putting it mildly."

"OK. I was an ass."

"You're getting warmer."

Jake chuckled. "You aren't going to make this easy, are you?"

"Easy? Why would I do that? Do you think this last week without you was easy? Do you think competing with your anger is easy? Do you think knowing I'm a target because someone wants revenge against you is easy to deal with? It's not!" She turned away, walking in the opposite direction. Jake kicked his loafers off, running after her in his bare feet.

"I wanted to tell you myself." For the second time in less than thirty minutes, he recited everything he learned over the past week, including information he had about Aimee and why she wanted revenge.

She wiped tears from her cheeks. "I'm sorry about Cuddy. So you didn't know he had a girlfriend or was planning to get married?"

"No, we shipped out the same day we all returned from leave. It's usually pretty quiet the first day back, and no one said much."

"And she thinks you're responsible?"

"I thought I was responsible." Jake kicked at the sand. "This past week, I had a lot of time to think. About what happened that night, about Kyle, about us."

"So did you come to any conclusions with all that thinking?"

Jake chuckled. "As a matter of fact, I have." He took her hand, pulling her to a stop. "First, I need you to know you were right, about Kyle. I wanted to blame him for everything, but that wasn't fair. I know he's changed, and I know I need to make things right with him."

"We all have scars in our past, and he's doing his best to raise Sofia."

"I know."

"I was wrong to go see Kyle and not tell you. I'm sorry, but I'm glad you figured it out, and I'm happy for you...for all of you."

"Don't apologize. You made it all possible," he said. "And your brother and your uncle."

"What do you mean?"

"Your brother Chase came to see me in Vegas. He set me straight, I guess you could say." Samantha's giggle was music to his ears. "I also went to see Pastor Murphy."

"You did?"

"Yes, and my counselor. I'm ready to move on from all of it."

"Just like that, huh?"

"Just like that." He closed the distance between the them. "But I can't do it without you." Jake rubbed his thumb over the ring on her hand. "I put this ring on your finger, and I want it to stay there. I love you, Samantha, and I need you in my life, not just today, but forever."

"I waited for you to call, text, anything, Jake. What happens when you get upset the next time? I don't know if I can keep doing this."

"There won't be a next time. My counselor thinks I have signs of PTSD. We're working on it, but I need you, Samantha. I need you now and forever. I love you so damn much...God, I've messed up and I know it...but I can't lose you. You are my life, baby. The reason I live and breathe. Just say you forgive me. Tell me we can be together forever." Jake waited out the silence, but he was growing impatient. "Please say something." He squeezed her hands, willing her to speak.

"I...uh..."

"I want to marry you, Samantha. Today, tomorrow, next month, or next year. It doesn't matter when. I want you to be my wife so we can spend the rest of our lives together. We have a whole future ahead of us. We are a family, you and me, and someday we will make a family of our own. That's what I want, Samantha. I want you and the whole package. All of it."

"Jake...I..."

Releasing her hands, her turned her toward the water, wrapping his arms around her, her body shuddering, snuggling into his embrace. Inhaling, he breathed in the salty tang in the air mixed with the jasmine in her hair. He listened to the sounds of the waves rushing forward, swirling onto the sand. "I'm not perfect. I know I messed things up more than once, but I still want to give you the world if you'll let me."

Extracting herself from his arms, Samantha turned to him. "I need you to promise me something, Jake."

"Anything. Name it, and I'll do it."

"I need you to promise me that regardless of what happens from this day forward, you are going to be there for me and the…for me, and that you won't walk away and go drown yourself in booze or get angry because something doesn't go your way. I don't want you to hide your pain from me; I want you to share it with me because that's what two people in love do. They are there for each other in good times and bad. And during those bad times, they help shoulder the burdens—it's what you did for me when I told you about my past. It's what I want to do you for you, but you have to talk to me and share your life with me. Can you do that?"

The moon reflected in Samantha's eyes, which were full of pained determination. She had opened up to him about her past, but he hadn't been honest with her about his. She had no concept, no frame of reference of what his childhood was like or what he dealt with in the army. He had wanted to shield her from it, but it wasn't fair to her, and he had almost lost her because of it. "All of it. I promise all of it, Samantha."

"How do I know?"

Jake took her hands in his again. "Trust me."

Samantha chewed on her cheek as the seconds passed. Jake waited. He was asking a lot from her considering what had happened this past week. *Trust me, baby. I won't hurt you again.* The seconds turned to minutes as she just stared at him, indecision flashing in her eyes.

"I…" her voice trailed off, and she looked away for a brief moment before facing him again. "I do trust you."

Jake looked up to the heavens, relief washing over him like a waterfall. "I promise you I won't break your trust ever again. I'll never hurt you again. I love you, Samantha." He tried to pull her into his arms, but she resisted.

"Why me?"

"What?"

"Why do you love me?"

Jake smiled. "That's easy, baby. You're smart, you're forgiving, loving, kind, compassionate, and affectionate. You challenge me, support me, and I know you love me." He brushed her bangs from her eyes. "You're one of the most courageous women I know. You can be stubborn, but your determination makes me love you even more." Jake brought his hands to her face, caressing her cheeks with his thumbs. "You are considerate, putting others before yourself. You are generous both with volunteering your time and giving to others." He bent down and kissed her lips, the quick taste only driving his hunger for more. "And you are the most beautiful woman in the entire universe."

"You forgot sexy," she said, biting back a smile.

"How could I forget? Definitely sexy, and in more ways than one. When you throw your head back in laughter, you are the sexiest creature on earth. When you are deep in thought and that little crease forms between your eyes, you are sexy. And when I make love to you, and your eyes are heavy with lust for me, you're sexy..." He kissed her eyelids. "When your body responds to my touch with goose bumps, you're sexy..." He slid his hands to her collar bone and down the front of her T-shirt. "When your nipples perk up with a single gaze from me, I think I died and went to heaven." Moving his hands lower, he grasped her hips, gyrating against her, his hands roaming over her ass. "And I love your sexy ass, your sexy legs. Everything about you is sexy."

"What if I get fat?"

Jake chuckled. He knew what she was referring to, but she had yet to tell him. "You'll still be sexy to me, baby, because it's you, and I love you, inside and out," he said, capturing her lips in his.

Her arms wrapped around him, her short nails digging into his back as she opened to him, their tongues dancing, tasting, reconnecting in a renewed sense of urgency. He swallowed her moan, both of them dropping to their knees in the sand, but she pulled away. "Jake, I have to tell you something."

He kissed her lips again, then her cheeks, her eyes, her forehead. "What?"

She pushed lightly on his chest, forcing him to look at her. "It wasn't sup-posed to happen this way. The timing totally sucks, but you need to know."

"Does it have anything to do with why you were at the clinic?"

She nodded. "I'm pregnant."

Jake smiled. Hearing the words from her mouth sent a thrill of excitement through him. He started to chuckle.

"You think this is funny?"

"No." He tried to compose himself. "No, not at all, but I think you may have just made me the happiest man on earth."

"You're not mad?"

"Mad?" He took her face in his hands. "Not only am I looking at the most beautiful woman in the world, but she told me she's pregnant with my child." He kissed her again. "I didn't think it was possible to love you more than I had before, but I do. I love you, Samantha, with everything I have, everything I am."

"Then show me." She pulled off her T-shirt.

Jake unbuttoned his shirt while she slipped off her bra. Laying his shirt on the sand, he laid her on top of it, sliding off her shorts and panties. Her breasts were plump like strawberries, heavy under his heated gaze, her nipples prickling when a breeze passed by. With his finger, he made small circles around her nipples. She let out a soft moan, and he smiled, watching a slight smile creep across her face. Sliding his hand lower, toward her navel, he made a figure-eight before following his trail back up to her breasts. He wanted to seduce her, tease her, take his time to pleasure her to show her how much he loved her, but she looked so beautiful, and oh so sexy lying in the sand, the moon providing enough light to outline her silhouette. She was complete perfection, a masterpiece.

He kissed every inch of her face, savoring the taste of her skin, how it felt on his lips. Once he reached her lips, he covered them with his, her taste one he could never get enough of. He pulled away, his eyes filled with lust and admi-ration, unsure how he could love someone this much. She licked her lips, her anticipation building as she squirmed beneath him. He lowered his head again, nipping at her chin and her neck and suckling on her collar bone.

"Jake." His name was but a whisper on her lips, her arousal evident in her soft moans.

Reaching her breasts, he pulled them into his mouth, swirling the taut peaks with his tongue. He lowered his head to her torso, where somewhere underneath there was a baby they had created together. He kissed every inch of her stomach, stopping only momentarily to rest his head on it, closing his eyes. Samantha ran her fingers through his hair, and he looked up at her. The young, beautiful girl he met that first night was now his, and with a baby on the way, they were forever connected.

The love he had for her had always been present, but tonight, it felt different: whole, complete, perfect. The thought of making love to her, here on the beach, knowing together they had created a lasting bond made his shaft hard, thick with a craving he needed to satisfy. Sliding his hand lower, he dipped his fingers in her slick heat, making her hips rise. Unable to resist her, he continued his descent past her naval, until he found the sweet spot between her parted legs, swiping his tongue over her saturated core.

A satisfactory hum passed over his lips as he tasted her sweet cream. Pressing his tongue against her hard nub, he bit gently, eliciting a gasp from her. Pushing her legs farther apart, he inserted his tongue, lapping up the juices of her arousal.

Her hands came to his head, her palms fisting his hair as she pushed his face further into her core. He let his tongue linger back to her nub and inserted two fingers inside of her, teasing her with slow rhythmic strokes, coaxing her to the height of an orgasm as her walls began to tighten around his fingers. He was harder than steel, his shaft almost painful, his balls aching.

He pulled away, quickly standing to pull his jeans off before crawling up her body, using every muscle to restrain himself as he teased his shaft against her, wetting it just enough to enter her inch by achingly slow inch. He barely recognized the deep throaty groan as his own when he hit the tip of her cervix. He stilled momentarily, catching his breath before entering her again. He hovered over her, kissing her, sharing the taste of her arousal.

Lifting his hips, he pulled out slowly, allowing her to feel every inch of him. When only the tip of his shaft remained inside, he entered again, penetrating in long languid strokes, driving to the depths of her core. He broke the kiss, pulling back, caging her between his arms. Pushing the bangs off her forehead, he stared into her eyes, the depth of their love reflected in them.

"Jake," Samantha whispered his name, but he was speechless, in a state of awe because of her. She was beautiful in so many ways. Her head arched back, her body tensing, her core pulsating, gripping his shaft with the force of a vise.

Jake couldn't move, wanting the pleasure to last forever, but he couldn't hold back, unloading himself inside of her, his body trembling, a tear streaming down his cheek, matching those in her eyes. He never imagined he could love a woman as much as he loved her.

Chapter 24

$\mathscr{S}$hannon stopped in front of a small boutique along Madison Avenue in Manhattan, effectively bringing the foursome to a complete stop. Samantha looked up at the sign, *Eva's*, all in pink glittering letters. "Have you been here before?" Samantha asked Shannon.

"This is where I bought my wedding dress when Clay and I got married. We don't have an appointment, but we can look around. I'm not sure if Eva is here, but if she is, I'm just warning you, she's a little different."

"Different how?"

"You'll see," Shannon giggled. "You'll either love her or hate her."

Monica rolled her eyes, obviously understanding what Shannon was referring to. Dana and Samantha followed, along with Cam and Manny. Two others she didn't know stood outside the building. She didn't like it, but she understood it was necessary now, and as long as they kept her and the baby safe, she accepted it.

Dana and Samantha followed Shannon and Monica past the white counter and further into the store. White walls, white carpet, and white gowns that seemed to run the length of the entire block catapulted them into a fantasy world. She might have liked the place if not for the noxious perfume odor and the overbearing music blasting from the invisible speakers.

"When did you start chewing your fingernails," Dana asked.

"Today," Samantha said. "Just nervous. We never told his family how soon we are getting married."

"Don't you think that's rather important for them to know?"

"Probably."

"Shannon." An older woman's deep, raspy voice came from somewhere among the white dresses. A slender woman emerged and embraced Shannon. Her hair was black and hung down to her waist, her nose was pointed, and her black eyes were glittered with gold and fake eyelashes that curved upward and touched her brows. Her long fingernails were squared off at the end, colored in a dark pink with black stripes. She wore a pink jumpsuit with a black belt and black-and-pink zebra-striped pumps with at least a five-inch spiked heel.

"I guess this is what Shannon meant by different," Dana whispered, trying not to laugh.

"I guess." Samantha continued to watch the two women in front of her.

"And who do we have here?" the older woman who must be Eva asked, peering over Shannon's shoulder.

"You remember my mother," Shannon said.

"Of course." Eva embraced Monica, kissing each cheek.

"And this is Samantha. She's engaged to my brother, Jake, and that's Dana, our friend."

"Well…" Eva walked over to Samantha and circled her. "I would love to work with her."

"Since this is Samantha's first time shopping for wedding dresses, we thought we would just browse today to give her some ideas."

"Nonsense, we will do it now." Eva was still circling Samantha, a deep crease in her brows. "She has a small waist," Eva said. "And she's short."

And I'm right here! Samantha wanted to say but she held her tongue. Dana covered her mouth, stifling her laughter, and Samantha elbowed her.

"A trumpet or mermaid style would be best for her shape. Come, let Eva work her magic." Eva gestured for the them to follow her.

"I told you she was a little different," Shannon said. "But she's the best."

"Who knows, maybe by the time we leave here, she'll address you in the first person." Dana bumped her shoulder into Samantha's.

"That's Eva," Shannon said. "She does that to everyone."

When they entered the next room, Eva clapped her hands, and both Samantha and Dana stopped giggling and stood up straighter. Another woman appeared, rolling out a rack of dresses, and Eva began shouting orders to her. Samantha felt sorry for the meek girl, who couldn't seem to do anything right for Eva. Though Shannon seemed to love Eva, Samantha was leaning toward the "hate her" category.

"Sit." Eva gestured toward the sofa. "The bride should be the center of attention. Once I decide on the best fit for you, we can take some measurements."

"Once she decides?" Samantha looked at Dana with her brows raised.

Dana took Samantha's elbow and led her to the sofa. "Sit!" she said, mimicking Eva with a giggle. Samantha couldn't hold back her laughter, and Eva shot her a malicious glare. Samantha elbowed Dana but didn't try to hide her laughter.

"Maybe Eva is short for Elphaba. At any moment, her broomstick may appear, and with any luck, she'll fly far, far away," Dana whispered.

Samantha laughed again, only to receive another glare from Eva. Dana and Samantha refused to sit as Eva instructed them. She looked behind her at all the gowns hanging on racks in the store. "Why don't I just browse through the racks of dresses over there?"

"The racks?" Eva sat up in her chair. "I don't sell gowns 'off the rack.'" Eva turned to Shannon. "Did you not tell her this?"

"What are all of those dresses then?" Dana asked.

"Those are for display only. Every gown sold from my store is specially designed for each bride. A seamstress will spend months creating it to your measurements."

"Months?" Samantha asked.

"Yes, months. You can't expect perfection from something off the rack." Eva scolded Samantha with a shake of her head. "You are marrying Jake Morgan, aren't you?"

"What does who I'm marrying have to do with anything?"

"Morgans don't buy off the rack."

"OK." Shannon stood, holding out a hand in each direction, trying to break through the tension. "Maybe we should come back another time."

"I'm booked out for the next two months."

"No problem," Samantha said. "We're getting married in two weeks, so I don't think we will be needing your services."

"Two weeks?" Shannon and Monica both gaped at her.

"You can't possibly plan a wedding in two weeks!" Eva said.

Samantha walked over to Monica and put her arm around her. "Sure, I can. She did it, so I think she is the best person to tell me everything I need to do."

"Why, that's unheard of! You will never get one of these dresses in that amount of time."

"Yeah. I'm sorry I wasted your time." Samantha dropped her arm from Monica. "I'm more of an 'off the rack' kind of girl anyway."

Eva gasped, and Dana burst into another fit of laughter. Samantha nabbed Dana's elbow, leading her out of the store, both of them bending over in laughter. The heat from the afternoon sun were stifling but a welcome relief from the snooty bitch inside.

"Who are you, and what did you do with my friend?" Dana said through her laughter.

Samantha couldn't stop laughing. She wasn't sure what came over her. She was usually not so bold, but that woman was making her crazy.

Shannon and Monica exited a few moments later. "I tried to warn you she was different."

"I'm sorry, Shannon. I know she's a friend of yours."

"I wouldn't say she's a friend, more of an acquaintance."

"Obviously, she was only considering Jake's money and how much she would make off a sale," Monica said. "We didn't even look at the dresses she had rolled out, but I would bet they were the most expensive dresses in her store."

"I'm sorry," Shannon said. "She really is the best, though you about gave me a heart attack when you told her you were getting married in two weeks, until I realized you were joking."

"Oh, I'm not joking, Shannon."

"No!"

"Oh, yes. So let's find that dress because if I go home empty handed, Jake's going to end up picking it out, and that will be a disaster."

Samantha returned to the apartment, carrying a handful of bags matching those that Cam and Manny were carrying. Jake met her when the elevator opened, taking the bags from Cam and Manny. "Is there a wedding dress in one of these?"

"And then some," Samantha said. "Your mom and sister like to shop."

"I know. So is that a yes?"

"It's getting altered, so it's not here, but yes, I found one."

"Can I see it?" Jake asked, taking her bags and setting them in the entry way inside the apartment.

Samantha laughed, shaking her head. She rose to her tiptoes and kissed him. "No, you can't see it."

"Did you tell them?"

"Yes, they know we are getting married in two weeks. I couldn't really gauge your mother's reaction, though. I got the sense she wanted a big wedding, but she couldn't argue with me because of how fast she got married." Samantha plopped down on the sofa, dropping her head back.

"You're probably right, though I think your uncle is good for her. You look tired. Are you hungry? Thirsty? Do you need me to rub your feet?"

Samantha lifted her head, quirking an eyebrow toward him. From the moment he approached her on the beach until today when she went shopping with his mother, sister, and Dana, they had been together, and he had been doting on her every minute. She knew he didn't want her to go shopping, or leave the apartment. She saw the concern etched across his brow; she endured the twenty questions about when and where and with who; and she understood the quick text messages flying across his phone. Through all of that, he never showed any anger, and she embraced the smile and the sweet kisses he gave her on the way out the door.

Jake sat on the coffee table in front of her and lifted her foot, slipping her sandal off. His strong hands dug into her arches and the balls of her feet. "Ooh, that feels really good." She let out another contented sigh. She had been enjoying every minute of him spoiling her with breakfast in bed, foot massages, and back rubs. When he'd taken Friday off from work and spent it with her, they watched a movie, and talked for hours. She quizzed him on everything from past girlfriends to office politics. Even with the mystery woman still lingering over their heads, he managed to find a balance, seeming to relax more, while still keeping a tight rein on her. She accepted it, willing to do anything to keep their baby safe. "When do you plan to talk to Kyle?" she asked.

"I cleared my schedule to fly out early Thursday morning. Did the doctor say anything about flying?"

"She said it was fine for now, but probably not during the last trimester."

"Then I would like you to come with me. We can stay the whole weekend, if you want."

"No. I think I'd like to come back on Saturday. I need a day to recover in case I get sick." Samantha kicked off the sandal on her other foot and lifted it onto his lap.

"Cal called. He asked me to stop by The Hub. Would you like to come with?"

"No, I have things I need to do."

"Oh. Are you planning to leave the apartment?"

"Nope."

"Are you going to tell me what you're doing?"

"Nope."

The creased brow returned, and she smiled at him.

"I'm not going anywhere, I just have things to do here, I promise."

"OK. I won't ask any more questions."

She smiled. She had a surprise for him for his birthday, and with Shannon, Dana, and his mother's help earlier today, she should be able to pull it off if Cal followed through on his end and kept him away long enough.

"Max stopped by today. It appears we hired a rather exceptional new employee to run our marketing and communications department."

"Oh yeah?"

"Yep. She finished redesigning our website, somehow capturing our story in a series of words and pictures."

"She sounds like she's pretty good."

"Better than good. She's the best. But how did you do it?"

Samantha pulled her feet from his lap and sat up. Taking his face in her hands, she kissed him. "You make it easy. You are kind and generous in so many ways, from veterans causes to children in need. You carried on your grandfather's legacy of philanthropy. He has to be smiling down on you right now."

Jake stood up, walking into the kitchen. Samantha followed him.

"Why do you do that?" she asked.

"Do what?"

"Walk away when someone is complimenting you?"

"I don't like to brag about that stuff."

Samantha wrapped her arms around him, dropping her head back to look up at him. "It's not bragging. You should be proud of all you have accomplished."

"I don't like to talk about it, but I'm impressed with how you narrated a story without being boastful."

"I'm glad you liked it."

"I loved it, and I love you." He leaned in, devouring her lips, making her insides tingle.

"You better get going," she said, breaking away from the kiss.

"Are you trying to get rid of me?"

"Not in a million years. I know you have to go, and the sooner you go, the sooner you will be home."

"True, because when I do come home, there will be a repeat of last night."

"I'm counting on it."

Jake gave her a quick kiss. He bent over, kissing her tummy like he had earlier that morning when she left the apartment. "See you later, little man."

"How do you know it's a boy?"

Jake stood up, tapping his temple. "Dads know these things."

Samantha laughed. "What if it's a girl?"

"If she looks anything like her mother, then I suppose I'm going to have to lock her up, home school her, make her attend college classes online, hire her on in the company where I can keep a close eye on her—or better yet, she can work remotely—and maybe when she's thirty, I'll let her live on her own."

"Oh my God!"

"What? I know what boys want with beautiful girls like you."

"And you don't want to give her a chance to find a love like ours?"

Jake placed his hand over her cheek. "You make an excellent point." He kissed her again. "But not before she's thirty."

Chapter 25

*J*ake entered The Hub just before four in the afternoon. A few of the regulars waved at him as he walked past them toward the main bar. He eyed the female bartender, realizing it must be the one Samantha asked him about. "Is Bill around?" Jake asked.

"Not today. Can I help you?"

"I don't think we've met. I'm Jake Morgan."

The woman who Samantha said called herself Rebecca stopped what she was doing. She smiled brightly. "I know who you are, Mr. Morgan." She winked at him. "Can I make you a drink?"

The wink annoyed him. It wasn't acceptable to him to have a female who worked for him, winking at him in such a suggestive manner. Samantha had told him Rebecca acted weird the night she and Jen were out, like a jealous ex-girlfriend. Though there was a sense of familiarity he couldn't remember seeing her before. "No, thanks. I'll only be here a minute."

She propped her arms on the bar, resting her breasts on them, displaying ample cleavage. "I heard you were getting married soon." Jake turned away, not interested in seeing the woman's breasts pouring out of her shirt. Not only was it inappropriate the way she was downright flirting with him, but it was a little creepy. He'd been around enough women to know how shallow she was, and if Cal didn't fire her in the next hour, he would do it himself.

"Excuse me," Jake said, not granting her a second look. He walked past the bar and back into the manager's office, slamming the door.

Cal jumped. "JT, you fucking scared the shit out of me."

"Who the hell is that woman behind the bar?"

Cal shrugged. "Her name is Rebecca. I don't know much about her. The manager says she's not the best, but not the worst either."

"Fire her."

"What? Why?"

"Samantha and Jen were in a little over a week ago, and she was rude to them, and now she just hit on me."

"As if that hasn't happened before?"

"Not that unabashedly and never from an employee. She's fired. You do it or I will!"

"OK." Cal raised his hands. "Settle down. I'll take care of it."

"Where is Bill?"

"I wish I knew. That's what I wanted to talk to you about. He missed his shift last night and he hasn't shown for his shift, which started at two today. He's not answering his cell phone or his door."

"He's one of our best," Jake said. "He's in the leadership development pipeline, isn't he?"

"He was, but a no-call, no-show two days in a row warrants termination," Cal said. "Unless something is wrong."

"Which is why you asked me here."

"Exactly." Cal tossed a file on the desk. "That's his personnel file."

Jake picked it up, paging through the documents. Bill was a six-year employee, starting as a dishwasher at one of the restaurants. His record was clear of any discipline, and he never had any attendance issues.

"His manager says he can only remember one time when Bill asked to switch a shift. His mom and dad decided to drive up from South Carolina at the last minute after the schedule was posted. He's a good kid."

"I know," Jake said. "And I remember Samantha telling me he was her favorite bartender." Jake sighed. "Did you call his parents?"

"I asked Shorty to call them and find out if they know anything. I called the local hospitals, and there's no one by his name registered."

"You said he didn't answer his door. Did you go to his home?"

"I went to his apartment, yes."

"Inside?"

"What do you think?" Cal snickered.

"Anything?"

"He may have had a guest. I found a pair of female panties on the floor and a condom in the garbage can. I think if Shorty doesn't come up with anything, we should ask his parents to file a missing person's report."

"They'll want to come up here, so take care of them: hotel room, money for expenses while they're here—whatever they need."

"I'll pass it on to Shorty."

"Is that all?"

Cal checked his watch. "Yep, that should do it."

"OK. I'll talk to you next week. Don't forget about my mother and Bauer's party Tuesday night."

"Noted. What do I get them?"

"Nothing, just be there."

Jake left a little more than irritated. Cal could have had that conversation over the phone, but he guessed he wanted Jake to see the kid's personnel file. He urged Tobin to drive faster, wanting nothing more than to get back to Samantha, to get home. *Home.* He repeated the word. It was only an apartment, but it was home. He drummed his fingers on his leg, toying with an idea. Deciding it could be done, he plucked his phone from his pocket, calling his old buddy from high school.

"You must have the wrong number," Drew said when he answered the phone. "Because most of my friends call me at least a couple of times a year."

Jake laughed. "I added you to the list of the invitees for the youth center charity dinner, but you never showed."

"Sorry about that. Met a girl, had a thing; you know how it goes."

"I do. I met a girl too. We're getting married."

"No shit? You?"

"Don't sound so surprised, but that's why I'm calling. How many crews do you have now?"

"Four, and we're going balls to the walls right now."

Jake grimaced. "I need a house remodeled in two weeks, along with a pool put in."

Drew howled through the phone. "You are fucking joking, right?"

"No joke. I'll pay double. Hell, I'll pay you triple. I'll hand over all creative authority to do what you want. I had some things in mind and had some plans drawn up a while back. They're old, but I can send them to you tonight when I get home."

"Triple, huh? She must be pretty special."

"She is," Jake said. "Can you do it?"

"Send it over. I'm not committing to a damn thing until I see it."

"You're a pal, Drew."

"I know, Jake. You've always been there for me. I wouldn't be able to do what I'm doing had you not loaned me the money to start my business."

"You paid it back. We're square."

"You didn't charge me interest."

"It's in the past. Right now, I need your help."

Jake ended the call as Tobin pulled up to the new apartment. Jake scooted toward the front seat, handing Tobin a hundred-dollar bill. "I won't need you tonight, buddy. Go take your wife out for dinner."

Jake jumped out of the car, sprinting toward the entrance. This past week had been mentally exhausting but exhilarating as well. Having Samantha back in his life, he was the happiest man in the world. He thought back to earlier that morning, remembering the birthday card she'd given him with the ultrasound photo inside. It was the best damn birthday gift he'd ever had. Knowing that his beautiful bride was carrying his baby, well that was…his mind drifted off, imagining a baby in one arm and Samantha in the other. "Surreal," he said to himself as he stepped off the elevator and walked toward their apartment.

Opening the door, he was greeted with a heavenly Italian aroma. "Samantha?"

"In here."

The blinds were shut, the lights were dim, and melodic music was playing from the speaker. He peeked around the corner, drawing in a breath at the sight in front of him.

Samantha smiled at him, setting a plate on the counter. "Dinner is served."

Jake couldn't look at his plate. All he saw was her, dressed in one of the lace bra and panty sets like she'd worn in Vegas. He told her he wanted one in every color, and this one was black, and damn, he was getting hard just looking at the curvature of her plump breasts, her protruding nipples trying to play peek-a-boo with him, down to her toned tummy where their future child rested. She turned and he groaned, showing him the thong panties, her bare cheeks taunting him.

"Stop staring. Your dinner is going to get cold."

"Samantha…" Jake cleared the frog from his throat. "Damn."

She opened the refrigerator, bending forward and grabbing two bottles of water. Jake adjusted himself, his painful erection ready to burst through his jeans.

She motioned with her eyes to sit when she placed the bottles on the counter.

Jake finally composed himself and sat, but he still hadn't taken his eyes off of her. She walked around him, and he couldn't stop himself from reaching out and grabbing her. He turned his stool, hauling her into his body. "You look amazing."

"What about the pasta?"

"That too."

"Wait until you taste it."

"I'd rather taste you."

"Uh-uh. You need to eat first."

She tried to pull away, but Jake didn't let her go. He kissed her, nipping at her bottom lip. She moaned, dropping her head back. Jake kissed his way up her neck, nibbling on her ear. "I plan to."

Chapter 26

$\mathcal{J}$ ake escorted Samantha into the Roosevelt Hotel Tuesday night, still pinching himself. The last few days they spent together had been some of the best of his life. The meal she made had surprised him. Not only was it good, it was delicious, and the fact she sought help from his sister because she wanted to do something for him made him love her more.

"Jake, stop that," Samantha scolded him, removing his hand from her stomach. "People will start talking if you keep touching me like that."

"I can't help it." He pulled her into a hug inside the elevator. "I find it hard to keep my hands off of you, especially when you wear a dress like this one."

"Try harder because I'm warning you, these hormones are in overdrive right now, and when you touch me, it makes me crazy, and I want to rip your clothes off."

Jake snickered, swallowing the roaring laughter ready to spew forth. She didn't need to warn him a bit. He was ready, willing, and able, any time or any place. He took her hand, leading her into the venue, a smile still on his face. "We're late."

"That's your fault." She swatted him with her clutch.

"My fault? If I remember correctly, I was taking a nice long shower when you joined me."

"I needed to shower, and you were taking too long."

"And what did you think was going to happen when you came up behind me with your naked body?"

"Hey, you two!" Shannon waved, rushing over to them. "Isn't this exciting? Look at all these people that showed up. I don't know half of them."

Jake scanned the room, looking for familiar faces. "Me either."

"You two go on in. I need to find my man," Shannon said with a giggle.

Jake rolled his eyes. Shannon didn't get out much, but when she did, she tended to overindulge in the wine. "Come on, baby, let's go mingle."

"Ooh, I see Charlie." Samantha started to pull him along.

Jake looked behind them, nodding to the two security personnel posing as partygoers, both dressed in suits. "You go. Cal is waving me over." Jake pulled her back to him, giving her a chaste kiss on her lips. "Stay close to Charlie."

"I will. And remember, not a word about the baby."

Jake smiled, nodding his head. They promised each other they wouldn't tell anyone until she reached her twelfth week, but he didn't have the heart to tell her his entire team already knew. He watched her walk away. The short silver dress hugged her gorgeous curves, reminding him of the dress she wore the first night when he realized who she was as she walked toward the podium. When she woke him last night in the middle of his peaceful sleep for another round of sex, he decided they were having at least ten kids because Samantha being pregnant was good for his libido. He only hoped her hormones stayed in overdrive for the next seven months.

"You look good," Cal said, handing him a drink. "Working from home suits you."

"It's who I'm working with at home that suits me."

Cal laughed. "Good for you."

"Any news on Bill?"

"Not yet. I told you his parents filed the missing person's report, didn't I?"

"Yes. Are they still here?"

"Yep. Shorty put them up at the Hilton in Midtown."

"Thanks for doing that." Jake brought his drink to his mouth, halting in midair when he saw Rebecca behind the bar. "What the hell is she doing here?"

Cal eyeballed her. "I was wondering the same thing. I fired her, just like you told me to. It didn't go down very well, and she started knocking over chairs on her way out the door. I didn't dare let her make me a drink though."

"I don't blame you. Where'd you get mine?"

"The other bar." Cal nodded across the room. "The other bartender didn't know anything about her. He said she just started yesterday."

Jake glanced over at her, and she smiled and winked at him. "What reason did you give her?"

"Policy violation."

"And yet she's smiling and winking at me." Jake took another sip from his drink. He couldn't look at Rebecca any longer. There was something that seemed a little off with her. He searched the room for Samantha, finding her in a group circle with Charlie and her friends. "Where are Shorty and Max?"

"They were going to stop by the police station, but it looks like they have arrived," Cal said, gesturing toward the entrance.

Both Max and Shorty approached them, determination on their faces. Sensing a hand on his shoulder, Jake turned around.

"Jake," Bauer said.

"Richard," Jake shook his hand.

"Any news on the vandalism?"

"I have an inkling we are about to find out."

Jake greeted Max and Shorty with a handshake. The somber looks on their faces told him something was wrong. He glanced up to where Samantha had last been, relieved to see she was enjoying herself. Charlie raised a bottle of water toward Jake, silently announcing he was sober. He knew he didn't have to worry about Samantha when she was with Charlie. Both he and Chase were as protective of her as Jake was.

"There's a detective outside in the hall. He wants to speak with you," Shorty said. "Is this a good time?"

"No, but I'll speak with him anyway."

"Mind if I join you?" Bauer asked.

At one time, Jake would have been furious with Bauer nosing in his business, but he wanted to solve this vandalism issue, and he was willing to accept Bauer's help. "Not at all."

Jake, Cal, and Bauer followed Max and Shorty into the hall. A man dressed in a pair of gray slacks, a white shirt, and a scally cap walked over to him. "Mr. Morgan, I'm Detective Cooper. I think we met earlier this summer at Tess's birthday party. I'm a friend of hers."

Jake nodded, thinking he recognized the gentleman from somewhere. "I remember now."

"This is my partner, Detective Lutz."

Jake exchanged pleasantries with the other detective and introduced his team and Bauer.

"You worked with Detective Grady over in Kansas City, I heard," Detective Cooper said.

"You know about that?"

"Once I talked to Cal about your missing bartender and I learned about the vandalism, I gave him a call to see if he had made any headway."

Jake glanced at Cal, raising his brows in question.

"There's an empty conference room down the hall. Let's talk there."

"How much did you tell them?" Jake asked Cal as they followed the detective.

"Everything. After what happened at the cabin last month, I figured maybe this time, we should let the police handle it."

"Good decision." Bauer slapped Cal on the shoulder.

Jake didn't agree at first, but he couldn't change it. It was done, and maybe in the end, it was the best decision. "Any news on Bill?" Jake asked when they all entered the room.

"We found him," Detective Lutz said. "In an alley about four blocks from his apartment. He'd been stabbed twice, once in the lower back and once in his lower torso."

"Jesus," Jake said, exchanging glances with Cal. "Is he going to make it?"

"No," Detective Cooper said, scrutinizing both Jake and Cal. "He's dead. We're waiting on the autopsy report, but based on the timeline, we are estimating it happened sometime late Friday afternoon."

"What timeline have you pieced together?" Bauer asked.

"Number one, he didn't show for his scheduled shift Friday at The Hub. Two, we found a cell phone next to him. He made a couple of calls to some friends and sent a text message earlier in the day. Their alibis check out."

"Was he dating anyone?"

"Based on what we found in his apartment, we believe so. We've bagged the items for evidence, but it will take a while to get any results or a DNA database match."

"I have a room full of men out there that could make your case a priority," Bauer said.

Jake crossed his arms, leaning against the wall. He was still processing what happened to Bill. He had just told Cal on Saturday that he was a good employee, destined for a leadership position. He was also the favorite bartender of Samantha and her friends, and he would need to find a way to tell her.

"I appreciate that, but after talking with Detective Grady, I think we may have caught a break."

Jake felt a surge of energy. They needed a break. All of this needed to end. He pushed off the wall. "What did you find?"

"As I said, Bill had a cell phone next to him, and I think he was trying to warn you, Mr. Morgan."

Jake placed his palms on the table, his apprehension making him ill. "About what?"

"We aren't sure. That's what we were hoping you could help us with. It doesn't look like the message is complete." Detective Cooper handed Jake a piece of paper. "The phone was dead, but when we powered it up, this text message to his boss was the first thing on the screen. I'm guessing he died before he could finish it."

Jake held the paper in front of him. Bauer and Cal peered over his shoulder.

Warn Morgan Aimee is

"Is this the same Aimee you mentioned to me, Jake?" Bauer asked.

"It has to be. But how did Bill know any of this?"

"How does Detective Grady fit in all of this?" Bauer asked.

"We think it might be the woman he was dating. Based on what Mr. Mitchell here told us, we contacted Detective Grady, and he sent us the information on Aimee Steinway. Interesting how her father died the exact same way Bill did," Detective Cooper said, eyeing both Cal and Jake.

Cal scratched the back of his head. "I may have left that part out."

"Because you thought your friend killed him?"

Cal shrugged. "I wasn't sure about anything."

Detective Cooper nodded. "Your friend was a large man, and I'm also assuming he was trained. Mr. Steinway's death and Bill's death are the work of an amateur. Aimee Steinway has some questions to answer. We've been talking to Bill's friends. It sounds like he was spending a lot of time with a coworker. We're reviewing your employee list now."

"We just need to find her," Bauer said. "Do you have a photo?"

"Her last DMV photo shows her to be about five-foot-eight inches, blond hair, and brown eyes." Detective Cooper handed Jake the photo.

"We've seen it," he said, taking the photo from the detective. He had only glanced at it, registering the hair color, height, and eye color in his mind so he knew who to be on the lookout for, but now he studied it a bit closer, creasing his brow. He had a sense of unease, like he should know her. "Cal, would his manager know which coworker he was spending time with?"

"I already sent him a message," Cal said.

Detective Cooper nodded toward the photo Jake was still holding. "That photo is from seven years ago. According to her sister, the last time she saw her, she had cut her hair short and it was brown. We aged the photo and shortened her hair and changed the color to brown. Do you recognize her now?"

Jake took the photo from the detective, the blood in his veins beginning a slow boil. *Samantha. Their child.*

"Jesus," Cal said. "That's Rebecca."

"The one you fired on Saturday?" Shorty asked.

"She's..." Jake started backing up toward the door.

"Fuck!" Cal shouted. "She's fucking here!"

A mass exodus from the conference room ensued with Jake at the lead, sprinting back toward the event room. The only thing on his mind was reaching Samantha and getting her the hell out of there and letting the others handle Rebecca. He rounded the corner, running through the doors, his eyes scanning the crowd, looking for Samantha's silver dress.

"By the bar!" Bauer yelled from behind him.

Jake looked over at the bar where he had last seen Rebecca. She was still there, and so was Samantha. Rebecca handed her a glass. "Samantha!" Jake called out to her, pushing everyone out of his way. His legs felt heavy, like he was moving in slow motion. "Samantha!" She turned, bringing the glass toward her lips. "Don't!" She lifted her eyes, finding his. Scrunching her eyebrows together, still holding the glass close to her mouth. "Put it down!" Jake yelled. The crowd began to part as Jake and everyone else behind him raced toward the bar. He was so close. "Put the drink down!" He scanned the area around the bar, finding members of his security team moving in toward Samantha, concern on their faces, obviously knowing something was wrong. Jake's gut coiled when Rebecca sneered at him, as though she had information he didn't. He knew in that moment if he didn't reach Samantha, his life would be forever changed. Rebecca bent over, reaching under the bar, just as Charlie came into his view.

Jake took two more steps and lunged, knocking the drink out of Samantha's hand and grabbing her. They tumbled toward the floor, and Jake quickly spun himself, taking the brunt of the fall with her landing on top of him. His head jolted back, hitting the hard, carpeted floor underneath him. He scrunched his eyes closed, unable to withstand the throbbing ache or see past the spinning circles of varying colors. He tried to open them, but his vision was blurry and the pain excruciating. He felt Samantha in his arms, quickly rolling her under him as a gun fired, blasting through the air.

"Jake!" Samantha screamed his name. "Jake!"

"Shh, baby," he said. "Stay down."

Jake opened his eyes. The pain was still present, but he had to get Samantha out of danger. Bauer was behind him, holding a gun, the thumbs-up announcing it was over. "Thank you, Jesus!" Jake gazed down at Samantha, pushing her bangs from her face. "You OK?"

She nodded, fighting tears. "Are you?"

"Better than ever." He kissed her soft, quivering lips.

"Ahem." Cal held out his hand.

Cal pulled him to his feet and they both latched on to Samantha, helping her up. "What the hell just happened?" she asked, straightening her dress.

Jake began to shake, the nausea he was experiencing not subsiding. He didn't know if this strange sensation passing through his body was an indication he might pass out or what it was. He pulled Samantha into his arms, burying his face in her hair, relieved she was safe and not hurt. He inhaled, trying to steady himself, but he felt his legs going weak. "You're shaking. Jake, talk to me." She rubbed her arms over his back.

"Let's move him to a chair," Cal said, grabbing him around his shoulder.

"Maybe I do need to sit a minute." Samantha tried to leave his side, but he pulled her back. "Don't go."

He squinted through his blurry vision. Her green eyes were misted with tears, her brow creased with concern. His mother and Shannon were right there too, though their voices were muffled. Jake sat down, bending over, heaving a breath, refusing to let go of Samantha's hand.

"It might just be an adrenaline rush," Bauer said. "He's going to be fine, baby girl."

"Is someone going to tell me what happened here?" she asked.

"Rebecca was really Aimee Steinway..." Jake started to say, then groaned when his head felt like it had might explode. He tried to catch his breath.

Cal placed his hand on Jake's shoulder. "Cuddy's former fiancée," Cal said, finishing for him. "She was working for us under an alias. The background check cleared, so whoever she found to help her did a good job," he said. "Bill, our bartender, must have figured it out, and she killed him."

Jake grimaced, not only from the discomfort in his head, but also from the callous way Cal had just told her about Bill.

"Bill? Bill from The Hub?"

"He tried to warn Jake before he died. It helped us make the connection."

Jake tried to stand, almost falling over when he did. Cal and Bauer caught him. "Hospital," he managed to say through rapid breaths.

"What's wrong?" Samantha asked. "Are you hurt?"

"Not me, you and the baby." Samantha's mouth fell open. Jake recalled his words, realizing his mistake. "Shit, sorry."

"You're pregnant?" Bauer asked, but before she could respond, his mother jumped in front of him, hugging Samantha.

"This is the best news ever." Releasing Samantha, she turned to Jake. "I'm going to be a grandma again."

"No kidding!" Bauer slapped Jake on the shoulder.

"Finally, something I knew before you did," Jake replied.

"I think we need to have that head of yours checked out."

"I'm..." Jake started to say. His eyes rolled to the back of his head, and his world went black.

Chapter 27

Jake took ahold of Samantha's hand, helping her from the vehicle, taking the small bag she handed to him. He peered at the dilapidated building in front of him, recognizing this visit was past due. He had wanted to talk to Kyle two weeks ago, but after the incident at the Roosevelt, he was sidelined with a severe concussion, unable to travel. Samantha entwined her fingers with his. He gazed at her, admiring the woman she was. After he hit his head, he didn't wake for twenty-four hours, and when he did, she was lying next to him, dressed in a pair of scrubs, her mascara smeared, her hair messy, but to him, she was the most beautiful sight he'd ever seen, and from the moment she brought him home from the hospital, she never left him alone. Today would be the first day they would be separated for any period of time.

He wasn't sure what he would have done without her. She didn't let him go to the office, instead hiring a courier to deliver documents back and forth between their apartment and the office. She took his calls, rearranged his schedule, and gave orders to anyone who called. He wasn't sure what decisions she made, but he didn't care. His team would have told him if something was amiss, and so far, no one had. In a matter of days, she'd earned the respect of his vice presidents and directors, taking charge of his weekly meeting. She reviewed the weekly dashboard report, reading it to him so he wouldn't strain his eyes reading it himself.

He gave her control, loving her more when he watched her in action. He even faked not being able to read something a few times, just to get her close to him, and as soon as she would bend over him, he would take advantage of her. She caught on after the first few times, but it didn't stop her from continuing. She cooked for him too, as did Shannon. His mother was a daily visitor until she and Richard left for Las Vegas two days before he and Samantha did.

"Are you ready?"

Jake nodded to her, leading her up the sidewalk. She looked as beautiful as always, and in three days, he was going to pledge his love to her in front of his family and friends. Samantha had asked his mother for help, and along with Shannon and Dana, and all four of them working closely with Kyle and Ammo, and the rest of his friends, the rooftop was ready for the intimate ceremony they had planned.

Samantha pulled him to a stop. "Jake."

"What?"

"Why are Cam and Manny here?"

"Because I asked them to be."

"Why? Rebecca, or Aimee, is dead. There aren't any other threats. Why are you still using them?"

Jake tugged her hand, drawing her closer. He caressed her now-pouty lip with his thumb. He still felt a little angst, his heart pounded, and he wanted to shove his fist through a wall when he thought about what could have happened. Rebecca was found with enough GHB on her to kill his entire family, but Samantha was adamant she'd watched Rebecca fill her glass with Sprite. Though the glass she had in her hand had broken upon impact, Richard's friends had done what they could to salvage the evidence. One of the broken pieces of glass contained trace amounts of GHB, and based on the liquid volume analysis, it was a lethal dose, enough to kill Samantha and their unborn child. Though he'd promised no more secrets, he'd made a calculated decision not to tell her. Withholding the information caused her no harm. It wasn't a secret; it was just better left unsaid.

"Because I decided I'm not taking any more chances with you or the baby, and though I'm cleared by the doctors to travel, I think we both know, as do my doctors, I'm not as quick mentally or physically as I used to be."

"You decided?"

"Yes, I did."

She stared at him with those beautiful green eyes, stern at first but quickly softening. She reached up, gently running her fingers through his hair. "OK. Let's go see your brother."

The conversation was easy: no arguments, no questioning. They had both endured enough agony and suffering to last ten lifetimes, leading to a mutual understanding that their unborn child was at the center of every decision. Of course, for him, Samantha was in that same center. He'd almost lost her to a madman and a crazy lady, and he would never take anything for granted again. She would always be first. "Speaking of brothers, I heard you talking to Charlie earlier. How's he doing?"

"I don't know. He's flying in with Cal. They decided to take the red-eye, so we won't see them until tomorrow. But I think he's still struggling."

Jake had thought Bauer shot Rebecca, but in fact, it was Charlie. He'd seen Jake running toward Samantha. As he approached the bar from the side, Rebecca pulled out a gun. No one knew who she was going to shoot—maybe Samantha, maybe Jake, maybe more of them—but Charlie saved them all from the deranged woman with one shot to her forehead. Samantha had told him about the encounter she and Jen had had with Rebecca and how strange she acted when questioned about the tattoo. When Jake and Cal went to the morgue with her sister, they had seen it for themselves. It was a dog tag—Cuddy's dog tag, to be exact. He hadn't seen it when he was at the bar, but maybe if he had… he couldn't think about what might have happened. He couldn't control it now.

Jake had paid for all of Angela's expenses to take her sister home. Before she left, he gave her an envelope containing information on a trust fund he'd started for Lance's child. Though he no longer blamed himself, it was the least he could do for a fallen comrade and his friend. He encouraged her to tell Cuddy's family, but Cal was right: it wasn't his business. He had no control over the situation; he could only hope she would do the right thing.

"Auntie Sam! Uncle Jake!" Jake smiled upon hearing Sofia's squeals. She and Kyle were bounding down the stairs. Samantha quickly jumped ahead of Jake, scooping Sofia into her arms. Sofia wrapped her tiny arms tightly around Samantha. She squeezed her eyes closed, whispering something in Samantha's ear that made her laugh.

Sofia held her arms out to Jake, and Jake took her from Samantha, enfolding her in his arms. The last time he held her, he didn't know she was Kyle's child. She gave Jake a hug and a kiss. "Are you all better?" Sofia asked.

"I am," he said.

Sofia let her arms fall to her side. "Do you think after I go shopping with Auntie Sam that you could color with me?"

"I would love to color with you. And since your cousins are arriving today, what do you think about you and your dad staying at the hotel so we can all color, and maybe we could swim too."

"Can we, Daddy?"

Jake looked at Kyle. He had a wide grin on his face, the type of grin Jake remembered from their childhood. "You bet."

"Let's go, Sofia. Dana and Ammo are waiting for us in the limo. We need to pick out your dress." Samantha took her tiny hand in hers. Sofia skipped all the way toward the curb where the waiting limo was parked. Samantha turned back to Jake, blowing him a kiss.

Kyle put his hand on Jake's shoulder. "I'm glad you're better. I have some soda and snacks waiting upstairs if you still want to talk."

"Sounds great." Jake followed Kyle inside the apartment, and it was just as Ammo and Samantha had described it to him.

Kyle opened a can of soda, poured it into a glass filled with ice, and handed it to Jake. "I'm glad you came. Can I show you something?" Kyle waved at him to follow.

Jake set the bag he was carrying and his glass on the table. He followed Kyle down the small hallway and into what had to be Sofia's bedroom. Everything was adorned in pink, and now he understood why Samantha had painted her toenails pink. Kyle picked up a frame next to Sofia's bed and handed it to Jake. "This is why I took that picture of you two. When I told Sofia about my illness, she started asking a lot of questions about family. I wanted her to know she had more than me. I never meant to scare Samantha or to give you an impression you were being followed. I only wanted a picture to give to her."

Jake handed it back. "Thanks for telling me. Speaking of pictures, Samantha asked me to give you something." They walked back to the dining room and Jake pulled a gift-wrapped box from the bag.

Kyle took the package, taking his time to examine the wrapping. He ran his finger along the bow before pulling on it. The slow perusal of it made Jake wonder when he'd last received a gift. Kyle carefully peeled away the tape and removed the wrapping without tearing it. He folded it neatly, setting it on the table. Unwrapping the tissue paper, he gasped. "Wow."

"Yeah, she's very talented."

"I asked her to take some pictures of me and Sofia, but I didn't expect anything so nice."

Jake walked around the table, peering over Kyle's shoulder. Samantha had created a collage of photos of the two of them. Sofia and Kyle were smiling in every single one of them, except for the one where she was kissing him. Samantha usually only took landscape photos, but she had someone managed to capture more than the faces of Kyle and Sofia, she had managed to capture the moment, and the first time she showed Jake the photos, he felt like he was in the moment, right there with them, laughing like they were. The love Kyle and Sofia had for each other poured out of their eyes and their smiles. Jake only hoped he would find that same kind of love with his own child. "She didn't know if you would like the color of the frame, so if you don't, she will order a different one."

"It's perfect," Kyle said, running his fingers along the wooden frame, etched with his and Sofia's names and the date the photos were taken. "Much more than I expected. You sure are lucky to have found someone like her."

"I know. I'm more than fortunate."

"So it sounds like most of the family will be here tonight." Kyle walked over to the living room and held up the frame. "How does this look?"

"I think that's a perfect spot."

"Could you grab a hammer and some nails? Right side of the kitchen sink, second drawer down."

Jake did as he was told, noticing how clean everything was. The drawer was organized neatly, though there was only the hammer and a small plastic container with nails and screws. He removed the tools, bringing them over to Kyle. Like they were when they were kids, they seemed to be in sync. Jake pounded the nails in the wall, and Kyle hung the photo, both of them stepping back to admire their work. "That sort of felt like old times," Jake said.

"You mean like when we would weed Mom's flower bed and stand back and look at our work?"

"Or mow the lawn?"

"Or clean our rooms." Kyle laughed.

Jake smiled, the moment so different than what he envisioned when reuniting with Kyle. He walked back to the kitchen and put the hammer and container away.

"All the rooms are ready, and the rooftop looks like a magical place right now," Kyle said when Jake returned.

"Thanks for helping Samantha and Mom with all of the arrangements."

"No problem. It was nice to see Mom. She sure looks happy with Richard. He's Samantha's uncle?"

"Yep. He forced me to invite her out to his place for dinner. End of story."

Kyle laughed. "Well, I'm glad she found someone."

Jake ran a hand through his hair. He had tried to prepare his words before he arrived, but with Kyle staring back at him now, he struggled to get them out. "I...I hated you for a lot of years."

"I hated myself."

"I didn't know." Jake ran a hand through his hair again. "What you did back then...to our father...was exactly what I wanted you to do." He didn't remember crying since he was a teenager, but in the last three weeks, there had been tears, once at the intensity of making love to Samantha, and again when Samantha and their child survived Rebecca's attempt on their lives. Jake blinked fast a few times, hoping the tears would go away, but they remained. "If I had known I might lose my only brother because of it, I never would have wished for it."

Kyle pulled Jake into a hug, patting his back. "You didn't lose me, brother. I'm right here." Kyle sobbed against Jake's shoulder, and Jake hugged him back, squeezing him as tight as he could. The first time Kyle had told him about what he'd done, his sister and Chase had been there, and he remembered something breaking free inside of him. He didn't know what it was—perhaps the chains that had once barricaded his feelings for Kyle had broken. Whatever it was, he felt a sense of peace now.

Kyle stepped back from Jake. "We have some lost time to make up for. How long will you and Samantha be staying in town after the wedding?"

Jake wiped his eyes. "We'll be here through Monday, then head back to New York. We talked about a cross-country road trip to visit all the amusement parks. We considered Hawaii too, but I think we'll stick closer to home," Jake said. "Maybe next year after the baby is born, we can be more adventurous."

Kyle's grin made Jake smile. "She's pregnant?"

"Nine weeks. We had decided not to tell anyone, but apparently I blurted it out after I hit my head." Jake chuckled and walked back over to the table, removing an envelope from the bag. "Before I forget, this belongs to you."

Kyle took the envelope from Jake. "What is it?"

"Your share of Grandfather's inheritance. It's been sitting in a trust since he died." Jake watched Kyle open the envelope, fighting back his own emotions when Kyle read the document. "You can have it transferred to a bank here if you want, but Shannon, Mom, and I all want you to come home, to New York. We can connect you to the best doctors. Mom has a lot of networks with her charity work, and she's consulted attorneys about the insurance company denying your request for a transplant."

"I don't know what to say."

"Say you will. You being back there will give us more time to spend together. I may even let you wash dishes in one of the restaurants," Jake said, trying to lighten the somber mood.

Kyle chuckled. "I would like that, but first, I need to ask something of you and Samantha. I never baptized Sofia or named anyone as her godparents, but if it's not too late, I would like that to be you and Samantha."

Jake smiled. "Samantha is rather independent, and while most of the time she doesn't like me speaking for her, I think this is one time I can be one hundred percent sure she'd say yes. So the answer is yes, we would be honored to."

"Thank you. Being a godparent is different than being a parent. I know I don't have a right to ask you this, and it's not fair considering you are getting married and starting a family of your own, but if the time comes when I'm not here anymore, it would be my hope the two of you would raise her as your own."

Jake blinked away the tears blurring his vision. Samantha would give her heart away if she could. She would never walk away from Sofia. "We can talk about that when Samantha is here, but again, I know my soon-to-be wife, and I know she'd say yes. But before we get to that point, come back to New York. Let's focus on getting you healthy first. Sofia needs you."

Chapter 28

Samantha stared at herself in the mirror. The simple gown she chose was fitted, wrapping around her shoulders, but draping low across her back leaving her neck and upper back exposed. She had dreamed of this day since she was a little girl, with a big gown and flowers and hundreds of guests, but it was insignificant now. She and Jake were already bound together, and the wedding was only making it official in front of their family and friends. She would be Jake's wife. They would make a family and grow old together. When he lay in that hospital bed without so much as twitching a finger, she thought she'd lost him. She cried herself to sleep and prayed like she had never prayed before when the doctors had told her they wouldn't know the extent of his injury until he woke up and they could assess his condition.

"I don't think I've ever seen a more beautiful bride," Dana said, standing next to her.

"I don't think I've ever seen a more beautiful maid of honor." Dana looked gorgeous in her sleeveless navy-blue sweetheart mermaid dress.

"I agree on both," Charlie said.

"Me too," Chase said.

Samantha eyed her brothers in the mirror, both of them looking as handsome as ever. Her day was perfect just knowing she was marrying Jake, but having her brothers both here meant the world to her. Separated for too long, their lives had changed, but nothing could ever break the bond they shared because that bond was sealed in place by their parents, two strong people who put family first.

Chase came to stand in front of her. "We have something for you."

"You didn't have to get me anything. You being here is all I want."

Chase smiled, reaching up to brush a hair from her face. Removing a black box from his pocket, he held it in front of him. "After Dad died, I cleaned out his office. He'd kept Mom's wedding ring in a box in the left-hand drawer. I'm sure he wanted to keep it close to him. Anyway, for once, my little brother had a great idea." Chase opened the box, and Samantha gasped, holding her hand over her mouth. Chase removed the necklace and handed the box to Charlie. "We took it a to a jeweler and had the diamonds removed from the ring, then had them create this necklace for you. Now you have something old and something new," he said.

Chase put the necklace on her, then stood next to her, watching her in the mirror. Samantha rubbed her finger over the circle of diamonds with a larger one in the center.

Charlie appeared on the other side of her, catching her eye in the mirror. "We chose that shape because together our circle of love is complete."

Samantha sniffed, wiping her eyes. "Mom always used to say that. Her family was the circle of love."

"We remember," Chase said.

"Seriously?" Dana gaped at them with her hands on her hips. "She finally stops crying, and you two waltz in here, and now her mascara is smeared again!"

Chase and Charlie both smiled at Dana. "You better get out of here before she kicks your asses," Samantha said to them.

"OK." Chase hugged her, squeezing her close to him. "It doesn't matter how many name changes you have, you'll always be my little sis."

"You'll always be my big brother."

"This wedding stuff can be stressful on the bride." Chase bent over. "Hang in there, little guy. It'll be over soon."

"Did you seriously just talk to my stomach?"

"I was talking to my future nephew," he said.

"How do you know it's a boy?"

"Uncles know these things."

"You guys have no idea what it is. I hope you aren't disappointed when it's a girl," Samantha said.

Charlie laughed, gathering her in his arms. "Promise me one thing," he said.

"Anything."

"If it is a girl, try again until I get a little nephew. I need a fishing buddy."

Samantha laughed. "I promise."

"OK, now go marry that man of yours, but don't forget about us."

"I could never forget about you. Now get out of here before you make me cry more."

"Damn," Dana said. "Sexy and sensitive. A dangerous combination." Dana handed her two garters. "This should finish out the borrowed and blue. The blue one is yours to keep, the white one I'm loaning to you."

Samantha laughed. "Thank you, Dana. You are my best friend, and I can't imagine a life without you in it."

Dana finished putting one on each of Samantha's legs. "It's a good thing you don't have to, and that's all I'm saying. Otherwise, I'm going to cry, and I have to walk down the aisle with this really hot guy, and I don't want to be a blubbering idiot."

"I get it, but I still love you."

Dana kissed her on the cheek, wiping off the lipstick. "I love you more, chica, but I gotta go. Sofia's waiting for me. See you in a few."

Samantha took a deep breath and walked away from the mirror. She picked up the single white lily Jake had delivered to her. Though she loved the tulip flower, and it was her mother's favorite, this was a new beginning with Jake, and she wanted something that symbolized her devotion to him.

Richard knocked, poking his head around the door. "Are you ready, baby girl?"

"I've never been more ready for anything in my life."

"I remember you saying you wanted to go to Hawaii one day. When you get home, you will find an envelope at your apartment with all the details for a Hawaiian vacation package from me and Monica. You can use it whenever you like, and it comes with two full weeks of free babysitting."

"That is a generous gift, Richard. Thank you. I'm not sure either one of us will be able to leave the baby for that long, though."

"He will be in good hands."

"He? Why do all of you think it will be a boy?"

Richard chortled. "Intuition."

Samantha held his hands. "Thank you for the gift, but you have already given me more than I could ask for. You saved me. You helped me grow from a gawky teenager to the woman I am today. You helped me see the light when my world was so dark. You gave me my life, Richard, and without you, I never would have met Jake."

"I love you, baby girl." He wiped a tear from her cheek. "I wish your father could see you now. He would be proud of you."

"He's here." Samantha held her hand over her heart. "And you're there too. Thank you for walking me down the aisle."

Richard smiled at her, something he'd been doing a lot more of since he retired from the CIA and married Monica. "Jake has proven to me how much he loves you. I'm honored to do it, but if we don't get out there, he's going to be storming in here any second looking for you."

Samantha smiled. "I know. He reminds me of you that way. I've heard daughters are drawn to men who are like their father. You treated me like your daughter, and lucky for me, I think I found a man who is the perfect combination of both of my fathers."

Chapter 29

*J*ake paced incessantly, shoving his hands in his pockets, then taking them out. He couldn't remember a time when he'd been full of such nervous excitement. "Cal, do you have the rings?"

Cal rolled his eyes at him, crossing his arms over his chest. "For the eighth time, yes, I have the rings."

"Is the photographer here?"

"Yep," Max said.

"How about the dining room downstairs? Is everything ready?"

"Done," Shorty said.

"Security?"

"Done," Ammo said.

"You know, little man, you are about to wear a hole in that carpet," Shannon said. "You need to relax. Everything is ready."

"Relax? I don't recall you being relaxed on your wedding day."

"True, but I was the bride," she said. "Do you have your vows ready?"

"Vows? Doesn't the pastor recite those, and we repeat what he said?"

Shannon giggled. "I was at your apartment when Samantha asked you if you wanted to write your own vows, and you said yes."

"I did? Why don't I remember that?"

"Head injury," Ammo said.

"Too busy ogling Samantha," Shorty added.

"Counting the minutes until Shannon left," Max said.

"So he could go another round," Cal said, as they all burst into laughter.

"Oh. My. God. Is this what you boys do in here?" Shannon asked, gaping at all of them with her hands on her hips.

"We're men," Ammo said.

"Men who think with their dicks," Shannon retorted.

"And that's a problem?" Cal asked.

"You would answer that way, Mr. Dom," Shannon said, rolling her eyes.

"That's enough kids, but Shannon, it's highly plausible I was in another Samantha trance, so I don't have any vows."

Shannon patted his chest with her hands. "Then speak from the heart."

Jake's mother poked her head in the door. "We're ready, Jake."

The room emptied out, except for Cal. "You'll be fine, and Shannon is right, speak from your heart. I know how much you love that girl, so just tell her in your own words."

"Thanks, Cal."

"Let's roll," he said, mimicking Cuddy's words.

"Yeah, let's roll."

Jake checked his watch when he stepped off the elevator, noting it was five minutes before noon. He had five minutes to walk with his mother down the aisle then he would see his beautiful bride for the first time that day. Samantha had suggested getting married at ten in the morning, and he should have agreed because he was going crazy not seeing her. He felt a familiar tug on his hand. He smiled at Sofia in her beautiful pink dress, holding Dana's hand with her other while she continued to tug on his. She let go, holding her arms up to him. Jake lifted her up, and she wrapped her arms around him, kissing him on his cheek.

"I love you, Uncle Jake," she said.

"And I love you. I'll see you after this is over, OK?"

"OK."

Jake set her down, and Cal raised his hand, cuing the lone cellist. As the music started to play, Jake held out his elbow for his mother as they began their descent down the white runner. The chairs were white, decorated with blue and pink bows entwined around a single white lily. Shannon and Clay and their two boys, Timmy and Tommy, sat in the second row. The boys were already punching each other, much to Shannon's dismay. Ammo, Max, and Shorty joined Kyle in the next row. On the opposite side were Anna, Tess, and Jen, sitting in the second row with Dana's parents and Jen's sister right behind them. Samantha's two brothers took the front seats, nodding to him as he passed by. Jake hugged his mother, kissing her on her cheek and telling her he loved her. Walking up to the white archway where Pastor Murphy stood, Jake shook his hand, then turned, chuckling as Sofia held a basket of lily petals, giggling as she dropped them by the handful. His mother reached for Sofia when she was at the front, lifting her onto her lap.

Dana and Cal were next. His best friend whom he met at the youth center had been through more than most kids his age, but he'd survived, and he was looking handsome next to Dana, whose beauty was as big as her personality. He looked at the bows again, then the dresses Sofia and Dana were wearing. He chuckled, shaking his head, knowing this was Samantha's subtle way of reminding him their baby could be a boy or a girl.

The cellist began playing louder, a sign for everyone to stand. Jake stood with his hands folded in front of him, his knees feeling weak, drawing in a breath at the sight of Samantha. Her dress was fitted, showing off her beautiful curves, her skin glowing against the white satin. She wore the necklace her brothers had shown him that morning, forcing him to put aside the gift he had made for her to wear. She had her hair up, with small ringlets falling around her face and neck, and she was wearing a smile only for him. Their eyes locked, her smile never fading. Though her emotions had been all over the place during these first few weeks of her pregnancy, she was happy now—happier than he'd ever seen her.

Pastor Murphy said something, but Jake wasn't listening to him. Though the sun was shining and he could see their family and friends gathered around them, they were somewhere else, in their own little bubble. Taking her hand from Richard, Jake couldn't help himself. He leaned in, kissing her, making her and everyone else laugh. "You're beautiful," he whispered before the small crowd quieted down.

Pastor Murphy didn't bother chastising him for his behavior. He began speaking, and Jake went through the motions, unable to take his eyes off his beautiful bride. They were facing each other, holding hands. Jake rubbed his thumb over hers, wanting...no, needing to feel her, to make sure she was real.

"Jake, do you have your vows?" Pastor Murphy asked.

"Samantha, I didn't prepare any vows, so I'm speaking from my heart because today I give you my heart. I promise that I will take your hand and walk with you wherever our journey may lead. I promise to encourage your compassion because that's what makes you who you are. I promise to fill your dreams, share your sorrows, buy you wine with fun names, and eat your cooking." Everyone laughed at his humor, but Jake raised Samantha's hands, kissing her fingers. "I promise to be faithful to you, to always protect you, and to make you and our growing family my priority. I promise to love you forever, baby, and then I promise to love you more because one lifetime with you will never be enough."

"Samantha, are you ready for your vows?" Pastor Murphy asked.

Samantha pulled her hands from Jake and dipped her fingers into the front of her dress, removing a slip of paper from the left side, much to the amusement of his friends, whom he heard laughing. "I'm not a walking Webster like you," she said. "I need paper." Jake laughed, remembering the night she let him take her home. It was the first time he kissed her, and he knew then that she was the woman he wanted to spend his life with. "For the record, I wrote mine yesterday." She held the paper up, smiling and winking at him. She licked her lips, taking one of his hands in hers. "Jake, on this day, I give you my heart." Jake smiled when she opened with the same words he had.

"You're my best friend, my lover, my teacher, and my guide. I promise to be truthful with you and to communicate fully and fearlessly. I promise to accept your faults and strengths as you do mine. I promise to be faithful, patient, and forgiving, and I promise to always have a loaf of bread and peanut butter and jelly because I know you won't always like my cooking. I promise to be your partner in all things because together we are one." Samantha folded the paper as the small crowd still snickered from her peanut-butter-and-jelly vow. "Finally, Jake, I promise to love you forever, because without you I'm not complete."

Chapter 30

Three days later, Samantha laid her head against Jake's chest as they gazed out at the ocean from the patio off the master suite of the home Jake had purchased in Huntington. It was his wedding gift to her, and she loved every square inch of it. But it was more than the house. With Jake as her husband, this was home. They were one, exactly as she'd professed to him in her vows on their perfect wedding day, surrounded by family and close friends. After the ceremony, they celebrated with their guests over lunch, then to her surprise, Jake had everyone pack their things and load a bus for a short ride out of town, introducing them to a luxury hotel he'd just signed a purchase agreement for. He had kept it secret, wanting to surprise her. She realized in that moment that not all secrets are bad. Sometimes, you want to do something special for another person to make them smile or laugh, and Jake did that for her.

Samantha inhaled, breathing in the salty tang of the ocean air. She let it out, savoring the moment, wanting to stop time from moving too fast. The sun was beginning to disappear, and the gentle breeze warmed her face. She closed her eyes, imagining family barbeques, long walks on the beach, sitting in beach chairs, and watching the stars at night. The beach here reminded her of her home in California, where the sun would cast a shimmer against the sand, making it look like a field of tiny crystals. There would be a certain point in time when the sun would hit the water, the horizon would disappear, and she wouldn't be able to tell where the sun ended and the water began. At one point in time, she had captured those photos on her camera, but those photos were now lost, and she only had the memories.

But here, with Jake, she would make new memories. She was given a second chance, and in some ways, he was too. Though the demons still haunted him, he was fighting, and she was standing proudly next to him, supporting him however she could. They were one unit now, each supporting the other, and while they were both scarred, physically and mentally, they were stronger together than they were apart. They had yet to experience normalcy in their lives together, and undoubtedly, with a baby on the way, there may never be normal. Standing here, wrapped in the arms of the man she loves, in a home they would grow old in together, was her new normal. Anything else was but a speck of time, but this...this she wanted to last forever.

"I always dreamed of this."

"Of what?" Jake kissed the top of her head.

"Having a husband, a home." She turned to him, rising to her tiptoes to kiss him. "Thank you."

"I want to make all your dreams come true."

"You already have."

"*Ti amo*, Samantha." He took her face in his hands and kissed her, an intimate kiss, a promise of a life filled with love. "There's more to come, baby. A whole lot more."

~The End~

Acknowledgments

Finally! I didn't want this story to end and had a hard time letting go, but I hope you enjoyed Jake and Samantha's story! I have so many people to thank, but as always, first and foremost my husband, my lifeline and my pillar of unwavering support. Your encouragement has sustained me in more ways than one. Life gets busy, but you always make sure I have time to do what I love to do.

I know this last book took longer than I thought, so a huge thank-you to all of you who stuck with me on this journey. Your positive comments, book reviews, words of encouragement, and sharing and commenting on posts and tweets has been a lifeline. I appreciate the feedback from the editorial reviews and readers. The feedback you provide helps me improve my writing, and I tried to weave it once again into this novel (all eight versions of it!).

Life can get complicated; we sometimes lose touch with friends and family because of distance, or for reasons we don't always understand. We are only on this earth for a short time, so make the best of it. Reconnect, love, smile, and laugh, and most of all, do what you love to do!

Until next time…M. J.

About the Author

M. J. Brookes, author of the Stem Series Trilogy, lives in Minnesota. The wife of a military veteran who served in Iraq, Brookes holds a master's degree in management and has worked in the public, private, and nonprofit sectors.

An avid reader and storyteller from a young age, Brookes put her writing dreams on hold to focus on college and a career. Years later, during a period of unfulfilling work, she began penning the Stems Series as a creative outlet. A friend's enthusiastic response to the initial draft of *Stems of Affliction* motivated Brookes to publish her erotic romance, with *Stems of Inception* hot on its heels. Now *Stems of Completion* brings Jake and Samantha's compelling story to a close.

Brookes can be reached online at MJBrookesauthor@gmail.com or on Twitter @mjbrookesauthor. You can also find her on Facebook at https://www.facebook.com/mjbrookes.

Made in the USA
Middletown, DE
12 April 2019